THIS LIFE AND ALL THE REST

NEXT LIFE DUET BOOK TWO

BRIT BENSON

THIS LIFE AND ALL THE REST

Copyright© 2022 by Brit Benson

All rights reserved.

No part of this book may be reproduced, distributed, or transmitted in any form or by any electronic or mechanical means, including information storage and retrieval systems, without written permission from the author, except for the use of brief quotations in a book review and certain other noncommercial use permitted by copyright law.

This book is a work of fiction. Names, characters, places, and incidents are either the product of the author's imagination or are used fictitiously. Any resemblance to actual persons and things living or dead, locales, or events is entirely coincidental. Except for the original material written by the author, all mention of films, television shows and songs, song titles, and lyrics mentioned in the novel are the property of the songwriters and copyright holders.

Cover Design: Murphy Rae

Editing: Rebecca at Fairest Reviews Editing Services

Proofing: Sarah at All Encompassing Books

Bonus Content Artwork: Liliya Goncharova IG: @lilu_goncharova

 Created with Vellum

CONTENT NOTE

Please be aware, book two of the *Next Life* duet contains some difficult topics that could be upsetting for some readers.

Topics that take place on page are: vulgar language, sexually explicit content, graphic depictions of self-harm*, discussions of addiction, unprotected sex, physical injury/illness of a family member

Topics that are referenced but do not take place on page are: loss of pregnancy*, addiction relapse*, physical injury

*If you require a content-specific chapter guide for these topics, you can find one **on my website.**

FROM THE AUTHOR

Macon and Lennon, my sassy, tormented little babies.

They've given me hell. Sleepless nights, emotional stress, and sob-fests in my shower. But, fuck, do I love them.

I was scared to write the conclusion to this duet. I never expected book one to receive the attention that it did, and each new rave review heightened the expectations for Lennon and Macon's HEA. I wanted to do them justice, and to be honest, I didn't know if I was capable of pulling it off.

Thankfully, I think I proved myself wrong.

I'm so fucking proud of this book. I'm so proud of these characters and the way they've grown. I'm proud of this story. I truly feel I gave them the HEA they deserve.

I hope you love it like I do.

PLAYLIST

I Would've – Jessie Murph
happier – Olivia Rodrigo
Fever Dream – Jillian Rossi
Falling – Harry Styles
Landslide – Fleetwood Mac
The Way I Loved You (Taylor's version) – Taylor Swift
What A Time – Julia Michaels, Niall Horan
Lie To Me – 5 Seconds of Summer, Julia Michaels
Night Changes – One Direction
Hurt Somebody – Noah Kahan, Julia Michaels
Peer Pressure – James Bay, Julia Michaels
supercuts – Jeremy Zucker
skinny dipping – Sabrina Carpenter
Lover of Mine – 5 Seconds of Summer
Take on the World – You Me At Six
this is how you fall in love – Jeremy Zucker, Chelsea Cutler
Always Been You – Jessie Murph
Queen Of The Night – Hey Violet
I GUESS I'M IN LOVE – Clinton Kane

18 – One Direction
Dandelions– Ruth B
Your Love Is My Home – The Light the Heat

This playlist can be found on my website at www.authorbritbenson.com/playlists

*To rock bottom,
the journey back to the top,
and growth.*

Lennon

PROLOGUE

"Come on. Ruined lives? Bloodshed? You really think a relationship should be that hard?"
"No one writes songs about the ones that come easy."
-*Veronica Mars*, 2x20

4 Years Earlier

My eyes fill with tears, but I refuse to let them fall.

He doesn't want to talk to me? Take the hint? Fine.

Fuck him. Fuck all of them. I'm done being their punching bag. I'm done with all of it. I don't need them. All I need is myself, and I need a change.

I block Claire's email.

Then I block Macon's.

I start to block Andrea's contact on the app but stop. Right now, she's the fastest connection I have to my dad. I leave her unblocked for now, but I mute her and set her to text only. In five months, when he's home and retired, I'll block her.

Then I stand and rummage through Aunt Becca's drawers until I find a pair of scissors. I take them to the bathroom and look in the mirror. I grab my braid, hold it up over my head, and hack it off. I run my fingers through the strands. All that's left is a jagged, uneven bob.

I stare at myself in the mirror.

Maybe I'll dye it too. Maybe I'll go blonde. Or red.

I smile, and it's not fake.

A new Lennon for a new life. I've outgrown the last one.

ONE

Lennon

Present Day

My phone is ringing. Not the regular tone. Not the alarm.

I feel around the bedside table for it in the dark, knocking it on the floor with a thud. I leave it, close my eyes, and start to drift back to sleep.

It's ringing again. I groan and kick off the covers. The balmy air tickles my naked skin, hardening my nipples and bringing attention to my already sticky thighs.

"Who is it, *chérie*?" Franco mumbles from beside me, his French accent thicker in sleep.

"*Je ne sais pas,*" I say as I kneel on the floor and feel around for my phone. It stops ringing again. I huff. My fingers finally close around it, and I grin in triumph, standing back up and climbing back into bed before checking the Caller ID.

My heart stops and my brow furrows when I see the name. I haven't seen that name on my phone in a long time.

"*Qui est-ce?*" Franco asks again. I don't answer.

"Capri," he prompts, and I blink before forcing out the name.

"Claire."

"Your sister?"

"*Step*," I correct, just as the phone starts ringing again. I let it ring six times before I answer.

"Hello?"

Lennon?

"Yeah, it's me."

It's Claire.

"I know."

Lennon. You need to come home.

It's almost nine in the evening when I step off the jet bridge, wheeling my carry-on behind me.

I didn't have the mental capacity to pack more. I didn't have the mental capacity to do much of anything besides shower, throw a bunch of stuff into my carry-on, and try not to panic. Luckily, I've had a nine-hour international flight, plus a ninety-minute layover in Philly and a ninety-minute connecting flight to get my shit under control.

It doesn't matter. I probably won't be here long anyway.

My stomach grumbles as I walk toward arrivals, reminding me that all I've consumed in the last twenty-four hours is a few packages of airline cookies and several airplane bottles of vodka. I can't eat on an anxious stomach.

Apparently, I can drink, though.

I pull my phone out of my bag and turn it on, then immediately shove it in my pocket, so I can ignore any messages for a little while longer. As I walk past baggage claim, a familiar blonde head of hair catches my eye, and I heave a sigh of relief.

Then I see the sign she's holding, and I smile.

"CASSATT, MARY" is written in bold black marker on a piece of white poster board. I shake my head slowly as I step in front of her and tap on the sign.

"Mary Cassatt was known more for oils. Or printingmaking and pastels. Not a lot of watercolor. And she was mostly straight impressionism," I say flatly, but the humor in my voice is still recognizable to anyone who knows me. And Sam definitely knows me.

She rolls her eyes.

"Well, it was that or this."

She flips the poster board to show me the other side.

ART SCHOOL DROP OUT.

I bark out a laugh and her lips break into a grin. Her eyes sweep over me, then scan my face. Her smile drops off, and she reaches out and takes the handle of my carry-on.

"You look like shit, Len," she says frankly.

She's the only person close to me who still calls me Lennon. She'd stop if I asked, I'm sure. But I haven't. I don't question why.

"You fly ten hours in economy, and we'll see if you're fresh as a daisy afterwards."

Sam turns and starts walking, so I follow.

"You should have let me get your flight. I could have flown you first class."

"No thanks. I don't really want to be flying in style on the Senator's blood money. I'm good with economy."

"Ah, yes," she snarks, giving me a sidelong glance as I follow her to the short-term parking lot. "Your *integrity*."

"Look, I'm not saying anything about you. If he was my dad, I'd milk my trust fund for a Georgetown education and a life of luxury, too. But he's not my dad, so..."

I trail off, and Sam sighs.

"Yeah, I get it." She uses her key fob to unlock her BMW

with a beep, then pops the trunk and drops my carry-on into it. "It's just my internalized guilt. But you know I'm simply biding my time. The moment he drops his presidential bid, I'm blowing his shit wide open."

She slides into the driver's seat, and I get in on the passenger side.

"And when you do, I'll be on the sidelines with popcorn, ready to whisk you away to some place remote, if things get too shady."

"Aw, thanks, babe," she croons with a grin as she starts the car.

"I mean, what are friends for, if not to protect you from psycho, corrupt family members?"

Sam snorts a laugh in agreement, and I'm smiling for the first time in twenty-four hours, but it quickly disappears when she pulls out of the parking lot and points her car in the direction of our hometown. Reality sets in, and I have to rest my head back on the seat and control my breathing.

"You wanna go home first, or to the hospital?" she asks quietly.

She doesn't ask me how I'm doing. She knows already. I'm sure it's pretty obvious.

"Actually, can you take me to your house, instead?" I don't correct her for her use of the word *home*. That place hasn't been home in years. "I want to take a shower and consume something that isn't vodka before I have to deal with everything."

Sam nods and turns on the radio. I'm not worried about running into Chase or the senator. They're never home when Sam is home, and she'd warn me if they were. She must have arranged something with them last minute since she would otherwise be spending the summer in DC, working an internship. Sam and her family have an unspoken agreement

—when she's not at her college apartment, they leave the house in Franklin for her.

She opens her mouth, then shuts it again. I wait for the question, but it doesn't come.

"Just say it, Sam," I say, putting my head back on the headrest and closing my eyes.

"I was just wondering what you're gonna do when you see *persona non grata*."

Her tone is so matter-of-fact and in no way a reflection of the turmoil I feel churning in my belly. I try to match my tone to hers.

"It's not a big deal," I lie. "Not any different than when I see everyone else."

Sam scoffs, just like I knew she would. Bitch always sees through my bullshit. It doesn't matter, though. The lie was for me, not her.

"I still can't believe you've avoided contact for this long."

"It's not hard when there's an ocean between us and he's always deployed."

"Yeah, but he's not deployed now," Sam warns, and I release a slow exhale.

No. No, he's not.

"WANT ME TO COME IN WITH YOU?" SAM ASKS AS HER CAR idles outside the hospital entrance.

"No. Thank you, though."

She took me to her house, let me shower and take a fifteen-minute nap, then fed me leftover pizza before driving me here. *After* rearranging her schedule so she could pick me up from the airport. She's already maxed out her best friend good deeds for the day.

"You sure? I don't mind. I can wait in the waiting room."

"It's okay," I say honestly. "I think I need to do this alone, first."

She nods. "Text if you need me to scoop you up after."

I get out of her car and shut the door. I walk to the revolving door, then turn and give her a wave. She doesn't leave until I'm in the building.

Instead of walking to the information desk, I follow the signs to the ICU. There's a nurse at the desk and I tell her my name. Visiting hours are technically over, but Andrea spoke with them and convinced them to make an exception for me since I was flying in from Paris. Luckily, they didn't loosen the one visitor at a time rule, so I know I'll be in there alone.

I walk slowly, keeping my eyes forward, but I use my peripheral to count the doors. I control my breathing, fighting off the tears that are already forming.

I can do this.

For him, I can do this.

The sound of beeping and whirring monitors surrounds me when I step through the door, reminding me of the last time I was in this hospital, and I have to fight off the memories of that terrible night. I never wanted to be back here.

The curtain around the bed is drawn, and I'm so grateful for that. For long seconds, I stand frozen, staring at that curtain, warring with my emotions.

"You can do this," I whisper to myself, then force one foot in front of the other.

Instead of pulling the curtain back, I slip through the opening at the edge and leave it drawn, giving us a little bit of privacy from the outside. I let my eyes fall to his chest, first. It still looks strong. It looks healthy. I watch as it moves up and down steadily. I try to ignore the fact that it's a ventilator, and not his body making the motion. After another long set of inhales and exhales, I drag my attention to his face.

His pale, lifeless face.

The tears fall, then. One, then two, then a hiccupping sob.

I close my eyes against them and breathe in time with the beeping. I reach out and take his hand. I squeeze it, but it doesn't squeeze back. Another onslaught of tears. I wrap my other hand around his, so it's nestled safely between my palms. Then I open my eyes.

"Hey, Daddy."

TWO
Macon

THE CRYING WAKES ME UP.

I roll over stiffly and grab my phone to check the time.

Almost three in the morning.

At least she's consistent. I don't even need to set an alarm when she's here.

I sit up and drop my legs out of bed with a groan as pain radiates up the left side of my body. I turn on the lamp on my nightstand and reach for the bottle of ibuprofen I keep next to the bed. I pop open the bottle, shake four of the pills into my palm, and toss them back dry.

The crying continues.

"Shh, shh, shh," I say softly as I push myself up from the bed. "I hear you. I'm coming."

I fumble my way to the playpen sleeper in the corner of my room and find a very hungry, very angry little human peering over the side of it.

When she sees me, she stretches out one of her tiny hands and uses the other to steady her wobbly body while she bounces. Her face, wet and splotched red from her wails, now shows off the happiest little four-toothed smile.

I fucking love that smile.

"C'mere, Squirt." I scoop her up and prop her on my hip. "Let's get you some num-nums."

"Babababababa," she chants, nuzzling her face into my chest and shoulder.

"Yeah, yeah, we'll get you your baba," I tell her with a tired laugh. I shuffle out of my small bedroom and into my small kitchen, flipping on the hall light as I go.

"I thought you things were supposed to be sleeping through the night at this age."

She lets out a happy little squeal that I can only assume means, *yeah right, sucker, no sleep for you.*

Quickly, with sleep-drooped eyes and a squirming baby in one arm, I fix a bottle, then take the hungry little monster to the couch.

I change her first, then prop her on my lap and laugh at her little grabby hands before popping the bottle in her mouth. She can hold the bottle by herself now, but I like to do it. I like the way her little fingers grasp onto mine as she eats, and I like the way she watches me.

Sometimes, I'll sing to her or tell her stories, but tonight, I'm too beat.

Tonight, we just stare at each other.

She's got such long eyelashes, and these gray-green eyes that I swear can see right through me. She's fucking fascinating, actually. She's a work of art.

I watch her until she finishes, then I set the bottle on the coffee table, put her on my chest, and close my eyes to get a few more hours of sleep.

Bang bang bang.

"Uh-oh."

Bang bang bang.

"Uhh-oooh."

I crack one eye open and focus it on the noisemaker. She's using her empty bottle as a mallet and is currently going to town on my coffee table. I lift my eyes to the clock by the television.

Six a.m.

Jesus, where does this kid get her energy? I'm still exhausted.

Bang bang bang. "Uh-oh! Uh-ohhhh!"

"Ok, Squirt, I'm up."

I sit up and reach my arms up in a stretch, then run my hand through my hair. It's getting a little long. It's about time I see the barber and tighten it up again.

I push myself to standing slowly, wincing through the stiffness, then head into the kitchen. I don't have to pick up the kid. She speed-crawls behind me.

"You want eggies or eggies this morning?" I glance at her over my shoulder. She giggles and moves to a sitting position in the middle of the floor. "Eggies it is. Good choice."

I whip us up some scrambled eggs, keeping an eye on her as I do. She found the ball under the table that we lost yesterday, and she's fucking stoked. It's one of those annoying ones that makes noises when you hit it on the floor or bounce it. I'm definitely sending that thing back with her this time. I could murder the person who gave it to her.

I fix up her highchair tray with eggs and some bits of avocado, then fix my own plate. When I turn back to the table, I find she's used one of the kitchen chairs to pull herself up to standing and is acting like she's about to take some steps.

"Nope, nope," I say quickly, sticking my foot out and nudging her gently, so she falls back on her butt. She giggles, and I shake my head. "None of that, Squirt. No first steps allowed unless Mama is here."

She squeals and claps.

"Mamamamama," she says happily as I set my plate down and pick her up, sticking her in her highchair and strapping her in.

"We'll see Mama soon. Eat your breakfast."

We eat our eggs in relative silence. She hums to herself, and I scroll through some news articles on my phone, huffing every time I read something that pisses me off, which is often.

I look up from my phone to find that she's painted her cheeks, forehead, and hands green with avocado. She's the messiest eater. It's gross, but in a cute way.

"You're a slob." I laugh, and she flashes those little teeth on a grin, mouth full of egg. "I'm not going to be able to take you anywhere until you learn how to eat. It's embarrassing."

"Mamamama," she says again, giggling as food drops out of her mouth. There's avocado on her eyebrow. How the hell does that even happen?

"Mama is going to think I let you play in a dumpster."

I get up and grab a washcloth, wet it with warm water, then gently wipe off her face. More giggles, more chanting. When she's finished, I wipe her down again, then haul her out of the chair.

Diaper change, clothing change, baby shoes that make no sense because she's just going to kick them off in the car. I grab her diaper bag, shove the menace ball into it, then we head out of the apartment and down the stairs to the parking lot.

I'm still in the joggers and USMC t-shirt I wore to bed, but I swiped on some deodorant and threw on a baseball cap on our way out the door. I buckle her into her car seat then slide into the driver's side.

I crank the engine and turn on Fleetwood Mac's album *Rumors*. The kid may not look much like me, with her straight brown hair and greenish eyes, but I'll be damned if she doesn't have good taste in music. I'm starting her young.

I make the drive across town, listening to Stevie Nicks with the baby on accompaniment, her little feet kicking the rattles hanging from her car seat handle. A few times, she's even kind of on beat, but most of the time it's just noise.

When I pull into the driveway, my stomach twists, and I take a few moments to breathe through it, after turning off the car. Not too long, though, because the *Mamamama* chant starts in the back seat, and it's the kind of chant that tells me that if I don't move my ass, I'm going to be dealing with a very pissed off ten-month-old.

"Alright, Squirt, I hear ya." I sigh, hopping out and moving to the back to unbuckle her and lift her out of her seat. I prop her on one hip, sling the diaper bag over my opposite shoulder, then make the walk up the drive to the house.

She bounces in my arms and pats her hands on my face, leaning forward and giving me her version of kisses, which is essentially coming at you open-mouthed and slobbering all over your cheeks. Also gross in a kind of cute way.

The door is unlocked, so I let myself in. I kick my shoes off on the mat, then make my way toward the living room. I'm rounding the corner and heading toward the baby activity center when my eyes catch on a carry-on suitcase against the wall.

I stop short and stare at it.

Then I hear the soft padding of footsteps, and I know. Before I see her, I feel her. Then I smell her, and it pisses me off. Vanilla. My brain shouts *imposter* and my whole body tightens. I hold my breath as she appears in front of me.

Lennon.

I haven't seen her this close in years. She looks different, and it's not just the auburn color she's dyed her hair or the curves on her body that are more pronounced. She looks amazing. She's always looked amazing, but it's something else. Different from prom night, and different still from the London pub.

Despite the differences, she's still the same, too. There's just something decidedly *Lennon* about her.

She's in a pair of sweats and an oversized shirt with her hair piled on top of her head in a bun. Her one hand holds a mug of coffee and the other is scrolling through a phone, but the minute we're in the same space, her attention snaps to me.

She stops. Her eyes flare and mouth drops open, for just a split second, then her brow furrows and her lips purse.

In spite of myself, I let my eyes scan her. US NAVY shirt. US NAVY sweats. And she's barefoot, her toenails painted an emerald green. It makes my heart race and my anger spike. Glad to see she's made herself at fucking home.

I bring my eyes back to hers to say as much, but she's not looking at me.

She's looking at the mini-monster in my arms.

Evelyn's little fingers tighten in my shirt as Lennon takes a tentative step toward us. I try to relax my body, so she doesn't feed off my tension, but it's too late.

"Hey, Evie," Lennon says softly, her voice smooth and sweet and just how I remember it. I want to rush her and wrap her in my arms, but Evelyn whimpers and buries her face in my neck. The shock on Lennon's face pisses me off, and I scoff. Why is she so surprised? Evelyn doesn't know her, and that's Lennon's own fault.

"She doesn't like strangers," I say, my voice booming through the quiet space.

At that word, *stranger*, Lennon's shoulders stiffen. The spark in her eyes kicks up my heartbeat, in a way I haven't felt in years, but her lips stay flatlined, emotionless.

"I'm not a stranger," she says "I'm her sister."

"You're a *stranger*. You've seen her once in ten months. That's it. Then you come waltzing back around and expect her to, what, just embrace you? Nah, Len. That's not how this shit works."

Her eyes narrow as she studies me. She doesn't like the truth I just served up, but too fucking bad. That's what happens when you run away to the other side of the world and never return. You become *estranged*.

"It's *Capri*," she says finally, her voice low and commanding. I snort a laugh.

"Sure it is." I push past her and walk into the kitchen, just as my mom comes down the stairs.

"Hey, guys," she says with a smile, but her voice is tired and sad.

"Mamamamama!" Evie chants and bounces, reaching for our mom and making those little grabby hands. Mom laughs and gives me a quick hug, before taking Evie from my arms and peppering her with kisses.

"Hey, my sweet girl. Thank you so much for taking her last night, Macon. How was she for you?"

I smirk and move to the coffee pot to pour myself a cup.

"She's a little terror, but she's a good wingman," I joke, glancing back at the doorway and noting Lennon's absence. She's disappeared again. Figures. I look back at my mom and sister. "Got me like five numbers at The Outpost before eleven."

My mom rolls her eyes.

"You were asleep on the couch by nine," she says, and I shrug.

Eight forty-five, but I'm not going to correct her.

"Did you get any rest?"

"I didn't stay on the cot at the hospital, if that's what you're asking," she says with a sigh. "I was here in my own bed."

"But did you *sleep*?"

She doesn't answer, but she doesn't have to. The dark circles under her red-rimmed eyes say enough. She chews on her lip, and I watch as her eyes mist. I close the distance between us and pull her and Evie into a hug.

"He's going to be okay," I say as Evie giggles and pats my cheeks. "Trent is strong. He'll pull through."

Mom sniffles into my shirt.

"It's been days. What if...what if..."

She starts to cry, and all I can do is hold her and try to temper my anger.

My mom doesn't deserve this shit. Trent and Evelyn are supposed to be her happily ever after. Her second chance. She's been through enough heartache, and all I want to do is rage at whatever fucker is pulling the strings behind the curtain. They haven't even made it to their fifth wedding anniversary. Their daughter isn't even one yet.

Trent having a massive heart attack was never supposed to happen.

He's young and healthy. Young, healthy people with ten-month-old babies aren't supposed to have heart attacks and end up in comas.

"Dadadada," Evie starts to chant, which makes Mom cry harder, and I press a kiss to the mini-monster's head.

"We'll see your Dada soon, Squirt," I tell her, then lean back and make eye contact with my mom. "We will see him soon."

She forces a smile and wipes her eyes on her sleeve, then pulls away and gives Evie a kiss on the cheek.

"Has she eaten?"

"Fed her a Pop-Tart and some Dr. Pepper on the drive over."

Mom laughs like I hoped and rolls her eyes.

"She's got avocado in her ear," she deadpans.

"She's gross," I say with a shrug. "Take it up with the heathens raising her. I'm just the babysitter."

The mood has lightened, but I'm still on high alert. Listening for movement. Subtly sniffing the air like some sort of rabid bloodhound.

I shouldn't care that she's here. I knew she was coming. I had almost forty-eight hours to prepare, but my composure has been all but shot to fuck within fifteen minutes of being in the same space as her.

"When did she get in?" I ask quietly, trying to mask my emotions. I keep my eyes off my mom and dig through the fridge for a yogurt instead of looking at her.

"I'm not sure. Her friend dropped her luggage off here last night around eleven, but Len—*Capri*—didn't come home until around five this morning. I think she slept at the hospital."

I try to ignore the surge of anger I feel. *Capri*. What a joke.

"Her friend?" I ask, muscles tensing. If she brought that French fuck home...

"Oh, yeah. Sam. Samantha Harper. She picked Capri up from the airport, too."

I cock my head to the side.

"They're still talking?" I knew Sam visited Lennon for a while in England when she first moved. I learned about it after the fact. But last I heard, Sam was at Georgetown and Lennon was fucking around in Paris with hippy artists and that French dick.

"Apparently." My mom shrugs. "I'm glad she has a friend."

I snort, and Mom hits me with a glare.

"Don't start," she warns, her voice low.

I throw up my palms. *I'm stopping*, I say with the gesture, and she sighs and changes the subject.

"Are you going to the hospital today?"

"Yeah. I took the day off, so I'm going to go by now and then I can watch the squirt for you if you want to go this afternoon."

"Thank you, Macon." Her voice is heavy with both exhaustion and gratitude. I shake my head.

"You don't need to thank me, Ma," I tell her honestly. "I like watching her. You shouldn't have to do this by yourself."

She smiles softly and nods, then glances over my shoulder. I tense.

"Are you going to be okay?" she whispers, flicking her eyes from the doorway behind me to my face and back. "With her here. Are you going to—"

"I'm fine, Mom."

I can't tell if it's the truth. I don't know if the buzzing in my head and the tightness in my chest is going to get worse or better with Lennon's presence.

Just being around her for four minutes left me feeling more *everything* than I've felt in the last four years. And I've felt *a lot* in the last four years.

"I can handle it," I stress. "That shit is in the past."

The words are heavy and sour on my tongue. The moment I speak them, I regret it. But my mom's forehead smooths, and her lips curve up, telling me I've at least eased her concern for the moment. Good. She's got enough shit to worry about right now. My sanity teetering on the edge of a fucking cliff shouldn't even be on her radar.

"I'll be back this afternoon, okay?" She nods and gives me another hug.

I blow a raspberry on Evie's cheek and leave both the kid and my mom in giggles. My step is lighter until I walk outside and run smack into a soft, familiar body.

That's where the familiarity ends.

Vanilla.

Lennon huffs and rolls her eyes, then backs away without saying a word. She looks back at her phone and tries her best to ignore me.

I should walk away.

It's better for everyone if I walk away.

But I've never been good at doing what I should when it comes to her, and everything about her annoys me right now. The black skinny jeans and black tank top. The tiny tattoo on the inside of her upper arm. The black designer sunglasses she has perched on the top of her head, holding back her wavy auburn hair.

Capri. What a fucking joke.

I wonder if the Frenchman gave her the flashy rose gold bracelet on her wrist.

"Not even gonna say hi, Len?" I drawl. "You fuck off to Paris and now you're too good for your big brother?"

She was blank before, but the glare she hits me with is all fire. All passion. But is it passionate hatred or something else? We've always walked that line.

"I've been busy."

Her tone is flat, a direct contrast to the emotion in her hazel eyes, and I want to draw it out of her. My lips curve into a cruel smirk. *Busy.*

"Is that what you call bouncing on French dick in the City of Light?"

Instead of getting pissed or telling me to fuck off, she matches my smirk with one of her own and tilts her head to the side. My skin prickles.

"Why are you so concerned with whose dick I'm bouncing on, Macon?"

Her voice is sugar sweet, the kind that rots your teeth and turns your stomach. I fist my hands, fighting the urge to grab her and kiss the attitude right out of her smart-ass mouth. I shake my head slowly.

"Don't care who you fuck, *Lennon*," I say, keeping my tone detached and even.

I almost believe it myself.

I reach in my pocket for my pack of cigarettes and shake one out, placing it between my lips and lighting it up as I speak.

"I just find it interesting that perfect, wholesome Lennon

Washington flunked out of art school to become a freeloading, directionless Frenchman's whore."

I feel the crack of her palm on my cheek before I even realize she moved. My head whips to the side and stays there, staring at the pavement where my cigarette fell from the force of her slap.

I breathe deeply through the onslaught of thoughts and the raging boil of emotion in my stomach.

Lennon just slapped me.

Hard.

Guilt and excitement mix, but before I can make sense of them, she closes the distance between us, stopping just inches from my face as her voice, low and commanding, wraps around my body and causes the hairs on the back of my neck to stand on edge.

"You watch your fucking mouth when you speak to me. You don't know anything about me anymore. You don't know shit about what I've been doing in Paris."

Slowly, I turn my head and face her, keeping my expression blank, so I don't react to our closeness. The small space of air between us is charged, and I swear when our eyes meet, I'm zapped with a current.

"I just sold a painting for twelve grand," she states, smugness swirling with her fury. "I've got commissioned work lined up for the next year. And what have you done, huh?"

Her eyes scan my face, my hair, before falling on my left arm and studying the tattoos there. The surgical scar on my wrist tingles as her lip curls in disgusted humor.

It's the cruelest fucking smile I've ever seen on her pretty face.

"You joined the Marines," she says cloyingly.

She brings her finger to her face and taps her cheek in mock consideration. The pause is for dramatic effect, and I grit my teeth, preparing for the ax she's about to bring down on my fucking neck.

"Oh, that's right." She gasps dramatically. "And then you got kicked out of the Marines." She cocks her head to the side. "What happened, Macon? Get caught with drugs in your dress blues? You get high and screw a general's daughter?"

She waits as if she expects an answer, and it takes every ounce of strength in my body to grin like she hasn't gutted me with a rusty knife.

"Why are you so concerned with where I'm sticking my dick, *Astraea*?"

Her eyes flare for half a second and her lips part on an almost imperceptible gasp. The reaction kicks my heart up. The nickname. I try to read the emotions flashing through her eyes, but my attention catches on her mouth, and the way her teeth sink into her plush lower lip. On instinct, I reach up and free her lip from the bite with my thumb.

She doesn't flinch away. She doesn't step back. She doesn't even breathe until a horn honks from the curb, yanking us back to reality and cutting the connection.

We spring apart and look toward the sound.

I laugh. I can't help it.

The BMW that idles in front of my mom's house has tinted windows, but I know who's behind the wheel. I push past Lennon and walk toward my own car.

"I'll be at the hospital around noon," I say over my shoulder. It's a warning, so she has ample time to be in and out before I get there. I open my car door and look back at her. She's standing in the spot where I left her, her head cocked to the side as she studies me with a scowl on her face.

"What happened to nice, polite Lennon Washington?" I scan my eyes over her body like she's a stranger. She raises a brow and props her hand on her hip.

"She's dead," she says flatly.

I nod, trying my hardest not to show her my disappointment. My guilt. I let my eyes scan her once more, force a smirk to my lips, then climb in my car.

"Tell Senator Harper's daughter I said *hey*," I call out before slamming my door, cranking the engine, and peeling out of the drive.

My hands are tight on the steering wheel as I drive away, my heart pounding in my chest. My breath comes in pants and my forehead prickles with sweat.

Mother fuck.

I pull my phone up on the Bluetooth and call Casper.

"How'd it go?" he says when he answers. The concern in his tone just makes it worse.

"I need to get fucked up," I say through my teeth.

He's quiet for a minute, then he laughs nervously.

"That good, huh?"

"Fuck off. You gonna help me or not?"

I hear him sigh.

"Nicolette isn't going to like this," he says, but I can already tell he's caved.

"Let me deal with Nic." My body is already relaxing as I turn the car back toward my apartment.

"I'm just sayin, you're only five mo—"

"I'm aware of my status, Casper," I say quickly, cutting him off. "You in? I'll do it without you either way."

"Fine." He sighs. "I'll see you in twenty."

"Thanks."

I hang up and drive the rest of the way in silence, counting my breaths and working to loosen my grip on the wheel.

Fucking Lennon.

She better go back to Paris soon. I'm not going to be able to handle this much longer.

THREE

Lennon

I WATCH AS MACON DRIVES OFF IN MY DAD'S OLD 4RUNNER, the familiar taillights disappearing around the corner, long before my feet move from the spot where I'm frozen.

I vaguely remember Dad saying they had gotten a new car —something safer for the baby—but I didn't know he'd given the old one to Macon.

The realization makes me feel weird.

Jealous of the bond the two must have, one that I've obviously been oblivious to. Angry about how not five minutes earlier, Macon accused *me* of being a freeloader when *he's* the one driving off in a handout from *my* dad.

And... *warm*.

Strangely warm, in a way I can't understand. It feels like comfort. Like an ache I've harbored for the last four years has been soothed. I don't want my dad to be buddy-buddy with Macon.

But...

I'm glad someone, finally, is on his side.

I frown. Something about it doesn't make sense, but I can't pinpoint what.

Rarely does anyone speak to me about Macon. I shot down that topic of conversation pretty quickly in the beginning. I was told he'd enlisted in the Marines, only after he'd left on his first deployment.

Every mention after that was said as a peace offering. A subtle hint that it was safe to come home and visit if I wanted to.

I never wanted to.

It wasn't until Claire called a couple days ago that I was informed that Macon had been discharged.

Just so you know, she'd said, *he'll be here. He's home for good now. I don't want you to be blindsided.*

It was the first time in a long time I'd been grateful for Claire's interference.

"What the fuck was that?" Sam asks softly, making me jump. I didn't hear her climb out of the car.

I shrug, instead of answering. How can I when I don't know? My lip still tingles in the spot where he pressed his thumb.

He provoked me, and I let him. He wanted me angry, and I fell for it. Macon always has brought out the worst in me.

Astraea, he called me. And that ever-present smirk, like he's in on a secret joke with the universe, and I'm left on the outside, curious and confused.

For the briefest moment, I was pulled back to my previous life. Younger, and more naïve, and stupidly in love with a boy who broke me over and over again.

He was the boy who broke me, and I was the girl who let him, because I thought I could fix him.

I wasted a year and a half of my life mourning the loss of him, suffering in the damage of him. I spent the next year sifting through the wreckage, trying to find something worth saving.

But I pulled myself out of it. I built something beautiful

from the pain. I'm proud of what I've accomplished. I like who I am now.

I'm done sacrificing myself for someone who wouldn't do the same for me. I'll *never* make that mistake again.

He's also different, though.

He's gorgeous. He always has been, but it's cleaner now. More mature. His hair is shorter. I could tell from the way there was nothing curling out the sides of his backwards ball cap. His jaw is sharper and lined with stubble. The full sleeve of tattoos on his left arm didn't hide the fact that he's changed in other ways, too. He's larger. Harder. More sculpted. And even beyond the physical, something else about him feels different.

My heart and mind are racing.

"Ready to go?" Sam nudges my shoulder with hers, and I nod.

"Definitely."

I follow her to her car and climb into the passenger seat. I'm so fucking grateful she's here. She's always picking up my pieces, holding me together when she doesn't even realize it. I turn my head to tell her as much, but her furrowed brow halts my tongue.

"What?" I ask, even though I probably already know.

She gives me a sidelong glance and sighs.

"I'd be a shit friend if I didn't press the issue," she says. "You can always stay at my place. You don't even have to be around him if you don't want to. No sense in opening old wounds or whatever."

I huff out a hollow laugh. As if I'm worried about that happening.

Macon Davis is of no importance to me anymore. He's just some guy I used to know. My estranged stepbrother. An old relationship from an old life.

"It's fine. He doesn't live with Dad and Andrea, so I doubt

I'll see much of him," I reassure her. "And anyway, don't you have like some fancy-ass internship to get back to?"

Sam flashes me a sly grin and waggles her eyebrows.

"About that," she says slowly, keeping her eyes on the road as she drives me to the hospital. "I didn't want you to spend your birthday alone, so I might have played the whole 'daughter of a senator' nepotism card and got the entire month of July off."

"What? Really?" I turn toward her in my seat, and she laughs.

"Surprise, bitch! I had a place lined up in Paris and everything." She stops short and purses her lips. "Shit, I should probably cancel the reservation now."

"No," I say quickly. "Don't cancel it yet. I still don't know how long I'll be here. Once Dad wakes up, I'll head back to Paris. I've got too much work lined up. I can't stay gone long."

And I can't be *here* for my birthday. My mind won't stay quiet. My anxiety is heightened.

Sam hums but doesn't say anything. She understands. I'm sure she can imagine how much my skin is crawling. With each step out of June, my uneasiness grows.

I just need to get back to Paris.

Thankfully, Sam throws a new topic my way, and my chest tightens for a different reason.

"So, have you seen Evelyn?"

I purse my lips for a moment before responding.

"Yeah. She's afraid of me."

I sigh. Macon was right about one thing: it's my own fault. The way she clung to him in my presence made me want to cry. She feels safe around him, and I'm just a stranger.

"Well, maybe staying at Andrea and Trent's will give you some time to get to know her," Sam says, giving me hope. "She just needs to be around you some more. She'll warm up to you.

Babies are easy. Throw some snacks at it and wave some toys around, and you'll be the favorite in no time."

"Yeah, maybe."

Sam turns the radio back on and we finish the drive in silence. I'm in my head, and she lets me stay there, instinctively knowing what I need.

It was weird at first, my relationship with Sam. I'd never had a friendship that felt so natural.

I'd never felt like an equal with Claire. It was a one-sided relationship. I was always bending and compromising. I was subject to her whims, her emotions, and she never gave me space.

With Sam, it's the exact opposite. We accept each other. We don't try to make one another something we're not, and we fill in each other's cracks as needed.

I glance at her profile.

Her blonde hair is highlighted and styled to perfection. She's got black and gold Gucci sunglasses shading her eyes and diamond studs adorning her ears, and she's mouthing the words to the song playing through the speakers of her custom BMW coupe.

If you're going off appearance alone, you'd never guess that she's one of the most selfless, caring people I've ever met. She doesn't care at all about labels or material things; she's just playing a role until she doesn't have to anymore.

And that is why we click.

For years, I was the same. Playing the roles I was cast in just for the convenience of everyone else.

The *nice* girl. The *polite* girl. The *go with the flow to avoid confrontation* girl. The dutiful daughter. The supportive friend. The doormat girlfriend.

The day I decided to say *fuck it* and live only the life I chose, as the person I wanted to be, was liberating. I said goodbye to Lennon, hello to Capri, and no one in Europe knew me as anything different. I was able to cultivate an entirely new version of myself seamlessly, and it was exactly what I needed.

I want that so badly for Sam. I want her to shed the persona that's been forced onto her and finally show everyone the person she is on the inside.

Soon, she tells me.

And if I know her, I know she's going to say *fuck it* in an epic fashion.

FOUR

Lennon

England, 4 Years Earlier

AUNT BECCA AND I GET BACK TO HER HOUSE LATE.

We spent the whole day at Franco's. He gave me a welding lesson, then some friends of his and my aunt came by, and we made dinner. It was a nice day, marginally lightening the load of bricks that have been sitting on my chest for the past three weeks.

I reach up and run my hands through my now short hair. It's still jarring, and several times today, I almost regretted it. I almost unblocked everyone's numbers and sent more emails, too. I still might. I keep wavering between confident strength and fearful weakness.

I love my aunt Becca. I appreciate her friends. But in quiet moments like this one, where I'm left vulnerable to my own thoughts, my loneliness threatens to swallow me.

I'm so fucking scared.

I have no idea what I'm going to do, and I feel betrayed by everyone. Discarded. At a time when I should have the support of family, I've been cast aside in punishment for something I don't even fully understand.

My dad's anger, his reaction, was so out of character for him. In those moments before he dropped me off at the airport, he was nothing like the loving, caring father who raised me. He was agitated. Guilty. Uncertain and cold.

I dry myself off as I step out of the shower and wrap the towel around my body.

It's my second shower today. I might wake up in the middle of the night and take a third. Anything to calm the constant crawling of my skin and sate the constant desire to feel *clean* after weeks of filth. My body doesn't feel like my own, which makes it harder to be okay.

I'm pulling a pajama shirt over my head when my phone chimes from the app I use for international calls. My breath catches in my throat as I launch myself at my bed.

I've blocked everyone. Why is someone calling me?

It's a video call request, but I don't recognize the Caller ID. My fingers tremble as I accept the call.

Please be Macon. Please be Macon.

"Oh, thank GOD, you're alive," Sam yells from the other end. "I thought that bitch had you locked in the basement or something."

"What?" I breathe out a confused laugh. "Who?"

"Claire!" she exclaims. "You and Macon both just disappeared, and Claire wouldn't tell me shit. She's just being all smug and bitchy, so I threatened to fuck her up, and then I finally cornered your stepmom at her job and shook her down to tell me how to get ahold of you."

"Wait," I say quickly. "Macon's gone, too?"

"Gone. He's not with you?"

I shake my head slowly and force out the truth.

"I haven't heard from him since prom..." I whisper as tears

start to well in my eyes. "I can't call him. He won't return my emails. Claire said he was better off without me."

"That cunt," Sam says on a gasp, and I laugh even as I cry. "So, what happened? You're in England with your aunt? I thought you weren't leaving until after graduation. Are you coming back? Why the fuck didn't you tell me? I've been freaking out. And what the hell happened to your hair?"

I laugh again and swipe at my tears, then just stare at the screen. I don't even know where to begin, and that starts me crying all over again.

"Lennon, Jesus, what happened?" Sam whispers, and I shake my head.

"Sam... I fucked up. It's all so fucked up."

I cover my face with my hand and drown in the silence. Seconds tick by where she says nothing. The only noise is the faint sound of typing, and my sniffling and small, pathetic whimpers. I hate that I can't stop crying.

"Okay," she says suddenly. "I can be there tomorrow night. Let me talk to your aunt."

I drop my hand and stare at her, but she's not looking at me. Her face is illuminated by the screen of her laptop.

"What?"

She shuts her laptop and looks at me.

"Flight's booked, Len. Lemme talk to your aunt. I need to know if I can crash on her couch or if I have to find somewhere else to stay."

"Wait..." My brow furrows in confusion. "You're coming here? What about your dad? What about school?"

"Fuck my dad. And school is basically over. I've got the credits to graduate, and I was only going to walk because it's important for *optics*." She shrugs. "Let the senator spin it however he wants."

I open my mouth to tell her she doesn't have to come. To lie and say she doesn't have to worry about me, that I'm fine and will be okay, but I can't. When I speak, something entirely different falls from my lips.

"Thank you," I whisper, and she smiles softly.

"Lemme talk to your aunt, Lennon. I'll be there soon."

THE DOOR TO THE BATHROOM OPENS, LETTING IN A SMALL sliver of light from the other room, and Sam slips in.

I tried to be quiet. I didn't want to wake her.

She's been here a week, and I don't think she's gotten any sleep because of me.

She yawns and crosses the dark room, taking a seat next to me on the floor and moving the blanket draped over her shoulders, so it's covering me, too.

"Hey," she whispers, resting her head on my shoulder.

"Hey," I force out, my voice cracking from the sobs I was trying and failing to suppress.

"We're going to get through this, okay?"

Her words are so sure. I try to pull strength from them, but all I get is dead air. She wraps her arm around my torso and pulls me closer, embracing me tightly on the floor of my aunt's bathroom.

"I promise you. It's going to be alright."

Instead of responding, I fold my lips between my teeth and a new wave of tears start.

"I'm here for you," she soothes. "Me and Becca, we support you, okay? We love you. Whatever you decide, whenever you decide it, we're here for you one hundred percent."

I nod, and she hugs me tighter.

"Say you believe it, Len."

"I believe it."

"Good." She stands slowly, then reaches her hand out to

me. "Now let's go to your bed and spoon. Your aunt's couch is like sleeping on a fucking rock."

I snort out a laugh and put my hand in hers, letting her pull me to my feet.

"Thank you," I say, wiping my nose on the wad of tissue I've been clutching. She shakes her head and gives me a sad smile.

"You don't have to thank me for showing up, Lennon. I had a friend pull me up off the bathroom floor when I needed it. I'm glad to be that friend for you."

FIVE

Lennon

Present Day

"WE'RE HERE," SAM SAYS, ROUSING ME FROM MY PASSENGER seat nap.

I lift my head from the head rest and glance out the window. She's idling in front of the hospital entrance.

"Okay," I say quietly. She reaches over and grabs my hand, giving it a squeeze, and I send her a small smile. "Thanks for everything, Sam. Seriously."

"Psh." She waves me off with a grin. "I'll pick you up later? Just text, okay?"

I nod and give her a hug, then let myself out of the car, waving goodbye once more before stepping through the revolving doors and into the hospital lobby.

Just like last night, I make my way silently to the ICU. Every step is another rubber band around my chest, causing shallow breathing and a dull ache. I hum a Fleetwood Mac song to myself to try and keep from losing control.

I'm well-versed in anxiety. I know all the signs, know what to do to try and keep it from swallowing me whole. I'm not always successful. Sometimes I fall victim to my worries and fears. I hope this isn't one of those times.

I check in with the ICU desk. Show my ID, sign the sheet, and wash my hands. When the nurse buzzes me through the doors, I'm on my third loop through of "I Don't Want to Know," and I make myself stand just outside my dad's room until I can finish the song.

I don't want to know the reasons why.
Take a little time.
I don't want to know.

Then, I plaster on a smile I know he won't see, and I step through the door. The curtain is pulled shut, just like last time, and I slip through the opening and take a seat in the chair beside the bed.

"Good morning, Daddy." I force myself to smile, taking his limp hand in mine. "I don't know if you can hear me, or if you know I'm here." My words are mumbled and unsure. Awkward. "I'm not really sure what I'm supposed to do," I confess, "but I want to be around you. I hope that's okay."

I furrow my brow and try to push past the feeling that I'm talking to myself. Or worse. A corpse. I didn't really talk to him when I got here yesterday. I just cried, then fell asleep in the chair next to him. It's different now in the daylight. Everything feels more real, which is so much worse than the nightmare I was in last night.

The beeping of monitors is so constant and steady that it fades into the background, making my voice the loudest sound in the room. My heartbeat is the loudest one in my head, my thoughts a close second.

I haven't been the best daughter. I've barely seen my dad, a video chat maybe once a month. I've seen Andrea even less. I skip most holidays. I came back to Virginia for five days one month after Evelyn was born. Five days. I didn't even give him a week.

I take a deep breath and sit up straighter, keeping my eyes on our joined hands instead of his face or body.

"I saw Evie this morning," I continue, and I can't mask the sadness in my tone. "She's beautiful. And so big already." I pause and purse my lips before admitting, "and she's afraid of me."

I chew on the inside of my cheek as I relive this morning's encounter. See her tiny, chubby fingers grip on to Macon's shirt. Watch her whimper and hide her face in his chest.

"It's my own fault," I whisper. "Macon is right. I've only seen her once, and she was just an infant. Of course, she doesn't know me. But..."

I shrug and rub my thumb over the back of Dad's hand. It's colder than normal.

"I guess I didn't think it through. I wasn't thinking it would hurt. I don't know. I hate that she doesn't know me. Is she walking yet? I heard her say Mama."

My lips curve into a faint smile. Her little voice was so adorable. She was so happy. It was such a needed contrast to the gloom and doom that's clouding all of us right now. I wanted to go back into the kitchen just to hear it some more, to soak up more of her little baby magic, but I needed to get away from Macon, so I ran back upstairs to my old room.

"Andrea set me up in the guest room. It was nice of her. I was going to just stay at Sam's, but I'm glad I get to be around Evie and Andrea."

I take a deep breath.

I miss them.

I don't want to admit it, and when I'm busy in Paris with art and Franco and my new life, I can ignore it. I can almost forget another life existed at all before Paris. But here and now, I can't deny the longing in my chest. I miss them.

Being in my old room just makes it worse, which is one of the reasons I only stayed for five days last time. The purpose of the bedrooms has changed, but the feelings are still there. The memories are absorbed into the walls.

My old room is now the guest room, Macon's old room has been turned into Evie's nursery, and Claire's old room is Dad's office, which they put in once he retired from field service with the Navy. He still does something, some sort of government contract work, but none of us really know what.

"I brought us a book to read," I say, changing the subject. I drop his hand to pull the paperback out of my purse. "I got it from your bookshelf."

I study the book. It's worn, like it's been read before, probably more than once. I've never heard of it, but reading hasn't been one of my hobbies lately. I flip through the pages, finding a bookmark about halfway through.

"Oh...Do you want to just pick up where you left off?" I roll my eyes at myself, asking a comatose man a question. "Never mind. We'll start from the beginning."

I lay the book on the side of the bed and open it to the first page, making sure I can flip pages before taking his hand back in mine.

"Okay. I guess this is chapter one. You ready?" I pause a moment, then I start reading. "'What the? What about a teakettle?...'"

I'M AN HOUR INTO THE BOOK WHEN THERE'S A KNOCK ON THE doorframe.

I look toward the sound, but the curtain is still closed, so I can't see who is at the door. I pause my reading and stand.

"Yes?" I say, and I hear soft footsteps moments before the curtain is slowly pulled open, revealing two older men. Clipboards, white coats, slacks. Doctors? I give them a confused smile. "Hi."

"Ms. Washington?" one of them says. He's shorter and paler with graying hair. I nod.

"Yes, hi. Capri." I wince and shake my head slightly. "Well, Lennon, but I go by Capri."

"Nice to meet you. I'm Doctor Hendrick, the cardiologist working on your father's case. And this is Doctor Bashum. He's your dad's neurologist."

I cock my head to the side and turn my attention to the taller, darker man.

"Neurologist?" I ask, and he nods. "Why does he need a neurologist?"

"It's standard practice with patients like your father," he assures me. "Your father suffered a trauma, and it's my job to monitor his progress and assess when we can consider bringing him out of the coma."

"Okay." I suck my lip into my mouth and run my teeth over the soft skin.

"Can we speak to you a moment?" Doctor Hendrick asks. "We'd like to fill you in."

"Yes, definitely." I'm eager to know more and I'm sure it shows. "Please."

"How much has your mother told you?"

"Oh, um," I open my mouth to correct him, *step*mother, but I stop myself. It's not like it matters right now. "Not much. Just that three days ago he suffered a severe heart attack. He's in a medically-induced coma." I swallow hard. "We have to see what happens."

They both nod, then take turns explaining to me exactly what happened with my dad's heart. Words like *severe*, *cardiac arrest*, and *potential brain damage* mix together, causing my own chest to tighten and my head to fog.

They don't know what caused it. They've ruled out a brain bleed. There's no sign of chest trauma. He's healthy and active, blah blah blah.

"Now, generally after seventy-two hours, we can start to bring the patient out of their medical coma, but we've already spoken to Mrs. Washington, and we'd like to hold off for a bit longer," Dr. Hendrick says.

"Why?"

"Some of our tests have been inconclusive," Dr. Bashum says slowly, and my eyes widen.

"What? What does that mean? Is he not progressing? Is there brain damage? Is he going to die?"

My questions are rapid fire, my voice strangled, and I stare at the doctors' faces to try and read any sort of hint. Any sign. They give me nothing, and it makes me even more anxious.

"We're not saying any of that," one of them says. "It's too early to tell, which is why we'd like to wait until we can run a few more tests."

"Your father has the odds in his favor," the other says. I'm staring at my dad's chest through the panicked tears welling in my eyes. "He's young and healthy, and your brother started CPR within a minute of your dad's collapse."

My head jolts back.

"What?" I whisper, swinging my attention back to the man who was speaking. Doctor Bashum. He's blinking at me expectantly. "My brother?"

"Yes, your brother," Dr. Bashum repeats. "He was there with your father at the time of the incident. He started CPR and called emergency services immediately. The biggest factor in determining prognosis after a cardiac arrest is the time between the attack and when the patient receives medical care. Your brother resuscitated your father within minutes. Seconds, possibly. It saved his life."

The information hits hard. My mouth drops open and I finally let myself look at my dad's face. If I focus just on his eyes and forehead, I could almost believe he's simply sleeping. It would be like this never happened.

Macon saved my dad's life.

I clear my throat and say the first thing that comes to mind. "Stepbrother."

"Pardon?"

"Stepbrother," I repeat. "Macon Davis is my stepbrother."

SIX

Macon

"You sure you want to do this?" Casper calls from across the parking lot as I climb out of my car.

I nod and slip a cigarette between my lips. Casper cocks his head to the side.

"Thought you were quitting?" he asks, just as I light up and take a deep drag.

I laugh, blowing smoke out my nose.

"I'll try again after she leaves."

Just thinking about Lennon's blank expression pisses me off. She used to be filled with fire, and now she's ice.

You don't know anything about me anymore.

Ice and cruelty. But there's fire in there. I saw it, and just like before, I crave it.

Casper doesn't say anything else. I walk past him and head toward the building, and I hear him turn to follow me. I stop just outside the double doors, so I can take one last drag from my cigarette before stubbing it out on the brick wall and sliding it back into my pack, then I push through the doors and walk right past the office.

I should check the emails or the voicemail while I'm here, but I don't. I need to get in the ring before I fucking explode.

"Hey, I thought you were off today," Payton, one of the volunteers, says as I walk past.

"I am." I grin at her. "If you need something, figure it out yourself."

She laughs and shakes her head.

"How's Trent?" Her voice is softer this time, and I shrug.

"No real change," I tell her honestly. No news is better than bad news. "I'm heading over there in a bit. I'll report back when I know more."

Payton smiles and says she'll see me later, then disappears around a corner with one last lingering glance. Casper whistles low as he stares off down the hall, but I ignore him. Payton is attractive. Gorgeous, even. And she's made it more than obvious that she's into me. I choose not to feed into it.

Casper and I head into the gym and toward the locker rooms.

The rec center has changed a bit over the years. A real boxing ring has been installed, new equipment has been purchased, and several more art classes have been added. The volunteer staff has grown, too, and there's talk of building an addition in the next year or two.

One thing has stayed the same, though. It's still my refuge, has been even more so since I moved home for good five months ago.

We change quickly and I don't hold back my laugh when we walk to the ring. Casper is decked out—headgear, mouthguard, everything. If we had shin guards his size, he'd probably be in those, too, but all we have are youth sizes. I'm just wearing gym shorts and gloves, and the gloves are more a courtesy to him than they are for my comfort.

I need to feel it. All of it.

"Last chance to bow out," Casper says as we climb into the ring. "You're sure you're up for this?"

I nod as I stretch, grunting past the pain radiating up my leg.

"Don't go easy on me."

Casper sighs and mumbles something about how Nicolette is going to murder him. There's a slight possibly Nic might, but if he leaves me hanging, I definitely will.

I pound my gloves together twice and advance on him before he has a chance to change his mind. I get two body shots in before Casper can get a hit in, and when he does, it's obvious he's pulling punches.

I grunt in frustration then move toward a different strategy. I start tapping him, batting at the sides of his head with light, quick jabs just to annoy him. It works, and soon, he launches at me out of irritation.

"Fucker." He growls, hitting me with two jabs and a kick to the right side.

It's exhilarating. Each time a blow is landed, a little more of my tension burns away. I get lost in the dance, the game of guesswork and reading his body to anticipate the next punch or kick. I can taste the tang of blood when my lip splits, and my right cheek stings with the tell-tale signs of a bruise forming, but I welcome it all. This is what I wanted.

Mixed Martial Arts is something I picked up my first year in the Corps. I was angry, anxious, and trying desperately to cling to my newfound sobriety.

Trying and almost failing daily.

Then the Marine Corps Martial Arts Program gave me something else to focus on. An additional outlet. Something new to obsess over. I got good fast and even became an instructor before my plans were shot to hell. *Again.*

I haven't been able to go hard at this in months.

I couldn't, and then I wasn't allowed. Technically, I'm still not.

But fuck does it feel good to be back here without restrictions.

For a while, I pretend that my body is whole, that the aches and sharp pains are a result of the sparring match and not something entirely different. I forget about Lennon. I forget about my failures. I forget about the betrayals and disappointments.

Everything goes blank. It's just me, my opponent, and the ring.

Until, in the heat of the fight, Casper lands a blow to my left thigh and my vision goes black. I yell in agony and hit the mat with a fucking thud, clutching my leg to my chest.

"Shit." Casper drops to his knees next to me. "Fuck, shit, man. I'm sorry. What can I do? Shit."

I breathe through my nose and shake my head with my eyes clamped shut and my teeth gritted. The pain sets up a series of memories that I'd rather not see, and the sweat coating my skin from the workout turns ice cold.

Smoke and heat. Sand and blood. Fire. Gunshots.

Casper puts his hand on my shoulder, and I jump. I remind myself at the last second that it's him. I'm not in danger. I'm just an idiot.

The pain changes from stabbing to throbbing. It fucking hurts, but it's manageable. I open my eyes slowly and bring myself to a sitting position. I'm about to pull myself to standing when the gym doors open behind me.

Casper's eyes jump over my shoulder, then he drops his head back and whispers *fuck* at the ceiling.

I drop my chin to my chest. Fuck is right.

"What the hell are you idiots doing?" Nicolette shouts from beside the ring. I can hear the anger in her voice. "Have you lost your ever-loving mind?"

I hear the ropes shake and feel her approach, then she drops down on my other side. I hear a sharp smack and Casper grunts, then I feel her hands on my leg.

I open my eyes and watch as she gently prods and massages the muscles in my thigh, feeling along the scar that runs up the side. I breathe through my nose, anticipating the pain.

"You let him do this?" she scolds Casper. "What the fuck, Chris?"

"Sorry." He sighs and shoots me a glare.

"It's not his fault," I tell Nic, and she punches me in the arm.

"No shit." She narrows her eyes at me, scolding. "You're not ready for this yet, Macon. You're only cleared for stationary activities. Controlled exercises. You know MMA is too unpredictable. You're lucky you didn't reinjure yourself."

I drop myself down on the mat and bring my hands to my head, tugging a bit on my hair. I need to cut it. It's getting too long.

"Just give me some ibuprofen," I say, defeated. "I'll ice it and be fine."

Nic maneuvers my leg, so it's straight, then she lifts it and bends it at the knee, gently pushing it side to side. It hurts, but not in a *reinjured* kind of way. Just in an *I made a fucking dumb decision* kind of way. I got something out of this, at least. Pain.

"Up," Nic commands, and I roll to my side and slowly push myself to standing. "Walk."

I do as she says, walking from one end of the ring and back. I grit my teeth against the soreness, the ache more pronounced but not new. When she's satisfied that I didn't re-fuck my femur, she nods and stands.

"You're an idiot." She points at me, then swings her finger to point at Casper. "You're an enabler. You're both on my shit list."

She folds her arms across her chest, glaring at us with dark brown, angry eyes. Nic's eyes are so brown that sometimes they look black, and right now, under the gym fluorescents, with her light blonde hair and intimidating scowl, she could definitely pass as some sort of vengeful fallen angel.

I lean back on the ropes, fold my arms across my chest to mirror her stance, and flash her a grin.

"You still love me," I say smugly, and she rolls her eyes, completely unamused.

"Quit doing dumb shit, Macon," she says on a sigh. "Go throw a bowl or something, and I'll see you tonight."

Without another word, Nic turns and leaves the way she came. I don't know why she's here, but if she told me to work the wheel, then she's probably not going to my apartment upstairs. Everyone knows I like to be alone when I create. I've only been able to tolerate one person in my space while I throw or sketch, and that person might as well be dead to me.

The thought pisses me off again, and all the tension that I bled out while fighting comes back tenfold.

Capri.

What a mother-fucking joke.

"Thanks for your help," I say to Casper as I climb out of the ring. "See you later."

I make my way out of the gym, down the hall, and up the stairs that lead to my apartment, trying my best to keep my gait even. My body wants to limp, but I force myself to take even, balanced strides. It hurts, but it's a pain that I'm proud of.

I unlock my door and walk into my apartment, taking off my shoes and kicking the door shut behind me. I go to my bedroom and down four more ibuprofen, then pull off my shirt and pants, so I'm standing in just a pair of boxer briefs. I fold the clothes and set them neatly on my made bed.

I turn and look at myself in the full-length mirror on the wall, running my hand down my abs then twisting to see the definition that's returning to my thighs. I'm finally starting to tone back up.

The tattoos on my chest and arms no longer look misplaced, like someone took my art and put it on someone else's skin. It's crazy how quickly muscle deteriorates when you're forced to be inactive for an extended period of time.

I run my eyes down the long, angry scar on my left thigh, and on instinct, the scar on my left wrist aches. I don't know what it is about my left side, but it seems to take the bulk of my abuse. The wrist, the leg, the sleeve of tattoos.

The heart.

I scan my face, taking note of the swollen, split lip and bruised cheek, then run my fingers through my hair and remind myself again to get it cut tomorrow. I put on my standard throwing attire—a tattered pair of jeans and an old band tee with the sleeves ripped off—and make my way to my studio.

When James and Hank decided to renovate part of the upper level of the rec center and turn it into an apartment, they chose to put the primary bedroom in a corner of the space with two walls of large windows.

When I moved in, I made the guest bedroom the primary bedroom and turned the primary bedroom into a studio. It's a little big for what I need it for—a couple work tables, my pottery wheel, and a single desk for sketching—but the natural light is unmatched, and the closet is the perfect storage room.

When I walk in, I don't even have to flip on the light because the summer sun is shining brightly through the windows. I grab a block of clay from the closet, glancing briefly at the pieces in various stages of completeness lining the shelves along the wall. Some are ready to ship, some are still drying, and some need to be brought downstairs to start the firing process.

It would be convenient to have a kiln of my own in the

studio, but for now, I don't mind using the rec center's kiln. Besides, the stairs are good for my rehab.

I choose a playlist from my phone, setting it to stream through the Bluetooth speaker. It's a compilation of indie folk-pop songs, and I choose not to acknowledge why, of all the playlists I've made, I selected this one.

I go about setting up my wheel, filling two buckets with water from the attached bathroom and laying out my basic tools, before finally taking a seat on my stool behind it. I stretch my left leg out and back a few times, getting it used to the sitting position, then I slam the clay onto the surface of my wheel and start to throw.

SEVEN

Macon

It's 12:30 when I park my car in the hospital visitors' lot.

I was so caught up with the wheel that I didn't stop until quarter to noon, so I didn't have time to shower. I just washed the clay off my arms and changed before rushing here.

My window to see Trent is a small one. Lennon was here this morning and Mom will be here this afternoon. I just want to be able to pop in and check on him. I've been reading article after article about heart attack recovery, but none of it really matters until we know more about his case.

I climb out of my car, lock the door, and make the walk up to the ICU on autopilot. It's only been a few days, but I feel like I've been making this trip every day of my life.

When I get to the desk where I'm supposed to sign in, the nurse tells me that I have to wait. Someone else is back there. I want to ask who, but I know already.

I check the clock. Nearly one. I forgot to eat. I'm debating running down to the hospital cafeteria to grab a sandwich when the door lock behind me buzzes, and I turn to watch as it opens and reveals Lennon behind it. She startles when she sees me standing here, but her feet carry her in my direction, and she stops a little more than an arm's length in front of me.

Her face is red, her eyes swollen. She's been crying. My heart fucking cracks. This has to be so fucking difficult for her. She already lost her mom, and now this?

"Hey," I say softly, then nod to the doors behind her. "I was just coming to see him, but I can come back if you need more time."

She shakes her head, her brows scrunched in the middle.

"No. He's not in there. They took him for some scans or something."

"Oh." I shove my hands in my pockets to keep them under control. "You know how long?"

She shakes her head again. "They said it could be a while."

"Okay," I say slowly, taking a step back.

I should turn and leave, but something about the way she's watching me makes me want to stay. The icy demeanor from earlier is gone, and It's addicting. I linger, keeping my gaze locked with hers.

I open my mouth, then shut it, because what do I fucking say? I don't want to risk interrupting this moment. I'd stand here locked in this stare off forever, if it meant I got to keep her like this. Not cold and detached. Not blank. *Real.*

Here in the hospital, the betrayal and heartache seem to pale in comparison to all the other shit we're dealing with, and the only way Lennon and I can exist in the same space is if our past is minimized to something tolerable. Forgettable, even.

Anything more, and we're match-lit gasoline.

The energy between us is so palpable. We're either going to murder one another or fuck each other senseless.

And then probably murder each other.

"Thank you," she says, finally breaking the silence.

It's whispered and her voice cracks. I furrow my brow, confused, and she smiles the smallest, saddest smile.

"Thank you for saving him."

It makes sense, then, so I smile back.

"I had to pay it forward."

I mean it as a joke, but her face falls immediately, and I regret it. I know how fucking terrifying it was for me when Trent collapsed. I never should have brought up the night of my overdose.

I close my eyes.

"I'm sorry. I shouldn't have s—"

My words are cut off when familiar arms wrap around my waist.

My eyes fly open, and I freeze, stunned, for one breath, then two, before I slowly bring my arms out so I can return the hug.

It's not awkward. Not even for a second. She fits between my arms, against my body, like she was meant to be there.

I inhale deeply through my nose, breathing in vanilla, and try to shake how wrong the scent is. The body feels right, and I let myself rest my cheek on her head. It takes all my strength not to bury my face in her hair.

"He'll pull through," I say against her, repeating the words I've said to my mom a thousand times since Trent's collapse. I don't even know if I believe them, but I keep saying them. "He's going to be okay."

When she drops her arms and steps back, my heart sinks. I fist my hands to keep from tugging her back against me.

"If he's okay, it's because of you." She runs her fingers under her eyes to wipe away the tears. "Thank you."

I nod, but keep my mouth shut.

Her attention drops to the bruise on my cheek, then my split lip, but she doesn't ask what happened. Just furrows her brow.

Then she fixes her eyes on my jaw, and her lips quirk to the side.

"You, um..." She reaches out like she's going to touch me again before letting her hand drop back to her side. "You've got something on your face."

I brush my fingers over my stubble and find a spot of dry, matted clay. I laugh.

"Clay," I say, and she smiles.

"You still do that?"

She tilts her head to the side, and the way her hazel eyes have brightened heats my blood. I can't form words, so instead, I nod again.

Her phone vibrates and she pulls it out of her back pocket to check it.

"My ride is here. I guess I'll see you..."

"See you later, Lennon," I say with a smirk, and her lips turn down.

"It's Capri now, Macon," she states.

I pop an eyebrow and cock my head.

"Sure it is."

Her nostrils flare, and I wait to see if she'll say something else. Anything. She doesn't. She pushes past me without another word, but not before I catch the way her hand balls into a tight fist at her side.

I bet her teeth are gritted, too.

There you are, Lennon. There you fucking are.

EIGHT

Lennon

Sam drops me off at my dad's house with the promise to be back in a few hours to take me to the rental car place, since she's got to go back to DC tomorrow. I told her I could ask Andrea for a ride, but Sam insists on driving me.

There are still two weeks left of June, which means two more weeks of internship until she's off for a whole month. With any luck, my dad will wake up soon, and Sam and I will be on a plane to Paris at the end of those two weeks.

I'll be back on French soil by July, and spending my birthday in Paris where I belong.

My brow furrows, feeling guilty for being here while also feeling guilty for wanting to leave. When I think of all the work I'm unable to complete while I'm here, my anxiety spikes. When I think of prioritizing work over the health of my father, it spikes further.

And when I think of my emotional well-being...

Walking through the front door, a crying baby and the smell of burnt food pull me from my inner turmoil.

"Andrea?" I call as I hurry toward the kitchen.

The crying grows louder, the smell intensifies, and the air is laced with dark smoke.

"It's okay," Andrea says, and when I step into the kitchen, I find her fanning the smoke detector with a dishtowel with one hand and clinging to a screaming Evelyn with the other.

"Shit, let me help."

I rush to her and take the dishtowel.

"Thank you," she says, then turns to open the window above the sink. I watch her, noticing a pan of charred pasta and tears on Andrea's face.

"Sorry," she whispers to Evie, rocking her from side to side and holding her carefully against her chest. "I'm sorry for scaring you."

I look away. It feels like an intrusion, so I turn my attention back to fanning the silent smoke detector. I make a mental note to check the battery later. With this amount of smoke, it should definitely be making some racket.

"You can probably stop that now," Andrea says, so I give her a tight-lipped smile and stop fanning, lowering my arms to fold the towel and set it back on the counter. "I, um, just got distracted."

"Yeah." I glance at the pan of burnt pasta. "You want me to make something so you can..." I gesture to Evie, who is still crying. Andrea nods with a wince and a forced smile.

"Would you? I was throwing some spaghetti together for her, but that's the last of the noodles. I just realized I forgot to grocery shop."

She laughs lightly at herself, but it's humorless and tired, like she's laughing to keep from crying again. She sways and pats Evie's back as she talks over the sounds of the baby's cries.

"If you could just heat up some of the veggies in the fridge, there's some microwavable toddler meals I can give her to tide her over until I can get to the store."

"Sure," I say, moving toward the fridge. Andrea takes Evelyn into the other room while I pull out the vegetables and something that looks like a TV dinner for babies.

"If you make me a list, I can get the groceries for you," I call out to her as I follow the directions on the package, popping the little baby meal into the microwave, punching in thirty seconds, and hitting start. "It's no problem."

"Are you sure?" Her voice is softer now that the crying has stopped, and I round the corner into the living room to find her sitting on the couch breastfeeding Evelyn. "I don't want to trouble you."

The way she's tiptoeing around me churns the guilt in my stomach. Would she be this way with Macon or Claire, or would she send them to the store with a grocery list without a second thought?

"I don't mind. I need to get some stuff anyway," I say honestly. "Shampoo and bodywash and stuff. I couldn't bring everything I needed in my carry-on." I sit lightly on the arm of the couch. "I'll have to take your car, if that's okay? But I really don't mind."

"Yes, of course that's okay." The genuine relief in her voice makes my eyes sting. "Bring me the pen and pad of paper from the kitchen counter. I've got a list already started. I'll just finish it off for you."

I wait while Andrea scrawls a few more things on the list and hands it to me. Evelyn looks like she's falling asleep, which means she probably won't even eat the food I heated up for her.

"Keys are hanging by the door, and my credit card is in my purse."

I nod, wave awkwardly, then head toward the door, grabbing the keys but leaving Andrea's card untouched. Dad's keys are hanging on the hook next to Andrea's and seeing them makes me want to cry. His car is sitting in the garage, untouched, waiting for him to come home. I bet it still smells like him. It's only been a few days.

The urge to ask if I can drive Dad's car is strong, but I hold back. It's just a car. It's not him, and it's not like he's dead.

Not yet, a small voice whispers.

I shake my head and squeeze my eyes shut in an effort to ignore that voice. We don't know anything, yet. Dad could be fine. He could have minimal-to-no-long-term damage.

We just have to wait and see.

I climb into Andrea's car, bring the seat back because she's 5'4" and I'm 5'9", and then I turn the car on and back out of the drive. The trip to the store seems to take longer than it used to. I find myself spending most of the drive scanning the houses, buildings, and trees to see how everything has changed. When I pass by the Franklin Youth Recreational Center, a deep pit forms in my stomach and my hands itch with the urge to turn the car around.

I don't.

I pass the rec center and drive right to the grocery store. It's not until after I've parked that I decide to walk the few blocks down the street back toward the center.

It's a hot, sticky June day, so by the time I reach the familiar brick building, my face and body are dotted with sweat. The air conditioning offers a welcomed chill when I push through the doors.

I poke my head inside the office to see if I can find James, but he's not there. The place looks tidier than I remember it being in high school. The lonely fern is gone, too. I walk out of the office and wander, taking note of all the improvements and additions that have been made since I was last here.

Everything looks brighter, like the paint on the walls has been freshened up, and there are pictures framed everywhere.

One in particular catches my eye, and I find myself staring at a photograph of Macon wearing the Marine Corps dress blues, standing between James and Hank.

He looks so different.

He's bigger in this photo, almost larger than life. A result of the uniform, perhaps. His hair is buzzed short under his white hat, his shoes shined and his clothing wrinkle-free. He's even standing straight, with his shoulders wide and his strong chest puffed out with pride. I've never seen him stand so straight—Macon was always a sloucher—but the crooked smile is all him. The mischievous glint in his eyes is there, too. I want to reach out and touch the photograph. I want to see if his clean-shaven face is as smooth as it looks. If his lips are still as soft as I remember.

The photo is older, from probably two or three years ago, before Macon was discharged. I wonder what the Macon in the photograph was like. I wonder if I would have felt the same about him. I wonder, had I come back sooner, if this Macon and I could have had a chance.

I scoff at myself.

It wouldn't matter.

This Macon is still the same Macon who abandoned me. Cleaning him up and putting him in a starched uniform doesn't erase the damage done.

I turn from the photograph and continue to wander the halls.

There's a boxing ring in the gym that I don't remember, and new retractable divider walls to separate the two halves of the basketball court, too. When I turn down another hallway, my heart starts to thud faster. Excitement, fear. I can't help but feel like I'm doing something I shouldn't.

I'm just looking for James. That's all.

I repeat that lie as I turn a doorknob and step into a room I haven't seen in years. It smells of clay, and the sight of pottery wheels fills me with adrenaline. There used to only be a handful of wheels for the pottery classes, but the number has more than doubled now. I can't know for sure, but the wheel at the front looks the same. It could be the one Macon used when he taught here.

I head toward the wheel, noting the old boom box sitting on a table next to it, but stop in my tracks when I see several pieces of pottery on shelves in the back of the room by a kiln. I walk toward them quickly. I might even run. I'm in such a daze, I can't tell.

Vases, bowls, mugs, a wine decanter, something that looks like a lantern.

Some pieces have been painted and are waiting for glaze, some have been fired only once. I pick up one of the vases to admire it. It's absolutely beautiful. I want to flip it upside down to look for the initials of the person who made it, but I can't. Can't or won't, I'm not sure.

Macon did say he still worked with clay.

This could be his.

Something here could have been made by him.

I'm working up the courage to turn the vase over when the door behind me opens, startling me, and I almost drop the vase.

"Can I help you?" a woman says as I whip around to face her. She eyes me suspiciously. "There aren't any more pottery classes today."

I put the vase down softly and step away. The woman looks to be about my age. Early twenties, probably. And she's pretty. Very pretty. Even in faded jeans and a blue shirt with **VOLUNTEER** printed across the front, she looks like she could be in a magazine. Her makeup is flawlessly applied, her caramel hair curled into perfect beach waves down her back. I give her a small smile.

"Sorry," I say quickly. "I was just looking around. I was looking for James."

The woman raises an eyebrow.

"James?"

"James Billings. The owner? I used to volunteer here. I wanted to say hello."

"Oh," she says, cocking her head to the side. "James and his husband are in Massachusetts, now. He doesn't own the rec center anymore."

"Huh." I wait for her to elaborate, but she doesn't. She just flicks her eyes from me to the pieces of pottery and back. "These are gorgeous," I say. "Who did you say teaches the pottery classes?"

"I didn't." Something in her tone makes me stand up taller. I narrow my eyes, telling her that I'm not one to sit back and take unwarranted bitchy attitudes from strangers. Not anymore. She's going to get back exactly what she puts out. I hold her gaze and watch as she starts to back down.

"We have three instructors," she finally says, and I take pride in the way I've unnerved her. "Payton, that's me—" she points to herself—"then Adam. He does most evening classes."

I hold my breath and wait for her to reveal the third instructor, letting it out slowly when the name she states isn't Macon's. I don't even register what the name is, just that it's not Macon Davis.

"—she does the afternoon and weekend classes with me."

I smile to hide just how frazzled I feel and keep my voice even.

"Thank you. I guess I should be going, then."

She moves out of the way and lets me pass, then trails me silently the entire walk to the front entrance. Just before I push through the doors to head out to the parking lot, her voice stops me.

"What did you say your name was?"

The question gives me chills. I turn around and flash her another smile. She's studying me like one might study flesh-eating bacteria under a microscope. With wary interest, but not fondness.

"I didn't," I say sweetly, then I push through the doors and walk back to the grocery store.

NINE

Lennon

It takes me an hour to complete the shopping because everything in the store has been moved around since I was last here.

It's been four years, but it feels like an entirely different grocery store. I give up trying to snag things by memory and end up going up and down the aisles one by one, until I've gotten everything Andrea wrote down.

I load the bags into the car and make the quick drive back to the house. When I walk in the front door with the first load of bags, I notice the silence and decide not to announce my arrival just in case Evie is asleep.

I make two more trips to the car, then put away all the fridge and freezer items. Then I work to put away the rest of the stuff. Most of the cabinets are the same. Pantry items, canned foods, paper products.

I move through the kitchen on autopilot, remembering drawers and cabinets I haven't opened in years. It's the weirdest feeling of nostalgia, knowing exactly where the spaghetti noodles are kept.

When I'm finished, I quietly head toward the living room.

"Andrea?" I whisper, not wanting to wake the baby, but also not wanting to scare anyone. "Andrea, I'm back."

I hear deep breathing, so I tiptoe around the couch, expecting to find that Andrea had fallen asleep with Evie, but instead, I find Macon, and I'm momentarily frozen in place.

He's asleep, sprawled across the cushions with his head on the arm of the couch and one leg on the floor, and he has baby Evelyn curled up on his chest like a little kitten. One of his big hands, the left one that's covered in tattoos, is resting protectively on her back while the other is bent up and propped beneath his head.

This scene. This sight.

It will haunt me.

Everything about it fills me with guilt and longing.

Even the rose tattoo on the back of his hand, inked with dark reds and deep greens in a fashion that almost resembles a watercolor painting, makes my eyes mist. The thorny vine that extends from the rose and wraps around his wrist is such a direct contrast to the way he's cradling that baby. Evie sleeps so soundly, without a single care or worry. She's safe and warm and loved.

And Macon is the one keeping her safe. Macon is the one loving her.

I bring my hand to my mouth, silencing the whimper that wants to escape, and slowly, I begin to take steps backward. His phone starts flashing on the coffee table, then, silently alerting him to a call that he will miss, and my eyes fall to the screen.

"Nicolette" is calling, and according to the contact picture on display, she's a Barbie-esque blonde in a tank top and joggers.

I bristle with jealousy. I wouldn't peg her as Macon's type, but—I glance away from the phone and back at him—I guess I don't really know him anymore.

The phone stops flashing, then starts again seconds later.

She's persistent. I wonder if he's blowing her off.

I roll my eyes and turn away, heading back toward the front door.

If Macon is blowing Nicolette off to snuggle with his sleepy, 10-month-old half-sister, she should consider herself lucky. He could be high and making out with someone else in the passenger seat of a sports car.

But I guess I'm the only one who got to experience that version of Macon.

And for better or worse, I can't decide how I feel about it.

"Where's the Wicked Bitch of the Eastern Seaboard?" Sam asks randomly as I climb into her car.

After sneaking out of Andrea's house, I walked to a downtown coffee shop and got an iced latte. I was hot, sweaty, and emotional. None of which makes me a very pleasant person to be around.

I let myself cool off in a corner, sipping on my caffeine, before finally texting Sam an S.O.S. I need to go get my rental car soon, anyway, and I told her we'd grab dinner together.

I shrug as I buckle my seat belt.

"I don't know. I haven't asked. My guess is in Richmond on campus."

"It's a *Sunday*, and it's *June*," she says, pulling out of the parking lot. "What the fuck is more important on campus on a Sunday in June than your comatose stepfather, who paid for your tuition? Didn't she just graduate?"

I shrug again and look out the window.

I know Claire was here the day Dad was admitted into the hospital. When she called me, I could hear Andrea crying in the background. I don't know how long she stayed, or why she isn't here now, but I haven't given it much thought, and I sure as shit haven't asked. I sigh and roll my head toward Sam.

"Honestly? I'm glad she's not here. I need a little more time to adjust."

"I get that. This is overwhelming enough as it is, and she's an ominous dark cloud."

Nailed it.

Sam and I pick up the keys to my rental car, then we drive to a nearby restaurant to grab some dinner.

We keep the conversation light. She tells me more about her internship. I talk about the commissioned pieces I have lined up and what I'm working on right now. She asks about Franco, I ask about her current love interest, and we end the evening with a long hug and a promise to talk in a few days.

She's driving back to D.C. tonight because her mom randomly decided to come back to town. Her flight lands first thing in the morning, and Sam wants to miss her. Of all her family members, Mrs. Harper is easily the least smarmy, but I don't blame Sam for wanting to avoid her.

Her mom might not have been the one causing the problems, but she's also never done anything to stop them from happening. In my opinion, that makes the senator's wife just as bad as the senator.

It's only nine when I get back to Andrea's house, but I manage to sneak up to the guest bedroom without being seen.

I might be stuck in Virginia, but my life can't stop.

I have emails to send, client inquiries to respond to. I closed my commissions before I got on the plane, but I've still received several emails a day asking about them.

I've been considering hiring a part-time personal assistant or looking into getting an agent. I don't really need help selling my work but having someone to help answer these emails and handle the contracts and invoices would be nice.

I check my website traffic. It's kicked up an insane amount

since my latest gallery show. Franco jokes that I should pay someone to give it a makeover now that I'm making money, but I'm proud of my little DIY online gallery. I taught myself basic coding to build it, and while it's not flashy or complex, it gets the job done. It's simple and humble, and I personally think it puts my pieces center stage. My paintings don't need flashy web-design to shine. They do that on their own.

I've started doing a weekly blog about technique and my creative process, and I'll have to draft a few blog posts soon, but I'm just too exhausted to do it now. If I look at the computer screen for any longer, my eyes might actually shrivel up like raisins and fall out of my head.

I send Franco a message filling him in on everything, then I shower and pass out with wet hair all before eleven.

My first full day back, and it's exhausted me in every possible way. My arms and legs ache. My mind is in a fog. I wake up crying twice in a cold sweat, chased in nightmares by demons I can't exorcise. I haven't cried over any of it in a long time. I thought that meant I'd healed.

But everything is made worse in this room.

Everything is made worse in this town, around these people.

My hand rubs at the small scars on my thigh, healed now, but forever reminding me of just how low I can fall.

I don't know how I'm going to last much longer.

TEN
Macon

I WORK THE MORNING AT THE REC CENTER.

I'm still technically "off" for a family emergency, but since I live upstairs, it's easy to do paperwork and schedules when I'm not at the hospital or watching Evelyn. I don't sleep well most nights, anyway, so work and pottery make for good distractions.

I'm finishing up the volunteer schedules for the first two weeks of July when there's a knock followed by the slow opening of my office door.

"Hey," Payton says brightly, stepping into the room with a smile. "You busy?"

"Just finished up the schedule, actually," I tell her, clicking out of the online program I use. "What's up? I already scheduled you all day on the 4th so you can't ask for it off now."

I'm smiling, but I'm serious. Payton is one of our best volunteers. The kids and parents love her, and she can teach almost anything. No way we can get through the 4th of July Fun Day without her.

"I'm excited for the 4th," she says with a laugh. "No worries."

"Good, because I've got you in charge of the water games. You're the only one who can handle the middle schoolers."

Payton rolls her eyes playfully, a tint of pink showing on her cheeks. We're dangerously approaching flirt territory.

"So, what's up, then, Payton?" I say, changing my tone to something more professional.

"Well, I wanted to let you know that someone came by yesterday," she says slowly, and the way she's studying me sets my teeth on edge. Is she trying to read my body language? Does she want to see how I'll react? "They were looking for James."

"Okay." I raise one brow and fold my arms across my chest. "And did you tell them that James is in Massachusetts?"

"I did." She nods, then purses her lips. "But she said she used to volunteer here."

My back goes ramrod straight, but I fight to keep my face blank and my voice calm.

"She? Did *she* give her name?"

"No," Payton says, shaking her head. "But she looked to be about our age. She probably would have volunteered with you, but she didn't ask about you at all." She shrugs, trying to mask her interest and failing. "And she kind of looked like the woman in yo—"

"Okay," I say, cutting her off, "thanks for letting me know. Anything else?"

"No, not really," she says with a confused smile. "Just that, when I found her, she was poking around in the ceramics room. She was touching all the vases and stuff in the back."

My composure slips, then. My eyes widen and my body goes stiff.

"Do you know if she went anywhere else? Maybe down to any of the other art rooms?"

"I don't know," Payton says slowly. "I don't think so? She left through the front doors after I caught her with the vase."

"Okay." I nod. "Okay, good." I'm already moving past Payton and toward the door, with one foot in the hallway, when I turn and face her. "Payton, did you happen to tell this woman who the owner is?"

"No..." She cocks her head to the side and watches me warily.

I flash her my best, most charming smile and her shoulders loosen immediately.

"Thanks, P. I'll see you tomorrow. And if you need anything while I'm gone..."

"...figure it out myself," she finishes with a laugh. "Hey wait! You still coming out for my birthday?"

I wave over my shoulder. "I wouldn't miss it!"

I hear her giggle. I don't turn around to wave goodbye or see her smile, though. I just walk as fast as I can without all out running to the last room at the end of the arts hall. The one with all the easels and paints. The Lennon Room.

That was a close fucking call.

I'm not ready to reveal my cards, yet. I don't know if I'll ever be.

I SHOW UP TO MOM'S IN THE AFTERNOON.

This has become our routine. I go spend an hour or two with Trent in the morning, then swing by the house to watch Evie, so Mom can spend the rest of the day at the hospital. I'm not sure how much longer she'll be able to stay off work, so as long as Trent is still hospitalized, I want her to have as much time with him as possible.

This whole situation fucking sucks.

When I stopped by to see Trent this morning, there were flowers and a book on the table that weren't there yesterday. *Lennon.* I was hoping she'd already been by, and those were my signs that she had.

I recognized the book, too, because it's mine. I've read it probably five times, and I accidentally left it at the house last time I was watching Evelyn.

I don't know what compelled Lennon to pick it up and bring it to the hospital but knowing she's reading it makes me feel a little lighter. A bit more connected to her than I was yesterday. It shouldn't feel as good as it does.

I park my car at the curb, noting an unfamiliar red CR-V with Louisiana plates in the driveway. It must be Lennon's rental. I hop out and walk by it slowly, peeking in the windows. No personality. No signs of life. Yep, it's definitely a rental.

I head to the house and let myself in without knocking, kicking my shoes off on the mat.

"Mom," I call into the house, heading toward the kitchen. "I'm here."

"She's in the shower," a voice says from the living room.

My nerves spike because I'm an idiot. I knew Lennon would be here. I knew I would probably see her, even though she did a great job of evading me yesterday. I don't know why my fucking body still decides to react this way.

Calm the fuck down.

I take a second to get my shit together, then walk into the living room. Lennon is sitting on the floor with Evie, and they're taking turns stacking blocks. From the looks of it, Evie's not afraid of Lennon anymore, and Lennon is loving it.

"She's warmed up to you," I observe, leaning on the wall and shoving my hands in my pockets.

"Yeah." Lennon says with a small laugh. "It didn't take too long, really. I just had to give her some snackies."

Her laughter makes my smile grow, and I can't seem to take my eyes off her.

"She does love snacks."

Lennon smiles at Evie and tickles her belly.

"A girl after my own heart," she says, making Evie giggle. "Must run in the family."

The last statement turns my lips downward, so I change the subject.

"I hear you were at the rec center yesterday." Her back straightens in a way that tells me she didn't think I'd find out. "Payton told me when I went in this morning to make the schedules."

"Oh," she says, focusing way more attention than necessary on the blocks. "You still work there?"

"I make the schedules and do some paperwork. Office stuff."

Lennon nods and flicks her eyes from the blocks to my face and back.

"The place looks good. I love the pictures on the walls. And I saw they added a boxing ring and some more pottery wheels."

I wait to see if she'll say anything else. If she'll admit to seeing anything else, but she doesn't.

"Yeah," I say after a moment, "I guess there is talk of an expansion, too. Maybe putting in a pool."

"Oh wow." She looks at me with a smile that threatens to knock me on my ass. "That's amazing. The kids will love it."

I don't even try to hide my pride.

"I think so. Since the town is growing, it only makes sense that the center grows, too." I take a subtle deep breath before asking the question that's causing anxiety to build in my chest. "Did you happen to see anything else? Check out any other rooms or anything?"

The wait between the end of my question and her answer feels like hours, when it's actually only a few seconds. Just enough time to stack two blocks.

"Oh, no," she says dismissively. "Payton kinda crashed my

party, and I felt like I needed to leave." She glances up at me. "Sorry, you know, if I wasn't supposed to be in there."

I shake my head and smirk.

"It's fine, Len. You're welcome to go by anytime. I don't think our art rooms are going to quite live up to your standards, but you're welcome to use those while you're here, too."

She opens her mouth, then shuts it. I watch her draw her lower lip between her teeth, and I wait for her to say something, anything. I don't even know what I want to hear from her, I just know that I like talking to her in this way. Where our defenses are down and we're not at each other's throats.

In this conversation, we could easily pass for two old friends catching up.

So, I wait for more. One inhale and exhale, then two. Then three. Evie pulls herself to standing by the couch as Lennon finally speaks up.

"Macon," she says with a sigh, just as Evie takes one hand off the couch and starts to move her leg, "I go b—"

"Nope!" I cut Lennon off when I jump past her and nudge Evelyn with my foot, pushing her back onto her diapered butt. Evelyn laughs and I waggle my finger at her. "None of that."

Lennon gasps, eyes wide with disbelief.

"Did you just kick her?"

"No, I didn't *kick* her," I say with a laugh, bending low and scooping Evie up. "I *gently* discouraged her from accomplishing any big milestones today."

Evelyn pats her hands on my face and slobbers up my cheek while Lennon watches, her head cocked to the side, her brow furrowed. I can tell from her expression that seeing Evie with me makes her feel *something*.

Jealousy, maybe.

I'd be lying if that didn't bring me a little bit of joy. That's what she gets for fucking off to France, instead of coming back home like she was supposed to.

"Why would you do that?" she asks finally, and I force myself to smile, making light of an otherwise difficult topic.

"The squirt's been trying to walk," I explain, pressing a kiss to Evie's forehead before plopping her into her little 360-degree play center. She loves that fucking thing. It's got a bunch of rattles and activity toy things, and she can stand and spin and bounce without the threat of taking any first steps.

I grab a tissue from the box on the coffee table to wipe the slobber off my face, then turn back to Lennon.

"But I think that's something Mom and Trent should be around for, you know?"

Lennon's face crumples when she realizes what I'm saying, so I shrug and look away.

"I'm just trying to encourage Evie to hold off a bit. To save her first steps for when Trent is awake and can see them."

"Oh, wow. That's, um..." She swallows and nods. "That's very thoughtful."

The surprise in her tone rubs me the wrong way, and I roll my eyes.

"Yeah, well, I guess I'm not such a heartless prick after all."

I walk past her and into kitchen, and I can hear her stand and follow.

"I didn't say you were, Macon."

"No, you just were surprised, right?" I keep my back to her and open the fridge. "Heartless, selfish Macon Davis. He doesn't give two fucks about anyone but himself, yeah?"

"I didn't say that, Macon. That's not what I meant," she argues as I pop the top on my soda and take a drink. I swear she growls when I refuse to look at her. "Jesus, what the fuck triggered this?"

I bark out a humorless laugh, finally making eye contact, and her anger fuels me. I force a smirk and drag my gaze over her body, purposely lingering on places that kick my heart up a beat.

"When'd you get such a filthy little mouth, Lennon?"

She narrows her eyes at me as I take another drink of my soda.

"Does the Frenchman have a dirty mouth, too? What else did you learn in France, huh?"

"Don't do this, Macon," she says slowly, shaking her head. "Don't start. We were being civil."

"Civil." My lips curl cruelly, the word tasting like acid. "Is that what the French call fake as fuck?"

"Oh, fuck off, Macon."

"No, you fuck off, *Capri*," I say back, emphasizing her "name" with sarcasm.

I toss the full can in the sink, then turn and stalk toward the door. I need to get out of here. I'm itching for a cigarette or my wheel or a beating, but Lennon follows, hurling words at my back.

"It's been four fucking years. We're not kids anymore, okay? We're different people now. What did you expect? We'd just pick up where we left off?"

I whirl on her, stopping her in her tracks.

"Oh, no. I definitely don't want to pick up where we left off."

Her head jerks back as if I'd spit on her, and her scowl turns meaner.

"And whose fault is that?" she seethes through gritted teeth.

"The way I remember it, it sure as shit wasn't mine."

"Then your memory is just as warped as your attit—"

"My memory is perfectly fine," I say, cutting her off and closing the distance.

I scan her face, seeking out the anger I know I'll find in those hazel eyes. Her mouth is parted slightly, her chest is rising rapidly, in time with my own. My attention sticks on her lips before I finally drag my eyes back up to meet hers.

"I remember *everything*, Lennon. I wish I fucking didn't."

"What?" Her brows scrunch in confusion. "What does that even mean?"

"Forget it."

I look her over, settling my eyes on her auburn hair.

"Your roots are showing, *Capri*. Funny how that works, yeah? Not even a fancy French makeover can erase what's at your core."

I turn away without another word, grabbing my phone and shooting off a text as I walk outside. This time, Lennon doesn't follow.

I take my pack of cigarettes from my pocket, shake one out and place it between my lips. I check my phone again, sending another text, before lighting up and taking a deep drag.

Fuck, and I was doing so well with the whole quitting thing.

I know Jessica is off today. I don't want to call and bother her, but this is itching like it could turn into an emergency. I'm agitated as fuck, I'm pissed off, and I'm overthinking everything.

Who even is that woman in there? One moment, she's Lennon—my Lennon—and the next, she's someone I don't recognize.

I'm torn between wanting to kiss her and wanting to send her packing, and it doesn't help that I'm so keyed up, I'm not thinking straight.

I finish off my cigarette just as my phone alarm goes off, telling me it's bottle time for the squirt. I stub my cigarette out and drop it in the flowerpot Mom keeps on her porch. I'll snag it later and trash it properly on the way out. I twist my head slowly from side to side, trying to work some of the tension out of my neck, then I head back in the house.

Sure enough, Evelyn is starting to fuss.

Lennon has her in her arms and is swaying back and forth. It's doing a decent job of keeping her calm, but it won't last long. That baby gets hangry.

"It's feeding time for the monster," I tell Lennon.

"Oh. But Andrea just gave her breakfast not that long ago."

I move to the fridge and pull out one of the bottles Mom's got prepared for the day. She fixes them up for me when I'm watching Evelyn, since I can't do the whole breastfeeding thing. I take the bottle to the sink and run it under some hot water, warming it up.

"Yeah, she eats three meals of solids," I tell her, keeping my eyes on the bottle, rotating it under the faucet, "but she still gets like four bottles. She'll nap after this."

I take the bottle and test the milk on my wrist, then turn off the faucet and look up. Lennon is staring at me like I'm an alien, and Evie is sucking on her own fist.

"What?" I ask, rounding the counter and walking toward them. Evie starts bouncing in Lennon's arms when she sees the bottle, and the grabby hands and *babababa* chant start up immediately.

"Nothing." Lennon shakes her head, then hands the wriggling monster to me. "You just, I dunno, know a lot about taking care of this baby."

I snort, maneuvering Evie to one arm and giving her the bottle.

"She's not *this baby*," I say, as Evie wraps her hands around my wrist and lays her head on my chest. "She's my sister, and this is what family does."

I don't mean for the last part to sound as biting as it does. I don't mean to shade Lennon, but I do it anyway, and I feel like an asshole. I flick my eyes to her and consider apologizing, but the way she's watching Evelyn with longing makes me bite my tongue. Instead, I offer an olive branch.

"You wanna feed her?" I ask, and Lennon shoots her eyes to me.

"Really?" Her back shoots straight, then she screws up her lips. "What if I mess it up?"

I laugh and gesture for her to sit on the couch.

"You won't mess it up. She can pretty much do it on her own, anyway. I just like to hold her."

Lennon sits stiffly on the couch, and I hand Evelyn and the bottle to her.

"Relax, Len, Jesus," I say with a laugh. "You were just holding her and were fine."

"That was before she was eating. What if she chokes?"

I smirk. "Trust me, she'll be fine. Just take a deep breath, sit back against the cushions, and chill. She's gonna feel your stress."

I watch as Lennon nods and does exactly what I instructed. Deep breath in, then out, then she sinks back into the couch cushions and makes a conscious effort to relax her shoulders. It's hilarious, and I try my hardest not to laugh. I can't hide the amused grin, though, and when she sees it, she rolls her eyes and flashes one of her own.

"Good."

The sight of Lennon and Evelyn makes my chest tight and my throat dry. I open my mouth to say more, but my phone vibrates in my pocket. I pull it out and check the ID.

Jessica.

"I gotta take this," I say to Lennon. She flicks her eyes to my phone, then to my face and nods. I put the phone to my ear and answer as I walk through the sliding doors onto the back deck.

"Hey," I say to Jessica. "Sorry to bother you."

"It's not a problem," she says warmly. Just hearing the smile in her voice eases some of my building tension. "What can I do for you this fine day?"

ELEVEN

Lennon

I SNEAK A PEEK AT THE PHONE SCREEN JUST BEFORE MACON answers—Jessica—then I watch him through the sliding glass doors as he speaks to the person on the other end.

First Nicolette. Now Jessica. He has always been *popular* with women.

I study him as he paces back and forth, agitated and tight, but soon, his body grows loose. I watch as the tension in his shoulders disappears, and the irritated wrinkles on his forehead give way to lighthearted laughter and smiles.

Whoever this Jessica is, she certainly has a strange, calming effect on Macon.

I have to actively fight to keep my body from stiffening. I have to work to unclench my jaw. The jealousy and concern I feel surprise me. Jealousy, because the idea of Macon having a Jessica pisses me off in a way I don't want to admit. And concern because...

Well.

I recognized his body language when he first took that call. Jittery. Clenching and unclenching his fists. Rapid breathing. Short temper.

I remember what Macon would do when he got like that in high school. I learned quite a bit more about his habits from Sam, how they used each other. If Jessica is now filling that role...

I don't know which bothers me more—if she's an actual girlfriend, or if she's a dealer—and that makes me feel like a terrible person.

I don't want him to be using. Of course, I don't. But do I want him in love?

He hasn't seemed high at all since I've been back, but he's had years to get better at hiding it. He hasn't smelled like weed, either, but there are a lot of things he could be doing that don't have a scent.

And he was discharged from the Marines for a reason.

I'm still staring at him when Andrea steps in front of me, dressed in jeans and a t-shirt with her wet hair still up in a towel.

"Thank you," she whispers with a smile, gesturing to Evelyn, who is now sleeping on my chest. "Sorry you had to do that. I got caught up on the phone."

I shake my head and smile back.

"It's okay. Macon did it. I'm just the holder."

"He's here?" She looks around the room, then glances at the clock on the wall. "Shoot. I really lost track of time."

"He's outside," I say, then study her closely when I add, "talking to *Jessica*."

The way Andrea's brow furrows as she turns to glance outside worries me, but when I follow her gaze, I find Macon smiling and chatting like he doesn't have a care in the world.

Hmm.

Macon spots his mom through the window and ends the call seconds later, before coming back into the house.

"Morning," he says to her with a grin. "I've got her the rest of the day, if you want to head to the hospital."

"Well," Andrea says slowly, "I have some news."

Her hands are clasped together in front of her, and I focus my attention on that instead of her face.

"The doctor called. They want to wake Trent up. It could be hours or days before he actually comes out of the coma, but they want to start the process tomorrow."

I'm speechless. I'm excited, yes, but I'm scared. What if he wakes up and he's not the same? What if there's brain damage that they didn't expect? I can feel eyes on me, but I don't look up to meet them. I drop my attention to the floor and stare at the area rug, while rubbing my fingers gently over the sleeping baby on my chest, attempting to ground myself.

"That's great," Macon says. "Does this mean the tests are looking better?"

"That's what they told me," Andrea says, and I release the breath I was holding.

Okay. That's good. Scans and tests and whatever else are looking good. It could be hours or a week before he wakes up. I might be here for longer than I expected...

"...and then there will be rehab," Andrea says.

I finally look at her. She looks hopeful.

"Rehab?" I ask, and she nods.

"Physical therapy. His body will need to build back strength and coordination. Just for a few months, probably."

"Okay," I whisper. "Okay. This is good."

"Yes. It's very good." Andrea is grinning as she looks between Macon and me, her smile faltering just the tiniest bit when she says, "I'm going to call Claire and let her know."

She turns to leave the room, but I call out and stop her when a thought pops into my foggy brain.

"Andrea, would it be alright if I use Dad's office while I'm here? I have a few smaller pieces I need to work on, and if I'm going to be here a little while longer..."

"Yes," she says, her head nodding excitedly. "You can use

whatever you need. You can stay as long as you like." Her eyes mist, and her kindness makes my chest ache. "Is there anything you need me to get you? Supplies or anything?"

I shake my head slowly and force a smile.

"No. Thank you, but I can get it myself."

"Okay," she breathes out, head still nodding, smile growing bigger. "Okay, wonderful." She blinks a few times, then gestures to the hall. "I'll be back."

"You can use the center," Macon says once his mom is out of the room. "To paint, I mean."

"Thanks, but I prefer to paint alone."

I glance away from him when I say that. The words are true. I *do* prefer to paint alone. Even Franco knows not to disturb me when I work, and he's one of my closest friends. But a few years ago, with Macon, I felt the opposite.

A lifetime ago.

Now the idea of having him near me when I paint fills me with anxiety. It's an intimacy I haven't shared with anyone since him. It's one I now prefer to keep to myself.

Being around him right now is hard enough.

"And I'd rather keep my work somewhere less public," I continue. "You know, since they're commissions."

He nods slowly, watching me as if he's debating saying something more. I wait him out, but he must decide against whatever it was he was considering, because he turns and walks into the kitchen.

I hold my breath and stare at his retreating back.

So many emotions surge through me that my head swims and I feel dizzy. I want to go after him and make him say what he was going to say. I want to rage at him and demand answers.

Where did you go? Why wasn't I enough? How could you give up on us?

But I'm afraid of what he'll say.

I gave him everything once, offered my heart up on a silver platter, and what did that get me?

A fast-track ticket to rock bottom.

An emptiness I can't seem to fill.

A blackout date on the calendar, and a broken heart.

After Andrea leaves for the hospital, and Macon takes over Evelyn duties, I drive my rental to the art supply store in Norfolk.

I've missed driving. In Paris, I ride my bicycle or take the metro. Nothing quite compares to driving your own car on open American roads.

I'm typing up a list on my notes app in the parking lot when a video call rings through. It's late in France, so I'm surprised Franco is calling, let alone coherent enough for conversation. I answer with a smile, half expecting to find him very drunk on the other end.

"Hey," I say brightly, and he scoffs.

"*Hey*? Who are you answering the phone with *hey*? You've been in the States for less than a week, and already you're talking like an American."

Franco is lying in his bed, his dirty blond hair seeming darker against the stark white of his pillowcase. He's got that sexy bedroom look going for him, sultry eyes and plump lips, and he holds the phone just far enough away from his body, so I get a decent view of his naked chest.

I laugh and shake my head.

"I *am* an American," I say, and he rolls his eyes.

"Please, do not remind me." I swear he's making his French accent even thicker on purpose.

"This is prime socializing time for you," I say, changing the subject. "Shouldn't you be out drinking or dancing?"

Franco usually sleeps late because he likes to go out late. I'm the opposite. I love to wake up early. Even on sleepless nights, I'm up with the dawn. I work better when the day feels new and fresh. My creativity flourishes because the sunrise keeps my nightmares at bay.

"Ah, but I miss you. I wanted to hear your voice. The bed is cold without you."

I click my tongue and shake my head, amused. I don't even grace the comment with a response. He's so full of shit. There's no way that bed has been empty since I've left. I wouldn't be surprised if there was someone in it right now, angled away from the phone camera, just out of sight.

"How is your father?" he asks, and my smile falls a bit.

"As good as can be expected," I tell him. "They're bringing him out of his medical coma tomorrow, but it could be a few days before he wakes up."

"That is good news, yes?"

"Yeah, I think so." I purse my lips and cock my head to the side. "Actually, I think I might be here a little while longer than I planned. A week or two more."

"No, baby," he whines dramatically, making me laugh. He makes a pouty face, poking out his plump bottom lip and giving me puppy dog eyes. "Do not stay away from me anymore."

"Just until my dad is awake, and I know he's going to be alright. I was wondering if you could do me a favor?"

"Anything, *chérie*."

"Would you mind going to my apartment—"

Franco groans, as if I've physically hurt him, and I laugh again.

"My *appartement*," I correct, and he sighs with relief. Ridiculous. "...and ship me the piece I just started? It's been sketched out, but I haven't put paint to it yet."

"That deadline is not for another two months. You think you will be gone that long?"

"No, but you know how I like to have these things finished ahead of the deadline. Knowing I'm spending time away from it is giving me anxiety."

Franco nods and says something in Italian that I don't understand. I refuse to acknowledge it or ask for the translation, like he probably wants me to. My French has gotten better in the last year, so he'll switch to Italian sometimes just to throw me off. He knows it irritates me.

"I can probably ship it this weekend," he says finally. "Will that be alright?"

"Yes," I say eagerly. "Please don't forget."

I love Franco. He's a great friend, but he isn't the most reliable person. If I don't stay on him, *this weekend* could easily turn into *two weeks from now*.

"I will not forget, *chérie*." He runs his free hand over his jaw and his lips curl into a flirty smirk. "Though, I would be able to get to it sooner if your things were here..."

He trails off and raises an eyebrow, but I brush the comment off with a grin. He's been joking about me moving in with him for months. I try to tell him my presence will kill his nightlife, but he likes to tease anyway.

Truthfully, Franco likes the convenience of me, but he's not one for commitment. It doesn't bother me. It suits my needs just fine.

"Just promise you won't get distracted. It's important to me."

"*Je promets*," he says seriously, putting his hand over his heart.

"*Merci, mon amour,*" I say with a smile. "I will speak with you soon, okay?"

"*Bisou. Ciao.*"

"Bye," I say proudly, adding a little southern lilt to my tone, and he sticks his tongue out at me before ending the call.

I grab my purse and climb out of the car, locking the doors with the key fob as I walk into the store. I just need a few things for now. Luckily, out of habit, I packed my sleeve of brushes, so I grab a cart and push my way through the aisles. I spend more time browsing than necessary. Being surrounded by art supplies always makes me feel calm. At home.

After I dropped out of art school, I worked in a little art supply store in Paris for a while. *Un Tableau*. I love it there. If I hadn't started selling my paintings, I'd still be working at the art store. As it is now, I just pick up the occasional shift when I can. The woman who owns *Un Tableau* is brilliant and kind, and she told me I always have a job there if I need it.

Un Tableau is where I ran into Franco again, actually.

I hadn't seen him for about a year and didn't even know he'd been living in Paris, but he walked into my store one day and asked me out to dinner. I've seen him almost every day, since. He's introduced me to some influential people in the Paris art scene, which helped me get my first gallery show. I've earned my seat at the table, so to speak, but I definitely owe him for opening the door to the room.

I check out and load my stuff in the car after about an hour of wandering around the store. I'm on an art supply high, so I'm in a good mood on the drive back to the house. I go straight upstairs, purposely avoiding the living room, so I don't run into Macon.

I unload and set things up in Dad's office, moving around the room to find the best space with optimal lighting. I call Aunt Becca and talk to her for a while, filling her in on Dad, and letting her know my travel plans. When I hang up with her, I hear the muffled sounds of voices coming from downstairs. Andrea must be home. I check my phone. Seven p.m. No wonder I'm hungry.

When I get to the kitchen, Andrea and Macon are talking in hushed tones. When they see me, they break apart and do a shitty job of acting like they weren't just talking about me. I ignore them and head straight for Evie in her highchair.

"Hey there, little monkey," I say, booping her on the nose. The way she giggles dissolves the tension immediately. "You got a little somethin' on your face."

I swipe at the chunks of food she has hanging off her chin and she squeals louder.

"Yeah, she's disgusting," Macon drawls behind me, and Andrea laughs.

"Stop that," she says, swatting at his shoulder. "You were way worse at that age."

"He was worse at nineteen," I joke without thinking.

I slam my mouth shut just as Macon releases a surprised chuckle. The memory that rushes me is one that turns my cheeks crimson and my throat dry.

Messy eater.

I clamp my eyes shut against the emotions, the sudden burst of lust and longing, and keep my attention off Macon.

The entire kitchen is silent, even Evelyn, and the awkward tension is palpable.

That's what's so fucked about our family dynamic. Anyone else would clearly see this as a playful dig between stepsiblings. But with us? There's so much muddy water that everything is cloudy.

The silence in the room stretches, and I don't take my eyes off Evie. Then a phone chimes, and I see Macon move in my peripheral.

"Shit," he says, "I gotta go. I forgot I was supposed to meet Nicolette."

I feel my head jerk in attention, and my eyes shoot to Macon involuntarily. Andrea hugs him goodbye and tells him to "tell her hello," then he walks next to me and bends to kiss Evie on the head.

"See you tomorrow, Squirt," he says to her with a smile, dodging her grubby hands before she can pat his cheeks. He looks at me, and the smile is gone.

"Bye," he says. I nod and avert my eyes.

"Goodbye."

TWELVE

Lennon

I SPEND THE DAY AT THE HOSPITAL IN THE ICU WAITING ROOM. Waiting.

Macon is at the house with Evie all day, so Andrea can stay in the room with Dad. It upsets me a little, but when Dad wakes up, Andrea should be the first person he sees.

I keep myself busy by reading and sketching out ideas for my next painting. I know that it's unlikely Dad will wake up today. The doctor said it could be days. But I've spent so much time with entire oceans between my dad and me that just a few hospital walls feel like a huge improvement. And this way, when he does wake up, I'm seconds away instead of days.

Sam calls me when she gets off work around eight. We chat for a while, and she scolds me for not eating today, then threatens to order me food and have it delivered to the ICU waiting room. When I hang up with Sam, the sound of the double doors buzzing makes me jolt straight up to my feet.

Andrea comes walking through, her smile forced and her eyes tired.

"Hey," she says softly.

"Hey," I say back, shoving my phone in my bag. "Any news?"

She shakes her head slowly and adjusts the purse strap on her shoulder.

"I'm actually going to head back. Relieve Macon of baby duty and sleep in my own bed. The nurses will call me if Trent wakes up."

"Okay." I cover my mouth to stifle a yawn. "I'll come too, then. I'm hungry, anyway."

I follow Andrea out of the hospital and to the parking lot, then trail her in my rental. By the time we pull up to the house, all I can think about is eating something and passing out. I'm a few yards behind Andrea when she walks into the house, leaving the front door wide open for me.

I'm half dazed, so I don't pick up immediately on the strange, muffled conversation as I kick off my shoes and walk toward the kitchen. It gets louder, though, and I recognize the voices seconds before the situation unfolds in front of me.

Macon is angry and arguing with someone. His shoulders are tense and he's pointing while whispering heatedly with...

Claire.

I recognize her profile immediately, and my hackles rise. I haven't seen Claire in over four years. I've avoided her just as much as I've avoided Macon. I've gone back and forth during that time over which Davis sibling I hate more.

She looks the same, but more grown. She was always fashionable, but even I'm impressed with how "perfect" she looks. She's tamed her curls into magazine-cover quality ringlets. Her skin looks flawless, almost airbrushed. Her dress slacks and soft blue blouse are both sexy and chic. She's even wearing a pair of nude pumps.

She looks good, and it pisses me off.

I knew Claire would be coming back at some point in the

next few days. I'm surprised I haven't had to see her sooner but fuck if I don't feel like I'm walking into a goddamn ambush.

I'm hungry. I'm tired. I haven't prepared for this shit.

Macon whispers something else, and my eyes fall on the tense set of his shoulders before I hear Claire's voice.

"I belong here, too," she snaps back, far less concerned with keeping her volume down. "I shouldn't have to hide anything."

She puts her hands on her hips, and a visual of her in her childhood bedroom, bullying me to do something I didn't want to do, comes into my mind. It's the same stance, just a younger Claire. Back then, though, I didn't see the move for what it was. Selfish manipulation.

I was so naïve about so many things. I'm almost embarrassed by it now.

"You're starting bullshit," Macon says with a growl, and my eyes snap to him.

A muscle in his jaw ticks and his eyebrows are slanted harshly. I've seen him angry many times, but I've never seen this level of restraint from him. In high school, he'd have snapped. He'd throw something and storm out. He'd shout cruel insults. He'd probably be high.

Now? Now he's a force.

The controlled power that radiates from him sends a chill down my spine. His conviction excites me, and I have to breathe through the attraction.

"Now isn't the time for you to be playing immature games."

"I'm not playing games!" Claire says loudly, and Andrea surprises me when she steps in and takes Macon's side.

"Macon's right, Claire. Now is not the time."

I tilt my head to the side and watch as Claire's jaw drops and her brow furrows.

I move to take another step forward, then freeze, deciding

between interrupting or eavesdropping a bit longer. Do I remain a voyeur, or do I make my presence known?

I'm weighing the options when my eyes lock with someone else's in the room. My head jerks back in confusion and then cocks to the side.

"Hey, Lennon," Eric says awkwardly, halting the heated conversation taking place between Claire, Macon, and Andrea. "Good to see you."

"Yeah...?"

I drag my eyes from him to the others. Everyone is staring at me with different expressions. Andrea looks worried. Macon looks irritated. And Claire looks...scared? I look back at Eric and cut to the chase.

"What the hell am I missing?"

"Oh," Claire interrupts with a small, fake laugh, "sorry, Capri. We decided to come tonight instead of tomorrow."

She crosses the distance and stands next to Eric, like she's staking a claim, and in my confused state, I'm still not sure what she's hinting at.

"I hope it's okay that we take the guest room, since there are two of us?" Claire blinks, then slides one hand around Eric's waist and gazes up at him with a cheesy love-struck smile. "The drive was rough, and we're beat."

"It's fine," Eric says apologetically. "I told Claire we don't have to stay here—"

"Stop it, babe," Claire cuts him off with another fake laugh. "Capri doesn't mind sleeping on the couch, do you, Capri?"

Claire smiles back at me as she drags her hand up Eric's chest and splays it over his t-shirt covered pec. I stare at it, my eyes finally registering the diamond on her left ring finger, and then I laugh.

I flick my eyes from Claire's engagement ring to her face, which is twisted up in confusion from my reaction.

She wasn't expecting me to be amused? What did she want? Anger? Tears? That pisses me off more than anything else.

Why the fuck does she want to hurt me more than she already has?

Take the hint.

You're being pathetic and it's embarrassing.

I shake my head against the onslaught of thoughts, fighting against the spiral of memories that usually follows.

I will not let her see me break.

I glance at Eric, and the poor guy just looks like he feels terrible. Like he regrets whatever role he's played in this fucked-up family reunion. I roll my eyes and put him out of his misery.

"Don't worry, Masters," I say flatly, "I think we all know you had nothing to do with this."

Claire huffs, so I look back at her.

"I don't care where you sleep, Claire. Just kick my shit out of your way, yeah? You've always been so good at that in the past."

With that, I turn on my heel and stalk back out of the house.

I'll get a fucking hotel, or I'll call Sam and see if the Senator's McMansion is safe to crash at, or I'll sleep in my fucking car. I don't even care. I'll figure it out later.

I just need to get the hell out of here.

My fingers tighten around the steering wheel of my car as I pull onto the road. My skin itches and my stomach churns.

I need a fucking drink.

THIRTEEN

Macon

"Real fucking nice, Claire," I say on a sigh as I watch Lennon breeze out the front door without looking back.

"What the hell did I do?" she says, faking innocence that fucking Masters falls for. He rubs her shoulder gently, and she leans into him. "I don't know why she's upset. I didn't know she'd still be harboring feelings for him."

"Claire," my mom says, shaking her head, "I doubt it has anything to do with that."

Claire huffs and shrugs Eric off before walking to the kitchen island and throwing herself onto a stool.

"Well, I don't know what else it could be. I didn't do anything wrong."

She's so fucking unbelievable.

"Claire, you show up at nine p.m. after she's been at the hospital all day because her dad is in a coma," I say, ticking off points on my fingers and trying like hell to keep my voice even, "and you kick her out of the room she's been staying in so that you can sleep in it with your fucking fiancé, who also happens to be Lennon's ex-*whatever*. And you've done all of this after years of nothing but bad blood. No warning. No pleasantries. Fucking nothing."

"Well, whose fault is that?" she snaps back.

I run my hand through my hair, once again noting that I need to get it fucking cut, and squeeze my eyes shut against my frustration.

I'm exhausted, and I still have a few hours before I can crash. I don't have the energy to deal with Claire's bullshit, but if I don't do it, Mom will, and she needs that like she needs a kick to the stomach.

"You could have handled that better," I say slowly. "You cornered her, when she's already uncomfortable, and dared her to react. Now you're shocked that she bit back?"

"I'm not going to tiptoe around her," Claire nearly shrieks.

"Keep your voice down or you'll wake Evie," I scold. She scowls at me, but her next words are hushed.

"I have every right to be here, Macon. More of a right than her, even, because I've *been* here. I didn't abandon my family."

I glance at my mom.

Her brow is furrowed, and she's frowning at Claire, but she says nothing. There's no point. Claire won't listen to it, anyway. I look at Eric, and I want to laugh because he looks so fucking uncomfortable.

If this guy wants to save his future, he'll jump ship and find someone less vindictive and self-righteous to tether himself to.

"You tell yourself whatever you need to feel better, Claire," I say before giving my mom a hug. "I'll see you tomorrow." I turn to Eric with a smirk. "Welcome back, Masters."

Masters mumbles a thank you, and Claire says something snippy as I walk past, but I don't acknowledge either of them. I check my watch and head to my car. I've got to make an appearance at the bar for Payton's birthday celebration, and

I'd like to be in and out before everyone is blitzed out of their fucking minds.

The bar is packed, shoulder to shoulder, when I walk in.

It's not surprising, even for a weeknight. The Outpost does a great job with specials and entertainment, so it's never empty. The music is loud, all the pool tables are in use, and the band playing on the stage sounds great.

Before doing a sweep, I head straight for the bar. Mackie sees me after a minute or two and walks toward me, fixing my drink on the way.

"Davis," he greets loudly with a grin. "If you're here for P, her group is in the back."

"Thanks," I say, taking the glass he hands me. "Yeah, I'm here for Payton," I confirm, leaning over the bar so he can hear me. "Who all is back there?"

"Everyone," Mackie says. His grin grows and he laughs. "Your girl has the town wrapped around her finger. You'd never know she didn't grow up here."

Mackie graduated the year before me. I would have been in his class if I hadn't been held back in elementary school. He did a few years at the community college, but I'm not sure what he studied. All I know is he's the face of The Outpost now, and he's a damn talented bartender.

I smile back at him and nod, then raise my glass to say thanks once more before I push my way to the back room of the bar.

"Macon," I hear a voice yell, and I turn to the side to see a smiling Payton approaching me. "You made it!"

She wraps her arms around me in a hug, and even though she's tiny, I have to square my feet to keep from tipping over.

"Payt," I say with a laugh, "you lightweight. How are you already drunk?"

"Hush," she says playfully, standing back up and pointing a delicate finger at me. "It's my birthday. I can do what I want. C'mon!"

She grabs my hand and pulls me through the crowd until we're standing amongst a large group of Payton's friends, most of whom are rec center volunteers, or people I've known since high school.

Even Nicolette is here, nursing a bottle of beer and laughing. When she sees me, she waves and raises her drink in the air, so I do the same. I just saw her last night, so my feelings aren't hurt when she doesn't trip over herself to come talk to me.

I do my rounds, making sure to say hello to everyone before I dip out early. It's a lot of high fives and small talk. Some jokes and side hugs. Drunk person interactions. I don't mind being around drinking. It doesn't bother me like it probably could, but I have to be in the mood for it, and right now, I'm fucking not.

I told myself I would stay for two hours.

I make a good show of it. I even go back up to the bar to have Mackie make me another drink, but as my watch hand ticks closer to my deadline, it takes physical restraint not to just say fuck it and leave now. It's not until Payton mentions Casper that I realize I haven't seen him yet.

"Casper is here?" I ask her, and she smiles glassy-eyed at me over her cocktail.

I'm going to have to double check which friend is keeping an eye on her tonight.

"He is," she says brightly, then pops up from where she was leaning on the wall and takes my hand again. "C'mon, I'll bring you to him."

I chuckle. I'm perfectly capable of finding him myself, but I let her tug me around anyway. Miss Social Butterfly needs to get all her flutters out, or whatever.

She weaves me back through people to the other side of the bar near the booths, then pulls me in front of a table before sliding her arms around my waist. Normally, I'd gently remove her arms and step away, but I'm momentarily caught off guard when I see who Casper has been chatting up.

"Christopher," Payton chirps, "mister boss man was looking for you."

She laughs at her own joke as Casper smiles and raises his eyebrow.

"I'm right here, *mister boss man*," he says, then slides his arm over the back of the booth behind Lennon, who is sitting next to him.

"Just been catching up with an old friend. Payton, have you met Capri? She's visiting from France."

I watch Lennon's attention bounce between me and Payton, noting the way Payt's hanging on to me, and I swear I see Lennon's eye twitch in irritation.

I smirk, then make a show of wrapping my arm around P's body, resting my hand on her upper arm. Lennon's attention falls to the contact and sticks. I can practically feel my fingers burning under her gaze.

I'm about to rub Payton's arm, just to see how far I can push Lennon, when P relaxes into me and I realize what I'm doing.

I drop my arm and take a step back. Payton doesn't seem to notice.

"Oh! You were at the rec center," she exclaims, then slides into the booth next to Lennon. "I'm Payton! It's my birthday."

"Nice to meet you, Payton," Lennon says dryly, not even trying to feign interest. I have to bite my cheek to keep my smirk from turning into an amused smile. "Happy birthday."

"You guys know each other?" Payton asks, and Casper nods.

"Went to high school together," he says, flashing me a grin. "We go way back."

Payton whips her head to me like she's just made a brilliant discovery. I keep my eyes on Lennon.

"Macon!" Payton shouts, swatting at me playfully. "You know Capri too, then?"

I cock my head to the side and scan Lennon's face before answering. Her expression is blank, but her eyes are all fire, and suddenly, I want to find some gasoline.

"Nope," I say, popping the p. "I don't know anyone named Capri."

Casper chuckles and Lennon releases an annoyed scoff. She rolls her eyes and looks away, but I bring her attention back to me by leaning into the booth and grabbing her hand that was resting on the table.

I want to throw her off guard. I want to make her feel as unsettled as she makes me.

Her eyes go wide, but she doesn't pull away as I lift her hand to my lips.

"I'm Macon," I say, never breaking eye contact as I press a kiss to the back of her hand. "It's nice to meet you, *Capri*."

Her mouth drops open slightly, but she doesn't say anything. I rub my thumb over her palm before slowly releasing her. She places her hand in her lap and swallows before saying, "you too."

I fist my hand that was just touching her skin, flexing my fingers as if I can trap the feeling of her in my palm. I raise my drink and take a sip, hoping the cool liquid will tame the rising heat of my body temperature. It doesn't.

"Capri was just telling me how she needs a place to stay," Casper says. "Apparently, the place she was staying is now infested with vermin."

I choke on my drink as Lennon laughs, then she watches me with wide eyes as I catch my breath through my smile.

"Vermin?" I choke out, and she shrugs.

"It was the nicest way to put it," she says, full lips curled into a flirty smirk that I'm sure mine are mirroring. "I'm waiting to hear back from a friend."

She lifts her drink to her mouth and presses the glass to her lower lip. I watch as she sips, her eyes never leaving me.

"Who's your friend?" Payton asks, oblivious, and my shoulders fall slightly when Lennon looks away from me to answer the question.

"Her name is Sam. I'm waiting to see if I can crash at her place."

My back stiffens, and I flick my eyes to Casper. He's staring at me, sending me warning signals. Lennon didn't drop the last name, and I'm certain that was intentional, but Casper and I know who she's talking about.

There is no fucking way I'm letting her stay at Senator Harper's house.

I hear Payton ask a question, and when I tune back in, Lennon is explaining that her "friend" is supposed to be texting her back soon when she knows if her parents' house is free.

"I asked her if she wanted to stay with me," Casper says, "but my little apartment is too small for her paintings, and she's allergic to cats."

"You paint?" Payton perks up, and Lennon nods with a smile.

"I do," she says proudly. "Watercolors, mostly. Abstract impressionism."

"She's kind of famous," Casper says, and Lennon laughs, bumping his arm with her own.

"Hardly," she says, rolling her eyes.

"Check this out." Casper types something into his phone, then turns the screen to Payton. "That's her online gallery."

Payton scrolls through some of the images, her eyes wide in awe. I don't bother looking. I've seen them all already.

"Oh my gosh, this is amazing," Payton says. Lennon shrugs.

"My website design is simple, but the paintings are good," she says with a laugh. "They don't pay me to design websites."

I perk up at that comment.

"You designed the website?"

Lennon's eyes shoot to me, and she nods.

"Built it from the ground up. Took me almost three weeks and a few gallons of coffee, but I did it."

I don't take my eyes off her, but I bite my tongue on the desire to compliment her work. I know about the website. I know every single tab, image, and blog post. But I didn't realize she built it herself, and I'm surprised. I shouldn't be. Lennon never did know how to fail at anything.

Casper interrupts my eye contact when he leans into the table conspiratorially and cups one hand over the side of his mouth like he's about to tell a secret.

"She's got a commissioned painting for a popular British popstar," Casper mock-whispers, and Payton gasps.

"Who?" Payton shouts, and Lennon shrugs coyly before taking a sip of her drink.

"She's sworn to secrecy," Casper explains. "See? She's famous."

"That's so cool!" Payton looks to me with her eyes wide with excitement, then back at Lennon. "How much do you sell these for?"

"Depends on a few things. If it's a commission, I'll usually talk with the client to get an idea of what they want, then I price based on size, how long I think it will take, the difficulty level. Stuff like that."

Lennon sounds so professional, so focused, but there's an element of excitement behind her words that tells me she loves what she does. Painting is something she's always been passionate about but could never pursue.

If she had come back from Europe and went to college here like originally planned, she'd have been a finance major. Painting would have remained a hobby she did in secret.

Moments like this, it's hard for me to be angry that she never came back. I've spent four years pissed off that she stayed in Europe. Angry that she backed out of her acceptance at VCU and started art school in London. Pissed off even more when I heard she dropped out of art school and moved to Paris.

But fuck me, right now, I can't deny that she's doing exactly what she was meant to do.

How can I fault her for finally being selfish? I should be happy for her, but I can't do that either.

"What was the most you ever sold one for?" Casper chimes in, and I send him a glare. He just grins like a fucking idiot.

"Twelve grand," Lennon says proudly. Payton whistles.

"Whoa. Good job."

Lennon and Casper laugh at Payton's awestruck behavior, then Payton sits up taller in her seat and grins at me.

"Did you know that Macon se—"

"Stay with me," I say quickly, cutting Payton off.

Casper chokes on his drink and Lennon looks shocked.

"Excuse me?" she says, then shakes her head. "No, no way."

"Why not?" Casper interjects. "Macon has loads of space. No cats. And he's just a few blocks from here."

"No," Lennon says again. "If I can't stay at my friend's, I'll get a hotel."

"The closest hotel is, like, forty-five minutes away," Payton says sweetly, and I nod.

"And you probably can't paint in a stuffy, old hotel," Casper adds.

"You can use his studio!" Payton shouts, clapping her

hands together. "He's an artist too. He's got an art studio in his apartment and everything."

She whips her eyes excitedly between me and Lennon.

"She could use your studio, right, Macon?"

"A studio?" Lennon says curiously, cocking her head to the side. I nod slowly, biting my lip to hide my smile. Got her. It was almost too easy.

"Great natural lighting," I tell her. "South-facing. Huge windows."

I say the words slowly, dragging them out, like foreplay. I'm seducing her creative mind with the architectural elements of my in-home art studio. I know she's dying to see it for herself.

I watch her face as she considers it, and I know she's going back and forth in her head, trying to talk herself out of it.

She opens her mouth, to accept or decline I don't know, when her phone vibrates in front of her. She picks it up and types in her passcode. Casper reads the message over her shoulder, and I can tell by the way her shoulders fall and his smile grows that my place is now her best option.

"Sam's house isn't going to work," she says, and twists her lips up to the side.

"Stay with me, *Capri*," I say, emphasizing the name with just a hint of sarcasm, so the phrase before it doesn't gut me.

It's too close to before. Words written. Words ignored.

Lennon narrows her eyes at me, either at the way I say her name or my nod to our past. It doesn't matter which. We're here now.

"I don't want to cramp your style," she says, lowering her eyes to my drink. "I'm not really into the party scene."

Casper snorts another laugh, covering his face with his hand.

"What's so funny?" she asks, looking from Casper to me. I smile and raise my glass.

"This is Dr. Pepper and lime juice," I tell her. "I don't drink."

"At all?" she asks, and I shake my head.

"Three and a half years clean and sober," I tell her proudly.

I want to reach into my pocket and show her the recovery medallion my sponsor gave me when I hit three years, but I don't move. I don't want to spook her. I just let her absorb the information I gave her.

"I don't want to upset your girlfriend," she says after a moment, and I shrug.

"No girlfriend."

Lennon flicks her eyes to Payton, as if waiting for her to dispute my claim, but Payton stays quiet. Payton might not want it to be true, but she knows I'm single.

"No girlfriend. No partying. No cats," I say, placing my glass on the table and making a show of checking my watch.

"But I do have to be up early to babysit my adorable little sister, so if you're going to crash at my place, you gotta make a decision fast."

She's quiet, and I try like hell not to look eager. My heart is pounding in my chest. This could be the dumbest fucking thing I have done in a long time, but I have to follow through now.

Casper gives Lennon a nudge with his elbow.

"Go on," he teases. "You were just yawning like five minutes ago. Go crash at Macon's. He's your best option."

I know the minute she caves. She looks back at me with the same hazel eyes I see in my dreams, and grimaces.

"You sure you won't mind? It will only be for a few days."

"I don't mind," I say honestly.

I say my goodbyes and Lennon follows me out of the bar twenty minutes later. The silence is awkward as we walk to the parking lot. I follow her to her car, and she stops in her tracks when she sees me move to the passenger side.

"You need a ride?" she asks, and I grin.

"I walked. But I figure I should ride with you, so you know where you're going."

She doesn't reply, just unlocks the door and climbs in, so I do the same. She starts the car and silently follows the few directions I give her. I watch, amused, as her brow furrows more and more the closer we get to the rec center, until we're pulling into the parking lot and she's parking next to my car.

She twists in her seat and stares at me.

"Explain."

"I live in the apartment upstairs," I tell her, unbuckling my seat belt and climbing out of the car. "C'mon, I'll show you."

She hops out and walks quickly to catch up to me.

"I didn't know there was an apartment upstairs," she says, and I shrug.

"It didn't used to be much. James renovated it a few years ago, and I moved in when I came back." I unlock the side door, let Lennon in, then lock it again. "This way," I say, then head toward my stairwell.

We're quiet as we climb the stairs, and she waits patiently behind me while I unlock the door to my apartment.

"Here we are."

I usher her inside and then kick my shoes off at the door. She does the same, then trails me through the apartment and into the kitchen. She stops and looks around, and I wait for her to say something.

"It's nice," she says after a moment. "Really nice." She turns to me and raises an eyebrow. "And *clean*. I thought you said you didn't have a girlfriend?"

I scoff playfully and push past her.

"*I* keep it clean," I tell her. "No girlfriend, no housekeeper. Not even my mom. I do it." I gesture for her to follow me, then lead her to the living room. "I function better when my space is tidy."

"Me too," she says quietly, and I have to bite my tongue against the urge to say *I know*.

"Living room, kitchen, bathroom," I say, pointing in various directions so she knows where things are, then head into the hallway. "Bedroom," I say, knocking lightly on the door, "and studio."

I turn to face Lennon and push the door to the studio open slowly. I swear she's holding her breath and trying her best not to look excited. I fixate on her facial expressions, the brightness in her eyes and the twitching at the corners of her mouth. When I turn on the light, her reaction is so fucking gratifying.

Lennon swallows hard and her eyes go wide as she takes in the space. Even in the middle of the night, my studio is impressive.

I watch as she walks toward my wheel and surveys the workspace. She walks to my drawing desk, her hands hovering over the surface, like she wants to touch everything, but she won't let herself. When she gets near the closet, I speak up, bringing her attention back to me.

"You can set your stuff up in here tomorrow when you get it from the house," I tell her.

She nods, then shuts her eyes and sighs.

"Damn it," she mumbles, dropping her head back. "I don't have anything. I left all my stuff there." She lifts her head back up and looks at me. "I guess I'll be back soon."

She turns toward the door, but I stop her.

"Why? Just get your shit tomorrow."

"I don't have anything to sleep in," she says, and the way she stares me down feels like she's daring me to smirk. To make a smart-ass comment. Something sexual and suggestive. It's on the tip of my tongue, but I like throwing her off balance.

"I'll give you a shirt," I say with a shrug.

No smirk. No double entendre. She almost looks disappointed.

"I've got a pair of sweats you can borrow, too." I shrug again. "It's no big."

She twists up her lips and studies me, my skin heating under her gaze. I don't speak. I wait her out, letting her think it through. It should be such a simple thing, but it's not. Nothing is simple with us.

"Okay," she finally says. "Thanks."

I shrug a third time, the picture of fucking nonchalance.

"You can have my room, too. I'll take the couch." I push past her into the hall, hooking into my bedroom. "I'll switch up the sheets real quick for you."

"No, Macon," she calls, following me into my bedroom.

The moment she crosses the doorway, I can feel her. It's like the air changes. Everything smells like roses, now. It'll be permanent.

Mother fuck.

When the fuck did she change back? Vanilla was easier. Roses?

Mother. Fuck.

"You don't have to do that. I can sleep on the couch."

I'm already stripping the bed, though, and she huffs when she realizes I'm not stopping.

"It's easier for me this way," I tell her, and it's not a lie.

I drop the bedsheets on the ground in a ball and move to my dresser, grabbing a pair of USMC sweat pants and a matching t-shirt from the drawer. I toss them at Lennon, and she catches them awkwardly, hugging the mess of fabric to her chest.

"Go change. Take a shower if you want. I'll have this done in a second."

I turn my back to her, making the bed up without looking at her. I feel her eyes on me, though. I can practically hear her thoughts, but I don't acknowledge it. Instead, I put the fitted sheet on my mattress and focus on getting my own shit under control.

Having her in my bedroom is going to fuck me up, but letting her sleep on the couch will be worse.

If she's on the couch, there's nothing stopping her from sneaking out on me. At least if I'm the one in the living room, I'll know if she leaves. This time, I won't be caught off guard.

I can feel the energy shift when she steps out of the room and heads to the bathroom. It's like all the air follows her, and when the shower kicks on, my legs collapse. I sit on my mattress and put my head between my knees.

Fuck, fuck, fuck.

Why the fuck is this so hard?

My phone rings, and I pull it out of my pocket and put it to my ear without sitting up.

"Hello?"

"Macon, I'm worried about Lennon," my mom says quickly. "She hasn't come back to the house and she's not answering her phone. I know what Claire did was uncalled for, but do you think she would leave? Do you think she'd go back to Paris?"

I sit up straight and choose not to point out the way Mom slipped up and said Lennon. It feels so much more authentic than Capri.

Capri is a lie. Lennon is the real thing.

"She's with me, Mom," I say, and Mom's silence makes me nervous. "She's in the shower."

"Macon," she says, her voice full of worry. "Do you think that's smart?"

"She's just staying here for a bit." My exhaustion is evident in my tone. "Probably just until shit cools down with Claire. Lennon's going to use my studio and crash here. That's it. Nothing else."

A long pause follows. I can hear Mom's breathing.

"Are you sure you're going to be okay?" she asks finally. "What about last time?"

"That was years ago," I tell her. "I'm in a better place now. I'll be fine."

The words are true. I *am* in a better place now.

I'm not fresh out of rehab and having my last ounce of hope shattered.

This is my apartment, not some dirty alley outside of a pub in London.

I'm sober and stable. I'm not heartbroken anymore.

And more importantly, as wrong as it may feel, I tell myself that's Capri in my shower. Not Lennon.

"I'll be fine, Mom," I say again, repeating the words and stressing them.

Hoping like hell my mom believes them more than I do.

FOURTEEN

Lennon

By the time I'm out of the shower, it's after midnight.

I towel dry my hair and dress in Macon's clothes before leaving the bathroom and tiptoeing into his bedroom.

It's empty. I don't see him or hear him, and I don't like the disappointment I feel. I try to ignore it.

Macon's USMC shirt and sweats are too big in some places and snug in others. He's built like a triangle while I'm more like a pear. Plus, he's over six foot and I'm 5'9". Still, despite the fact that the clothes obviously aren't my size, they're still heartbreakingly comfortable.

I don't want to like the way Macon's clothes feel on my body. I don't want to like anything about him at all.

I fold my dirty clothes and set them on top of the dresser, before standing in the middle of the room and surveying it.

It's different in the ways you'd expect.

He's not nineteen anymore. Of course, his bedroom reflects that, but it's still very Macon. Black accents. A stack of sketchbooks and a jar of pencils. There's a large flatscreen TV mounted on the wall and a record player with a shelf of vinyl records in the corner. There are no clothes scattered on the floor or dirty dishes on the nightstand, but the room still smells like him. Spicy and minty. But no weed.

Three and a half years sober.

The thought makes me smile seconds before my lips turn into a frown.

Three and a half years sober, yet still four years of silence.

I thought I could fix him, but it turns out, he just needed me out of the way. He grew up, got clean, and made a life, all without me.

You could argue that I did the same, but it would be a lie to say I did it voluntarily. I was forced to rebuild. I made my decisions without him because I had to. He made his choices without any concern for me, and my life is a result of that.

Don't get me wrong. I have a good life. My art career is flourishing, and I love Paris. I have friends. I have happiness.

But is it what I thought I wanted?

Four years ago, had I been allowed to make my own decisions, my life would look a hell of a lot different.

I release a hollow laugh. Maybe I should thank Macon for that.

I sit gently on the bed, give myself a little bounce, then drop so I'm lying on my back. The mattress is like being hugged by a cloud, and I groan.

God damn it.

I don't want to be comfortable here.

I sit back up when my phone rings, and I'm surprised to see Franco's name on the screen.

"Good morning," I say with a smile. "What are you doing awake?"

"*Bonjour, ma chérie,*" he greets sleepily. "I was just missing your voice."

I roll my eyes. He's such a liar.

"Did you go out last night?"

"I did, but all of these people are dull," he says, waving his hand in the air. "I came home early. When will you be home? I miss you."

I laugh, and it feels good. Franco always knows how to make me feel special. Even though I know he is likely entertaining someone else in his bed, it doesn't bother me. My feelings for him aren't like that.

We've had sex, yes. More than once, and sometimes regularly, but there's no romantic connection there. We comfort each other in a different way.

"You don't miss me, Franco," I tease. "You have plenty of people to keep you company."

"Ah, but you are the one I want," he says. "Come home, *mon bijou*. Come back to me."

I open my mouth to respond, but a throat clears behind me, and I turn around to see Macon leaning on the door jamb with his arms folded across his naked chest.

My mouth goes dry immediately.

He has a pair of joggers slung low on his hips, and his entire left arm, shoulder, and part of his chest is covered in colorful tattoos.

I stare. I can't help it.

He drops his arms and stalks toward me slowly. His body is loose, but his face is tight.

"Sorry to interrupt," he says curtly, flicking his eyes from me to my phone screen and back. "I wanted to see if you needed anything before I go to sleep."

I blink a few times and shake my head no.

"I'm okay, thanks," I force out, and his lips twitch slightly.

It makes me angry.

He knows exactly what he's doing coming in here like that, flaunting his body. He wanted to throw me off guard, and he succeeded.

"Goodnight," I say, more sternly this time, and he smiles.

Damn those full lips.

He drags his eyes from my face back to my phone screen and the smile disappears.

"Hello," he says to Franco, "I'm Macon. And you are?"

I swear Macon's voice drops an octave, and when I glance at Franco, I can tell he's taken aback as well.

"I'm Franco," he says slowly, then he looks back at me. "Capri, I thought you were staying at your father's house."

"Not anymore," Macon answers for me. "Lennon's staying with me, and we've had a really long day and should probably get some sleep."

Macon runs his hand roughly over his bare chest and grips the back of his neck. I don't know if he's flexing his chest and biceps on purpose, or if they just look like that naturally, but I'm struck a little dumb. From the phone silence, I think Franco is, too.

I gather my wits and open my mouth to tell Macon to buzz off, but then my eyes fall on the clock tattoo on his pec and my mouth drops open.

Franco starts to speak, but I tell him quickly that I'll call him later, then hang up before shooting to my feet.

Macon takes a step back quickly, so I don't slam into him, but I don't take my eyes off the tattoo.

"What is this?" I whisper, narrowing my eyes and trying to make sense of the changes that have been made to the tattoo.

They feel important, they have to be, and it's making my brain fuzzy.

"What is this?" I say again.

"A tattoo, Lennon," Macon states, his tone dry as he walks backward toward the door. "The tattoo artist inked it up, so it fit in with the sleeve."

"No." I shake my head. "No way."

"Whatever you think it is," he says, stopping just at the doorframe, "it's not. Get some sleep."

With that, he turns and walks out, shutting the door behind him.

I stay frozen to the spot and stare at the doorway, running that tattoo through my mind.

The clock is still there. So is the script.

We are homesick most for the places we have never known.

It's a Carson McCullers quote, from a short essay she wrote in 1940. I learned that years ago on a drunken night when I was missing Macon and googled it.

But where the clock used to be on naked skin, it's now surrounded by a night sky with a random constellation, hovering just above, and partially behind it, stretching up to his shoulder and around the left side of his upper chest.

It's a rough rectangle with a line of stars connected to each of the four corners.

Virgo, probably.

I didn't think Macon would be into astrology, but he was born in September, so it would make the most sense.

The constellation and night sky are beautiful, but they're not what caught my attention. It's the actual clock tattoo that has given me pause.

The clock used to be broken. I remember it vividly. I've painted it an obsessive number of times. It was handless with a giant crack down the middle of it.

But now, where it was broken, it's been mended, touched up, so the crack resembles a reflection on the glass of a watch face.

And where it used to be handless, there are now hands. One long and one shorter, just like you'd expect on a traditional clock.

But instead of being just regular lines, they're paint brushes. Two of them.

Macon is an artist, yes, but his medium has always been

pencil on paper. Or clay. Sometimes charcoal, sometimes pastels. He draws, he sketches, or he throws.

Macon doesn't paint. I do.

Whatever you think it is, it's not, he said. *Get some sleep.*

I stay awake the rest of the night. He's lying. I know he is. Those paint brushes mean something. I just don't know what.

I don't know if I could handle it if I did.

FIFTEEN

Lennon

As usual, I'm up with the dawn.

I tiptoe out of the bedroom, not wanting to wake Macon, but he's nowhere to be found. The blanket and pillow he used last night are folded and stacked neatly on the couch, and the apartment is silent.

Almost.

The faint hum of music drifts down the hallway from the studio, and I fight every force I feel trying to tug me in that direction.

He's in there.

I don't know if he's sketching or working the wheel, but I know he's making art in some form, and the need to create alongside him is strong. Despite everything—despite last night and my fucked-up feelings and every ounce of bad blood between us—the artist in me longs to be inside that studio.

The core of me wants to be next to him, regardless of logic and lessons learned.

Lennon will always want Macon.

That's why I can't be her anymore.

I hurry to the door and slip on my shoes, then quietly let

myself out. I get to my car and breathe a sigh of relief. I let myself relax for a few inhales and exhales, then I turn the car in the direction of Andrea's and prepare myself for the next uncomfortable situation.

Even Stevie Nicks can't calm my nerves the closer I get to the house, but I have to get my things out of the guest room and office. And as much as I'd like to pretend Claire doesn't exist, I have to face her, too.

The last few days have made me realize how badly I want to be a part of Evelyn's life. I don't want to take the risk of her forgetting me again when I leave, and that means I need to get used to Claire.

No more avoiding family holidays. No more silencing calls.

I can still be a present sister while in France. I just have to make more of an effort.

I can do this.

For Evelyn. For Dad. For me.

I pull up to the curb outside of Andrea's house and try my best not to scowl at the car in the driveway. Claire would be riding around shotgun in a brand-new Audi SUV. No way in fuck it's hers, but I bet she drives it like it is. I'm sure she views the engagement as another possession she can manipulate.

I climb out of my car and walk slowly toward the front door, grateful that I changed out of Macon's sweats and back into my own clothes this morning, because it makes this feel less like a walk of shame. I give myself two breaths on the front porch before I knock, and thankfully, it's Andrea who answers.

"Oh, honey, you don't have to knock," she says quickly, moving over so I can step inside. "You can come in and out as you please."

"Thanks," I mumble, forcing a small smile. Andrea turns and walks into the house, and I do the same.

I can hear Claire and Eric talking in the kitchen, so when I step into the room, I'm not surprised to see them sitting at the counter drinking coffee with Evelyn propped in a highchair covered in something orange. My face must give away my disgust because Andrea laughs.

"It's squash," she says, moving to wipe off Evelyn's cheeks with a washcloth.

"Oh," I say with a fake smile. It wasn't Evie grossing me out, but I'll let Andrea assume. It's safer this way, anyway.

"I'll be right back," Andrea says, picking Evie up out of the highchair. "She needs a change."

Then she turns and exits the kitchen, leaving me alone with my ex-whatever and the bitch who had a hand in orchestrating one of the worst times of my life.

"Good morning, Capri," Claire says sweetly, and I don't miss how she moves her left hand, so the rock is in view.

God, was she always this insufferable?

"Good morning, Claire," I say, mimicking her tone, then I look to Eric. "Good morning, Eric. I trust you both slept well in the bed you kicked me out of?"

The way this grown man looks like a scolded puppy makes me want to both laugh and cry, but it's not his fault this family is fucked up, so I smile.

"I'm joking," I say.

He doesn't believe me. I turn back to Claire.

"I need to grab my stuff out of Dad's office and my suitcase from the guest room," I tell her, then pause for a breath. "Unless you already packed my shit and put it out on the curb?"

"Don't be so dramatic, Capri," Claire says with a huff and an eye roll.

Something about her so comfortably using my middle name sets my teeth on edge. It's like she's glad *Lennon* is gone, and it makes me want to come back just to spite her. Too bad the old Lennon is dead.

I smile, infusing my expression with every ounce of grace I

can muster, and tilt my head to the side to survey her. I scan her face and her hair slowly, the whole time sporting a blissful smile, and I do it silently. Just long enough to make her nervous. When her spine is rigid and her nostrils flare, I speak.

"Je suis désolé, ma soeur," I say. *"Faisons comme si tu n'étais pas une salope. Si cela vous aide à mieux dormir."*

Eric chokes on his coffee, his eyes wide on my face, and I can't hold back my laugh.

"Oh, I forgot you took French," I say honestly. "You'll have to tell me how I did. I know my French is still pretty rough."

He clears his throat and looks quickly to Claire and back.

"It was fine," he says, and I grin.

"What did you say?" Claire asks me, then turns to Eric. "What did she say?"

Eric shakes his head.

"She, um, said she was sorry."

Claire raises an eyebrow.

"I can tell you're lying," she hisses.

I watch the exchange with glee. Oh, poor Eric. He's always been too nice for his own good. Then I frown.

Jesus. Was this how I was with her?

"I'll go grab my stuff," I say airily while walking out of the kitchen.

I don't turn around to acknowledge them, and I'm in and out of the rooms within minutes. I can fit all of my belongings in my arms. It's precarious, but I'd prefer to only make a single trip to the car.

I descend the stairs slowly, then struggle a bit opening the front door, but when I get it without dropping anything, I have to suppress the urge to do a little dance in celebration.

When I get out the door, though, I see Macon stomping up the yard with a scowl on his face. He stops short when he sees me and surveys all the shit in my arms. His scowl fades as if he's just realized something, and then he closes the distance.

"Here," he says, snagging my carry-on and one of my bags of art supplies.

I don't say anything. I just let him help me carry it to my car and drop it in my trunk.

"You heading to the hospital?" he asks after I close the trunk, and I nod.

"I was going to try and see Dad for a half hour or so until Andrea comes by. I didn't want to disturb you this morning, so I let myself out."

He reaches into his pocket and pulls out a keychain, slipping off a key and handing it to me.

"Stop by my apartment first and drop off your stuff," he tells me. "I'm going to be here with Evie. Probably all day."

"Thanks."

I take the key slowly. Slow enough that my fingertips brush over his and goosebumps that I resent prickle my arms. I know he notices. The heat in his eyes when I look up is confirmation of that.

Movement at the house catches our attention at the same time, and we break our gaze to glance back at the front porch. Claire is standing there, arms folded, and she looks worried. I scoff, turn away from Macon and pop open my car door.

"I'll see you later," I tell him, and climb into the driver's seat. But because I'm feeling like a vindictive bitch, I call out to Claire before closing the door behind me.

"I apologized, yeah. I also said we can pretend that you're not an evil cunt if it helps you sleep better at night." She gasps angrily and drops her arms. "Or something along those lines," I say with a shrug. "Some things get lost in translation."

Then I slam my door, crank the engine, and drive off with a smile.

Claire can choke on a dick for all I care.

. . .

There's no change with Dad.

I was hoping to talk to a doctor while I was there, but I didn't get a chance to see one. I just read him a few chapters of the book and then left him with a hand squeeze and a kiss on the forehead.

After my visit, I head back to Macon's to get some painting done. I want to poke around his studio so badly. I want to snoop, but I don't.

Instead, I'm taken aback when I notice that Macon's drawing table has been cleaned up. The sketchbooks and pencils have been moved to a shelf, and in their place are two empty mason jars.

He must have done this last night, fixed me up a workstation, and it catapults me back to our afternoons in the high school art room. He'd lay out my paints and fill my jars, never once taking credit for it.

I half expect to see a sticky note on the table, but there isn't one.

I feel my heart warming, and then I push it back.

I remind myself that it's almost July. I close my eyes and allow myself a single memory. One of me chopping off my braid after learning the truth. Then I open my eyes and go about my business.

I figure out how to stream my phone playlist through his speakers, arrange my paints and brushes the way I like them, and I lose myself in the process.

The lighting in this studio is fucking insane, and I don't stop painting until the sun starts to dip low in the sky and I realize I need to eat something.

After cleaning up, I make my way out into the apartment and about scream when I run into Macon.

"I thought I was here alone," I say quickly. I splay one hand over my chest and try to catch my breath. "You scared the shit out of me."

"Sorry," Macon says slyly. "Me and Evie brought you some dinner, but your music was going, and I didn't want to disturb you. Mom called about an hour ago. There's no change with Trent, but she's going to sleep at the hospital, so we've got the squirt for the night."

"Oh."

I nod and look toward Evelyn, who is playing on the floor in Macon's small dining area between the living room and kitchen.

"Where does she sleep when she stays here?"

"I've got a little portable crib thing," he tells me. "I set it up in my room, but I'll keep her out here with me tonight."

He has a crib for her.

The information affects me in a way I wish it wouldn't.

The silence is weird, and when Macon realizes I'm not going to say anything, he moves to the fridge and pulls out some to-go containers.

"I ordered some food from The Outpost before I came home," he tells me, emptying the to-go containers onto plates. "It's taco night, and they have fucking amazing options, so I just got you a bunch to try."

He unpacks an assortment of beef, shrimp, chicken, and black bean tacos and pops each plate in the microwave. Then he opens a paper bag of chips and another container full of guacamole. He sets it all out on the kitchen island in front of me before picking up Evie and buckling her into a little travel highchair I didn't notice before.

It's so *domestic*. So stable and mature.

So different yet so perfectly aligned with the Macon I once knew.

I saw the good in Macon back then—I might have been one of the few who did—but the good was always buried beneath attitude and drugs and self-loathing. I never thought I'd get to see it laid out so blatantly on his surface.

It surprises me and renders me speechless. Goosebumps raise on my forearms, and I have the weirdest desire to cry.

"What?" Macon says, shaking me from my thoughts.

I hadn't realized how long I'd been quiet. I look from the dinner spread to him.

"What?" I repeat.

His brow furrows as his eyes bounce between mine.

"Don't tell me you've gone vegan or something, too?" He waves a hand over the plates of tacos. "I guess you could scrape the cheese off or something."

"No," I say, laughing lightly to try and hide how unsettled I feel. "I'm not vegan. Thanks for picking this up."

He nods, then fixes Evie's tray with a little deconstructed taco. She wastes no time in taking a fistful of food and shoving it in her mouth. I can't help but chuckle. She definitely diffuses tension without even trying.

"Okay, well..." Macon says, taking a seat on a stool on the other side of the kitchen island. "Eat. Tell me about Paris."

I sit and flash him a look like he's crazy.

"What do you mean?"

"What do you do? What's so great about it that you never come back home?"

I bristle at his tone.

"Paris is home," I say, and he snorts.

"Paris might be *Capri's* home, but Lennon will always belong here, and I think we both know who you are."

"Don't do this, Macon," I say with a sigh. "You don't know anything about me anymore. Quit speculating as if you do."

Just like how I don't know anything about him.

He keeps his eyes on his food for a few bites. He gets up and fills two glasses with ice water, setting one down in front of me before taking a sip of the other. He gives Evie a sippy cup filled with something from the fridge.

The silence stretches and I start to fidget.

The people pleaser inside me, the one I shoved deep down years ago, itches to apologize, but I keep my mouth shut. The part of me that will always have feelings for Macon wants to reach out and touch his hand, to comfort him. I don't do that either.

Getting close to him will only hurt me. Especially now. I've lost too much. I can't afford to backslide.

I've used up all my Macon Davis lives. I couldn't survive him again.

Just as I make up my mind to leave, he speaks.

"You're right," he says. "We don't know each other anymore. It's stupid to suggest we do."

His blue eyes lock with mine and the open vulnerability in them hits me right in the chest.

"Let's fix that. Tell me about Paris." He smirks slowly before adding, "I promise not to be a dick."

I tilt my head to the side as I survey him. What's he playing at?

"Why?" I ask. "You want to know why I dropped out of college to become a *freeloading, directionless Frenchman's whore*?"

Macon doesn't even flinch when I throw his words back at him. Not an ounce of remorse or shame, and it stokes my growing anger. His lips twitch at the corners as he sits back in his seat and crosses his arms over his chest, his silver wristwatch glinting in the gleam of the kitchen light. I keep my eyes on his, but the bulge of his biceps and chest are still visible, taunting me from the outskirts of my vision.

This would be so much easier if I wasn't attracted to him.

"I already know why you dropped out of college," he says after a minute, and I blink.

I don't roll my eyes like I want to. I don't let my mouth drop at his confident tone. I just blink. Once. Twice. Then I raise an eyebrow and wave my hand between us, gesturing for him to enlighten me.

"You never liked school. You did it because it fit your image."

He leans forward, folding his arms on the table, eyes never leaving mine.

"Goody Two-Shoes Lennon Washington couldn't fail at anything, which is why you took every AP class possible. But..." He shrugs. "You hated it. It only makes sense that you'd drop out of formal education the moment you had an ounce of freedom."

He stares me down, daring me to contradict him. He wants me to argue. He wants to double down on why he knows he's right.

And he is. To an extent.

As soon as I realized it was an option for me, I ran as far away from formal education as I could. But it took crashing and burning before I accepted it.

I don't tell him that.

I will never tell him that.

I can't let him know the power he had over me once.

When he realizes I'm not going to confirm or deny his theory, he sits back in his chair once more and hits me with a charming grin.

"Tell me about Paris," he says again, and because I need a change of subject—away from how well he knows me, yet how drastically he doesn't—I start talking.

I lean into everything that fits with Capri. I leave out everything connected to Lennon.

Macon is genuinely interested in hearing what I have to say, which unnerves me at first. He keeps eye contact. He interacts. He's an *active* listener. And it works.

The longer I talk, the more comfortable I feel, until we're laughing and smiling, and leaning so close over the kitchen island that it wouldn't take much to kiss him if I wanted to.

I tell myself I don't want to.

I talk to him about Paris and about *Un Tableau*.

About my little one-bedroom apartment in the 20th arrondissement of Paris. It's a sixth floor walk-up with non-existent air-conditioning and wallpaper older than me, but the lighting is wonderful, and the building has the most charming courtyard. I was only able to snag it because one of my old coworker's cousins moved to Germany. Before that I was in a three-bedroom with four people outside the city.

I tell him about my favorite brasseries and cafés, the bar I often go to with friends. I get lost in a story about my very first gallery show, and how I was such a nervous mess that I knocked over an entire table of beverages.

I don't tell him how lonely it gets, or how, most weekends, I choose to stay in and paint and get drunk alone. I don't tell him about the long string of lovers I can't seem to commit to. I don't talk about Franco, who is arguably my closest friend in the city but, despite his constant attempts, I keep my heart guarded from him.

I also don't tell him that the reason I had to get my own apartment was because I was tired of explaining away my nightmares.

I used to wake up in a cold sweat, sobbing and calling out for help. They'd get worse in the summer, right around my birthday, and the only way I was able to keep them at bay was to have another person in my bed. Even better if I didn't know that person, because then I wouldn't fall into a deep sleep.

The nightmares stopped about a year ago, but now that I'm back here, they've started again.

I don't tell him that it's all his fault.

I paint myself as a happy, successful American living in Paris. I make it sound like a light-hearted Netflix show, and for an hour or so, I let myself believe it as well. And I let myself believe that the reason I'm laughing and happy right now is because I like the topic of conversation, not because I like who I'm talking with.

Macon does the bedtime routine with Evie, putting her in the little crib in the corner of the living room. I offer to clean up the kitchen from dinner, and after he asks if I want to watch a movie. I say sure. He's just scrolling through the streaming options on his TV when there's a soft knock at the door.

He pauses and I watch as the confusion on his face morphs into dread. He pulls his phone out of his pocket and checks it.

"Fuck," he says to himself, then he looks at me. "Hold on."

He jumps up and walks to the door, then swings it open.

"What the hell, Macon!" a woman's voice yells, and she pushes past him into the apartment.

Macon immediately shushes her and steps in front of her, blocking my view, but I saw enough from my spot on the couch.

Nicolette. The girl from the phone screen.

"I'm sorry," he says quietly, "I took Evie tonight, and I forgot to call you."

"I've been downstairs waiting for thirty minutes," she seethes. "I had to call Payton to bring me her key because I got worried when you wouldn't answer your fucking phone."

"It was on silent," he says, his voice still hushed. "Let's just get together tomorrow."

My mouth drops open.

No, he is not trying to reschedule a fucking hookup. And he thinks he's being sneaky? I'm literally right here. I can hear and see everything.

"Macon, I have shit to do," she scolds. "You're not bailing on me again. I still have some time, let's just do it now. If Evelyn's in your room, we can do it in the living room."

"Nic, shut up," he says, then he mumbles something and Nicolette gasps.

"She's here now?" I hear her say. It's supposed to be a

whisper, but I can hear her just fine. "Macon, you are such a fucker."

She practically growls, then tries to push past him. He stops her, mumbles something else, then pushes her out the door.

He turns and walks back to me, and I make it very well known that I was watching. I can tell from his face that I'm not going to like what he's about to say, and I scowl at him.

"Just go," I say. He winces.

"I'll just be an hour," he says. "Evie should sleep, but—"

"Just go," I repeat. "We'll be fine."

He nods.

"Thanks," he says, then he turns and walks out the door.

I stare at it for a while, my anger fading into something worse. Something I swore I would never let him make me feel again.

Jealousy. Pain. Inadequacy.

I am once again the naïve, stupid girl who wasn't enough for the boy she loved. I'm the person who tried everything to be what he wanted and failed. I'm left behind. I'm discarded.

I feel myself retreating into memories of before. Before I picked myself up from the floor and changed my direction. Before I finally took hold of my life and became who I needed to be.

I sit down on the couch, put my head between my knees, and breathe through the memories.

I refuse to cry. I refuse to fall.

I choose anger instead.

SIXTEEN

Lennon

London, 4 Years Earlier

"You sure you're gonna be okay, Len?"

"I told you, I'm going by Capri now."

I finish lining my lips with the red liner, then add some lipstick. I smack my lips together in the mirror, and Sam laughs.

"Yeah, I'm not calling you Capri," Sam says firmly. "I fully support this whole reinvention thing. The hair. The attitude. Art school in London. You do what you have to do, and I'm cheering you on. But no way in fuck am I calling you Capri. It's too chic, and I'm claiming my best friend privileges."

She plops down on my bed and throws her feet up on the headboard.

"Besides, you can shed everything from your old life, but you're not shedding me. You're stuck with me, Lennon."

I roll my eyes, but I don't bother hiding my smile. Something about that makes me feel better, but I don't know why. I won't fight her on this. I'll give her her best friend privileges. God knows she's earned them.

"When do you have to leave?" I ask, changing the subject.

Sam's stayed with me as long as she can. She helped move me into my new apartment in London and get situated, but now it's August, and she can't put off college any longer.

She has to go back to the States, and I have to let her go.

I don't tell her it's gutting me. I don't tell her I can feel myself teetering on the edge of something scary. She's sacrificed enough for me. I have to figure out how to do this on my own.

Sam checks the time on her phone and frowns.

"My car will be here in, like, fifteen minutes."

The pit in my stomach grows, but I flash her a smile, then grab my glass of wine from the bedside table and finish it. She watches with a concerned expression.

"Don't do that," I scold her, and she throws up her hands.

"I'm not doing anything."

"You are. You're looking at me like you think I'm a ticking time bomb."

She's quiet for a minute, then she takes a deep breath.

"I think you might be, Len." My shoulders fall, and her frown deepens. "It's just... you haven't really dealt with anything, you know? It's like you've just shut off, and I'm worried."

I blow out a harsh breath, then pull my eyeliner from my makeup bag.

"I don't want to talk about this anymore, Sam."

I lean into the mirror on my desk and line my eyes with black instead of looking at her.

I'm tired of this conversation. Just because I'm not sobbing on her shoulder every night. Just because I decided that being sad isn't going to change anything. I don't want to mourn. I don't want to grieve. I don't want to hurt anymore. I want to live my fucking life.

Sam stares at me for another moment, then pulls her phone out.

"That's it. I'm staying."

"No," I say firmly. "You can't blow off college anymore. I will be fine. I can't use you as a crutch anymore." I drop my eyeliner on the desk and turn to face her. "You have done more for me than you know, but it's time for me to woman up and deal with this on my own."

"But that's the thing, Len, you're not dealing with anything. You haven't even talked about—"

"Stop," I blurt, cutting her off. "Just stop, okay? I don't want to fight before you leave."

She sighs, but then thankfully, she nods.

"I'm gonna miss you," she says with a sad smile.

"I'm gonna miss you, too."

"I'll come to visit soon, okay?" Her phone buzzes in her hand, and she looks at the screen. "That's my ride."

We stand at the same time, and I grab her in a tight hug. God, I'm going to miss her. She's kept my head above water this summer. Without her, I'm afraid I might drown.

"I'll see you soon, yeah?"

We break apart and she grabs her suitcase, wheeling it out of my room. I trail her to the door of my apartment. I don't know where my new roommates are, but I'm glad they're not here for my inevitable breakdown once Sam leaves.

"Text when you land," I tell her, and she grins.

"Duh." She hugs me once more before stepping into the hall. "Bye, bitch."

I laugh. "Goodbye, Samantha."

The moment Sam is out of sight, I walk back to my room, lock the door, and pull the vodka bottle out from under my bed. I unscrew the top and take a drink, wincing as it goes down.

Doesn't matter how much I drink, it doesn't taste any better.

I take a few breaths, then swallow some more, this time letting my eyes and throat burn. I drink until I feel dizzy, then I put the bottle away and strip out of my clothes.

I stand naked in front of my mirror, studying my body. I run my hands down my sides, flattening them over my belly.

I hate this body.

It doesn't feel like mine anymore.

It feels like a traitor. It's betrayed me along with everyone else.

Just once in my fucking life, I'd like to have control over something. I'd like to have a say in what happens to me. *Good, polite* Lennon Washington. *Go with the flow* Lennon Washington.

I followed every rule. I did exactly what I was supposed to. And what did it get me?

I pinch the skin at my stomach again, digging my nails in until they leave red, half-moon cuts. I drag my nails back up my torso and cup my breasts. I twist my freshly pierced nipples until they start to bleed, tears springing to my eyes. I cross my arms over my chest and grip the fleshy part of my biceps, sinking my nails into the skin until it hurts, leaving half-moons to match the ones on my stomach.

I know that the way I'm feeling isn't *normal*.

I might be depressed. According to the internet, I am. Aunt Becca got me the business card of a therapist, but I threw it away. Sam fished it out of the trash, so I burned it.

I don't need another person telling me what to do and how to feel.

I might be sick. Something might be wrong inside me, but I might also just be fed up with everything. Maybe I've stopped giving a fuck. Maybe I had to so I could save myself.

Maybe I'm not saving myself at all.

Part of me wonders if I'm starting to become my mom, but

I don't actually care about any of it. I don't want to care about anything.

Tears trickle down my face, and they piss me off. I swipe them away angrily.

I want to feel something other than sorrow. I want to feel something other than this hollow, paralyzing ache. I want to feel nothing.

I can't get rid of Macon's voice. I can't stop feeling his hands on me. At night, when I'm hovering just above sleep, I see visions of what was, what could have been.

Astraea. Sweet, sweet Lennon Capri.

You're mine. You've always been mine.

My heart races, and my panic rises as flashbacks assault me.

I close my eyes and see myself on the bathroom floor. I feel pain, sharp and deep, shooting through my body. I see Sam holding me in the backseat of the car, Aunt Becca cursing at other drivers from behind the wheel.

I hear people talking at me, pitying me. Pamphlets and advice and bullshit words meant to console me. Meant to soothe me.

And then, I feel empty.

I try to hold on to that feeling—the feeling of nothing, emptiness, oblivion—but it's yanked away, and replaced by unruly curls and piercing blue eyes.

I hate him. I hate him.

I love him.

I shake my head. I try to get rid of him, but he just won't go away. None of it will.

I move to my desk and open the drawer, reaching into the far back and feeling around for the hair scissors I bought last month so I could give myself bangs. Sam joked that bangs meant I hit rock bottom. I laughed it off. She had no idea.

I stand back in front of the mirror, this time ignoring my

naked body and zeroing in on my thighs and the array of cuts there. Some are starting to heal. Some are fresh. I use the scissors to scrape the scabs off a few of the cuts, making them bleed again, and then I find an untouched spot on my skin.

I brush my thumb over it softly. I grab my vodka bottle and take a drink, then close my eyes and summon Macon.

Just as he forms in my mind, I replace my thumb with the scissors, and I drag the sharp end slowly until it breaks skin. I know the right amount of pressure to apply now. Enough to hurt. Enough to bleed.

I open my eyes and stare at the fresh cut as the blood wells. I use my thumb to smear it, then push hard, sharpening the sting. When that doesn't hurt enough, I grab the vodka bottle and pour some over the cut. I wince at the burn and breathe through my nose.

I feel it, and slowly, the tears stop.

I pull a makeup wipe out of my drawer and gently rub it over the cut, then I pull on some jeans. They'll rub against it. It'll probably start bleeding again. I don't care.

I don't care about anything. I prefer it that way.

SEVENTEEN

Macon

It's almost midnight when I walk back to my apartment, but something inside me knows that Lennon isn't asleep.

I told her I'd be an hour, but it's been almost two. I bailed on Nic twice before tonight, so she insisted we make up for it. And I think she was punishing me, too. My leg throbs.

I open the door slowly and step inside, kicking off my shoes. My shoulders are tense. The energy in the apartment is charged, and not in a good way. I'm two steps into the kitchen when Lennon greets me with a bored expression, her carry-on sitting at her feet. I drag my eyes from her suitcase to her face.

"You goin' somewhere?"

"To a hotel." She stands from the barstool and grabs the handle of her suitcase. "I told you I didn't want to cramp your style."

Her tone is nonchalant, and her movements are fluid, but I can tell she's pissed. She takes a step toward the hallway, but I block her path.

"You're not cramping my style, whatever the fuck that means, and you're not going to a hotel right now." I reach down to grab her suitcase handle, but she yanks it back. "Don't be stubborn, Lennon. It's fucking midnight."

She hits me with an icy glare that burns my skin.

"I'm not being stubborn," she says coolly. "I'm removing myself from a situation that doesn't suit me."

I huff out a laugh, my eyes wide. A few hours ago, we were having a good conversation, and now this?

"*Doesn't suit you?*" I repeat incredulously. "What the fuck does that even mean? I don't have the right kind of French coffee for your morning cappuccino? The lighting in my studio not up to par?"

She tries to push past me, but I step in front of her again.

"What doesn't suit you, *Capri*, huh? Is this about your French fuck? What's his name? Franklin?"

I spit the words knowing full well they will piss her off, and she shoves hard at my chest.

"That *French fuck* is my *friend*," she says. "And he would *never* put me in a situation that made me feel so shitty."

"What the hell did I do to you now?" I hiss, and she flinches.

The flinch gets me right in the gut. It's like my question was a punch to her jaw, and I immediately feel guilty.

Lennon blinks a few times, then meets my eyes. Hers are emotionless.

"You said an hour," she says slowly. "You've been gone for two."

My jaw drops and I slap my hands at my sides.

"*That's* what this is about? Fuck, I'm sorry. I didn't know it would take that long."

I'm honest, but my words don't console her like I meant for them to. Instead, her jaw tightens in that familiar way and my blood heats.

"Yeah, well, I'm not your fucking babysitter, Macon."

She puts her hands on her hips and stares me down, anger evident in every inch of her body. Anger, and something else.

"I don't know the first thing about taking care of a baby and you just abandoned me with one."

"Is she okay?" I ask, glancing toward the living room. "Did she wake up?"

"No," Lennon snaps, "but that's not the problem."

I look back and study her. The agitation doesn't make sense. She's pissed. Fuck, I'm pissed, even, and I don't know why. I can tell she wanted me to just let her leave. She didn't want to talk about this, but I'm not leaving it alone. I can't.

There's something here...

"Then what's the problem?" I finally ask, putting just enough irritation in my words to push her over the edge.

"The problem is that I'm not here to cover for you so can go hookup with some girl for two hours," she whisper-yells, and it finally makes sense.

I am an idiot. But fuck if this doesn't excite me.

"What?" I say, cocking my head to the side, egging Lennon on. I take a step closer. "What are you so upset about? I thought you didn't care who I was fucking?"

"I don't, but I don't like feeling used," she says, her voice shaking just a little. "If you need to get your dick wet, do it on your own fucking time."

I laugh. I can't help it, and her nostrils flare. She's so hot when she's angry, especially right now. I haven't felt this high in years. She's jealous, and I'm feeding off it.

"I'm glad you think this is funny," she deadpans, then pushes past me to storm out of the kitchen.

I grab her bicep and spin her back to me, and she jerks her arm away but doesn't try to leave again. Her eyes are all fire, scathing with passion. My smirk grows. This is *my* Lennon. I knew she was still in there.

"You're jealous," I say clearly, and she grits her teeth.

"I'm not."

"Good," I snap. "You have no right to be. I'm not biting your head off for fucking the Frenchman."

Her head jerks back slightly, all but confirming my statement. Friend my ass. Friends with benefits, maybe. She's not even trying to deny that they're sleeping together, and anger surges through my body.

"Being jealous would make you a hypocrite," I say, taking another step toward her. "Did you think you'd be the last person I fucked? You think I'd wait for you while you're out screwing half of Europe? You think you're that special?"

"Shut *up*, Macon," she seethes through her teeth, and I smirk.

"Admit you're jealous."

"I am not."

"Seems like you are," I say, and her nose scrunches up in that cute little temper tantrum kind of way. "Seems like you care more that I was *getting my dick wet* than that I left you with Evelyn."

"Bullshit. You're wrong. I don't care who you date."

"Not dating Nicolette, Lennon."

I say it slowly and watch the smallest flash of relief pass over her face. I didn't imagine it, and it spurs me on.

"I think you're jealous," I repeat. "I think you care."

She shakes her head and forces out a raspy laugh. She tries for sardonic, but it just sounds fake.

"No," she stresses. "Never. That ship has sailed. Get over yourself."

I close the distance between us in two steps. She inhales sharply and her eyes flare, but she doesn't move away. The longer I hold eye contact, the more her face changes.

Anger morphs to anguish, then to longing. The closeness is enough to drive me mad, and I know she feels it, too.

She pulls her lower lip between her teeth, and on instinct I reach out, and tug it free. The feeling of my skin on hers, even the smallest amount, sets my body on fire.

"You're saying, if I kiss you right now," I say, caressing her lower lip softly with my thumb, "you wouldn't kiss me back?"

She shakes her head, the tiniest little jerk of movement. Not enough to shake off my thumb.

"No," she whispers.

I drag my thumb from her lip to her jaw slowly, and her eyes flutter shut as I wrap my hand around her neck, settling my thumb on her pulse point. Her heart is beating so fast. Just like mine.

I lean closer and dip my head lower, so my lips are hovering just out of reach. Our breaths mingle, and I swear I can feel her body vibrating, a taut rubber band threatening to snap.

"Are you sure?" I whisper, and she shakes her head again.

"No," she says, her voice no more than a hushed breath, and my restraint snaps.

We collide.

Lips and teeth and tongues.

The moment our mouths connect, I groan. Goosebumps erupt over my body. I bring my other hand to her neck, sliding my fingers into her hair and holding her to me.

Her whimper encourages me, our tongues tangling and massaging. Her breath is my breath. I can't get close enough. I can't touch enough of her.

Fuck, she feels so good. Sinfully good. Addictively good.

She sucks my bottom lip into her mouth and bites, making me groan again. I squeeze her neck, then grab her hair and tug her head back, so I can kiss the sensitive skin just below her jaw.

My dick is throbbing, and I know she can feel it with how we're pressed together. There is no room for breathing between us, no room for thinking, and that's exactly how I like it.

Her moans. The way she presses her lower body into me. The way she's kissing me in such a frenzy.

It's every fucking thing I've dreamt about for the last four years. I've missed her taste. I've missed the way she feels under my palms. Soft and warm and wholly mine.

I recognize this feeling.

It's like a dormant part of me has been shaken awake. My craving insatiable. My need for her stronger than ever. I want my mouth and hands and tongue on every inch of her body. I want to keep her here, against me, forever.

The way she fists her hands in my t-shirt kicks up my heartbeat, until it's beating so fast that it feels like it's going to pound out of my chest. Then she brings her fingers to my hair and her nails scrape against my scalp. I groan in pleasure, but she growls, frustrated, and I smirk against her lips.

Maybe I shouldn't get it cut.

"Fuck, Lennon," I say against her, dragging my hands down her back and gripping her ass. Her hands go for the waist band of my sweats, and she shoves them inside, wrapping her fingers around my hard dick and squeezing.

"Fuck," I grunt out, then walk her backward until her back hits the kitchen island.

I spin her around and drop to my knees, pulling her shorts down and rubbing her pussy with my fingers.

"Lennon, you're so fucking wet. You're so fucking wet for me."

She moans, and I spring to my feet. I need her. It's my only thought as I grab her hair, tug her back against my chest and shove my sweats down. I palm my cock with my other hand and swipe the head of my dick between her pussy lips. She releases the sweetest whimper.

"You want this?" I grind out, pulsing my tip at her opening. "If you don't want me to fuck you right here, stop me now. Otherwise, I'm going to shove my cock into this wet fucking cunt and fuck you until your cum is dripping down your thighs."

She whimpers again, a cry of need, and pushes her body back into me, so the head of my cock slips into her pussy.

"Shit, Lennon," I warn, barely holding on to my control. "Use your words, baby. Tell me you want this. Let me hear that sexy voice."

"Yes, Macon," she says, finally. Breathlessly. "Fuck me hard."

I slam into her.

We both moan when I bottom out, and she falls down onto her forearms. She's the most erotic fucking sight. Sloped back, ass out with my cock sliding in and out of her. I want to bend down and bite her plump ass cheek, but I settle for slapping it with my open palm instead.

"You're so fucking good," I tell her. "So sexy. So fucking good."

I've dreamt of being inside her again. Four years of beating my dick to visions of her. She flexes her pussy and I see stars.

"Fuck, yes, baby. Squeeze me like that," I grind out, and she does it again.

I pull out slowly, then slam back in. Her hips bang into the island, so I grip them with my hands, placing my fingers as a barrier before speeding up.

"Harder," she says, and I listen. I set a punishing pace. "God, yes, Macon."

Sweat dots my forehead, the sounds of our bodies slapping together, of my cock moving in and out of her wetness, make it hard not to come immediately. I grit my teeth against the tingle and dig my fingers into her flesh.

"Harder," she chokes. "Make it hurt."

The words hit me in the chest, and I almost stop, but then Lennon slams back into me, meeting my thrusts and snaking her hand between her legs. She starts rubbing on her clit, her pussy pulsating around me, and I know she's going to come soon. I do what she wants. I fuck her hard and fast.

I let go of her hip, so I can wrap her long hair around my hand and tug hard. Her head is tipped to the ceiling, and she uses her free hand to push her body back, bracing herself on the counter while I pound into her from behind.

"Keep rubbing on your clit, baby."

I move my hand from her hair to her neck and pull her up, so her back is pressed against my chest. I slide my other hand up her body and slip it beneath her shirt so I can pinch her nipple through her bra, but I stop when I feel a metal bar.

I brush my fingers over it and groan. So fucking hot.

"You got your fucking nipples pierced?" I say, and she laughs. I pinch, and she moans. "So fucking sexy. Let me feel you soak my cock."

Lennon opens her mouth on a gasp, her eyes screwed shut, and she turns her head to me, so I take her lips and swallow her moans as she comes. Her pussy tightens around me, and my thoughts fizzle to static.

Nothing has ever felt this good.

No drug. No fuck. No cheap thrill. Nothing compares to Lennon, and it's terrifying.

She's heaven and she's hell. She's my reward and my punishment. She'll ruin me again. I know it.

I hammer into her until her climax is over, then I press her back down on the island, pull out, and shoot thick ropes of glossy white all over her ass cheeks.

The sight will be burned into my brain.

Her round ass, marred red from our rough sex and painted white with my cum. I just had her, but I'm already hard again.

"Shit, you should see yourself," I whisper, rubbing my dick through her swollen pussy lips. "You're so fucking sexy covered in my cum."

She laughs, small and breathy, through her pants. Her

cheek is pressed to the counter, her arms lying limply at her sides. I've worn her out.

"Stay here," I say, patting the side of her thigh.

I pull my sweats up, then walk to the drawer of dishtowels. I pull one out, wet it with warm water, and use it to clean Lennon off.

"Thank you," she whispers, then pushes herself upright.

She bends down and picks up her shorts, making me realize that I'm still fully clothed. Her shirt and bra are still on.

"I'll be right back."

Without making eye contact, Lennon keeps her head down and walks toward the bathroom. When she shuts the door without looking back at me, my heart drops.

She's disconnecting. She's shutting down.

I was impulsive. I was thoughtless. I didn't take my time with her.

I told myself if I ever got her back in my hands, I would make it last. I would make up for the time lost. Instead, I didn't even take time to remove her clothes.

I fucked her from behind, fully clothed, bent over my kitchen island.

It was fucking hot, but from the way she's acting, it was all wrong.

Make it hurt, she said. Did I?

After a moment, the shower kicks on. I check on Evie in the living room, and she's still out cold. Then I sit back down at the island, and I wait. The shower stays on for thirty minutes. I spend that whole time worrying about all the ways I fucked up.

When the shower turns off and the door opens back up, steam billows out from behind Lennon. She's back in the clothes she was wearing before. Her hair hangs wet at her shoulders. Her eyes are swollen.

"I'm sorry," I say honestly. I stand and walk toward her, but she takes a step backward, so I stop. "Lennon?"

"We didn't use a condom."

Her voice is hollow, and I don't know how to respond. I don't even think I have condoms in the apartment. I didn't even think about it. I didn't think about anything.

Fuck.

"Shit," I say. "Okay. I'm sorry. I...I didn't come inside you," I say trying to comfort her, but I sound like an idiot and her face crumples. I feel like an asshole. "Are you on birth control?"

She nods, and her eyes start to gloss over.

"But that stuff isn't one hundred percent, Macon," she says angrily. "We were irresponsible."

"Okay," I say calmly. "I can take you in the morning and get the morning-after pill if you're worried."

She scoffs and brings her hands to her head.

"Jesus, why do I always make such dumb fucking decisions with you?" she says. "I'm supposed to be smarter than this. I cannot do this with you again. I can't."

"Lennon." I close the distance and put my hand on her shoulder. "Calm down. Everything is going to be fine."

"Don't tell me to calm down," she says, swatting my hand away.

She's crying, but she looks furious. I have no idea what's going on.

"What about STIs? Are you clean?"

My eyes go wide, and my mouth drops open in shock.

"Are you fucking serious right now?"

"Yes, I'm serious. I don't know who you've been with or what you've been doing."

"No," I say, trying not to sound offended. "I don't have any STIs. Jesus, Lennon."

She rolls her eyes like she doesn't fucking believe me, and my anger spikes.

"When was the last time you were tested?" She puts her

hands on her hips as she interrogates me, staring me down with angry, tear-filled eyes. "*When*, Macon?"

"When was the last time *you* were tested?" I spit back out of spite.

"Every three fucking months for the last four years," she says, and it's like a punch to the gut.

She's been pretty busy in Paris, I guess.

"Well," I whisper, "I'm so glad you're being responsible."

"Unless you're involved." Lennon's voice is muffled because her hands are covering her face. "Why am I so fucking stupid? How could I let this happen?"

"Lennon..." I say, opening my mouth, then shutting it.

What can I say? Tell her to trust me? Tell her I won't hurt her? Tell her it's different? She won't hear any of that right now.

"I can't do this with you," she says again. "I promised myself I wouldn't do this again, but I've only been here a week and I've already fucked up."

"Okay, I get it." My heart and pride are cracking into pieces. "We'll act like it didn't happen. You regret it. Fine."

"I regret *you*," Lennon whispers, and fuck if it's not a kick to the chest. "I can't feel like this again. I never should have come back here."

"Right," I snap, my voice shaking with my own emotions. "Leave, then. Runaway again. Go back to *Capri* and your French boyfriend."

"Quit acting like you're innocent. Quit acting like this isn't your fault, too, Macon," she says, her voice rising in volume.

"You're selfish. You take and take and take, and you don't care what it does to anyone. You don't care about the aftermath or how much you hurt people. I don't have space for your bullshit in my life."

She's like an erupting volcano.

A bottle of champagne that's been shaken before being opened.

She explodes, and I sway on my feet from the force of her words, from the hatred and the hurt behind them.

She used to be the only person who saw any good in me, but I guess she meant it when she said that person is dead.

I don't know if anything has ever hurt this badly.

Lennon glares at the floor as tears fall down her cheeks, her arms wrapped protectively around her torso. What's she protecting herself from?

Me.

There's so much I could tell her.

There are so many ways I could attempt to defend myself right now, but I can't. I don't. It's not the right time. It might never be. She wouldn't listen anyway, so I keep things brief.

"You need to demonize me to fit your narrative, fine," I say, my voice low and shaky.

I advance on her.

"You want to make me the villain in your story, so you feel better? To justify running off to Paris and saying *fuck you* to your family? Okay. But don't *ever* say I didn't care about you. You're the *only* thing I have ever cared about."

I reach out to touch her but drop my hand before I can make contact.

"Every single decision I've made over the last four years has been for you."

A sob escapes from her lips, and she screws her eyes up tight, but the tears keep falling.

"God, Macon, I wish you would have given me a say in some of them, then."

The sentence makes me uneasy. It feels ominous, but I don't know why. I put my palm gently to her cheek, rubbing my thumb over the wetness from her tears.

I want to kiss her. Even now, especially now, I want her.

"Nicolette is my physical therapist," I tell her, setting the record straight. One less thing for her to feel guilty about. One less thing for her to hold against me.

"Physical therapist? What? Why?"

Her eyes narrow with confusion and I drop my hand, clenching it into a fist at my side.

"Busted my femur about six months ago when my helicopter went down," I say, trying like hell to sound casual. If I think too hard about it, the flashbacks come. I don't need that right now. "Nic came by tonight because I've missed my last two PT sessions, and it's important that I don't miss a third. She's been doing me a favor and letting me do them in the evenings since Trent is in the hospital."

Lennon doesn't say anything. She just blinks at me slowly with her brows scrunched, trying to make sense of everything in her head.

"I'm not sleeping with her," I say clearly. "I've *never* slept with her."

I let her process my words. I wait to see how she'll react. If she'll ask questions. She doesn't. Her eyes dart to her feet and she bites her lip, but she doesn't say a word.

Evelyn starts to fuss in the living room, and we both look toward the noise.

"I'll be right back," I tell Lennon quietly. She nods.

I walk to the crib slowly. Each step taking me farther and farther from Lennon. My sense of dread spikes, then sadness. Because I already know what's about to happen. I know her better than she knows me.

I rub Evie's back, give her a pacifier, and walk slowly back to the hall.

Lennon is already gone.

Once again, she's chosen to leave me. She ran. Things get too hard, and she runs.

But I fucked it up this time. I provoked her. I was

downright mean with some of the things I said, and then I couldn't fucking keep my hands off her.

Talk about emotional whiplash.

I sped up when I should have gone slow. I devoured when I should have savored.

I walk back to Evie's crib and make sure the video monitor is on, then grab the receiver off the counter. I bought this about a month ago so I could do work in the office downstairs while Evie napped in my apartment. I'm fucking thankful for it now.

I grab my pack of cigarettes from the drawer in my kitchen, then take them and the baby monitor downstairs to the parking lot. I light a cigarette, take a drag, and tell myself it's enough.

It's not.

I know throwing and sketching won't do it either, so I take out my phone and call Casper.

"Dick," he rasps, "do you even know what time it is?"

"Sorry. You wanna box?"

"No." He groans, and I smile when I hear the rustling of bed sheets. "I do not want to fucking box."

I hear someone's hushed voice say something in the background, but I can't make out what.

"Sorry," Casper whispers on the other end. "I'll be back later."

"You got company?" I ask, and Casper snorts.

"Like you care." I'm grinning like an idiot. I can hear his keys jangle and a door open. "You can have an hour. That's it. And I swear to god, if you tell Nic—"

"I won't tell her," I say quickly. "Thanks, Casper."

"Fuck off, Davis."

He hangs up on me, but I heard the smile in his voice. I wouldn't have called him if I wasn't sure it was okay. In fact, I know he would be pissed if I didn't. Anytime I start to feel guilty, I replay the conversation we had a few years ago.

I was struggling. Emotionally, I was all over the fucking place. Mentally, I wasn't much better. Once, I even went as far as to buy a bag of bullshit from some junkie dealer in a back alley in Virginia Beach, but then I cracked and called Casper.

Any fucking time of day. Any day of the week. I don't care if it's fucking Christmas morning, and we're eighty years old in a nursing home surrounded by grandkids. You call me. I'll be there.

I wait in the parking lot, chain-smoking and watching Evie sleep on the monitor, until Casper pulls in, then we walk silently into the rec center and to the gym.

Once we're in the ring and the baby monitor is propped on a table next to it, he makes eye contact and I brace myself for whatever harsh reality he's going to toss at me.

"You have to talk to her soon."

I glance away, and he hits me upside the head with his gloved hand. I bat at him, but I don't hit back. I just bring my eyes to his like he wanted.

"I'm serious, Macon. You can't do this shit to yourself again, and you can't lose this opportunity. If she goes back to Paris before you talk to her, you're going to regret it."

I close my eyes and drop my head back.

He's right. I know he's right. But fuck, I don't know if I can. I don't know if it matters.

Lennon made her choice once. Who's to say that anything I've done will make a difference? Who's to say she'll actually care now? What if I just set myself up for failure all over again?

"Maybe I don't want to know why she did what she did," I say honestly.

"Then don't ask," he says. "Just fill her in on everything that's happened since. Show her what's changed. Show her what hasn't changed." He shrugs. "Give her a new choice."

I let his words settle. I roll them over in my head, but one thought keeps circling.

Would I really be giving her a *new* choice?

I'm still the same person, deep down. I've just cleaned up a little on the outside. I'm not sure if that will ever be enough.

"One hour," Casper says, interrupting my spiral. "You've got one hour."

He pops in his mouthguard, slips on his other glove, then pounds his fists together. When he speaks, it's mumbled around the plastic.

"Hit me, fucker."

EIGHTEEN
Macon

"Is she here?" I ask my mom as I hand her Evelyn.

"I thought she was staying with you," Mom says, eyes wide. "What happened?" She looks at the clock on the wall. It's 6 a.m. and Lennon is MIA.

"She left late last night," I say honestly. "We kind of got into it."

"Macon," my mom sighs, leading me into the kitchen, "do you think she's gone back to Paris?"

"No," I lie. I can't be sure of anything right now. "She wouldn't leave while Trent is still in the hospital."

My mom grabs her phone off the kitchen counter and dials. Evelyn reaches for the phone with a grin, so I give her leg a little tickle to distract her. The squeal of laughter she lets out makes me smile despite the shitty situation.

I need a fucking drink.

The phone rings several times before going to an automated message. Mom hangs up and her brow furrows.

"Maybe she went to a hotel," she says to herself.

"Did Capri run off again," Claire asks from the doorway behind me.

I don't even turn to look at her.

"Well, that's no surprise," she continues, then pushes past me and grabs a coffee cup from the cabinet. "She decided a long time ago that she's too good for us."

"Shut up, Claire," I say, rolling my eyes. "Just for once, could you keep your bitchy thoughts to yourself?"

"Oh, funny," she hisses at me. "Does self-righteousness always come with sobriety? What did *you* do for her to run?"

"Don't start with me," I say. "Don't act like you give two fucks if she's gone. You don't want her here. You haven't wanted her here for years."

Claire opens her mouth to argue, but Mom throws her hand up, cutting her off.

"Both of you stop," she says, her voice cracking. "My husband is lying in a hospital bed in a coma. We don't know if he'll wake up. I have a ten-month-old child to take care of. I shouldn't need to parent my adult children, too."

Mom's tears have always crushed me. I hate seeing her cry. I've gotten better over the last few years, but right now, I feel like that same fucked-up teenager who always let her down.

"I'm sorry, Mom," I say, pulling her and Evie into a hug. Evie pats my cheek and slobbers me up with a baby kiss. "We'll do better, okay?"

I look at Claire and raise an eyebrow.

"Yeah, Mom, we will," Claire says softly. "Sorry."

Masters joins us in the kitchen, sliding his arm around Claire and kissing her temple. She smiles up at him, and I have to force myself not to scowl.

There's a knock at the door that makes us all sit up straight. There's only one person who would be knocking on the door right now.

"I'll get it," Masters says, before lumbering out of the kitchen.

I strain to hear what's happening as he opens the door.

Muffled conversation that I can't make out, but I already know who is about to round the corner with Eric. I don't even look up from my coffee mug when he comes back to the kitchen with our guest in tow.

"Capri," my mom breathes out.

She rushes to her, and I glance up just in time to see her pull Lennon into a hug.

"Honey, where have you been? Where did you stay last night?"

Lennon's eyes shoot to mine, and I shake my head once, letting her know that I didn't tell my mom *everything*.

"I got a room at a motel out of town," she says, looking back at my mom with a forced, tired smile.

"How are you going to paint?" I ask, and she startles.

All her stuff is still in my studio. No way she can paint in a dumpy-ass motel. She doesn't answer. Just shrugs.

"Why can't she paint at the rec center?" Masters pipes up. Helpful Boy Scout as always. "I doubt the owner will mind," he jokes, looking at me with a friendly grin.

I flare my eyes at him, trying to tell him to shut the fuck up, but he tilts his head like he's confused.

"Oh, who's the owner?" Lennon asks.

I stare Masters down. He opens his mouth, then shuts it. He looks from me back to Lennon, but before he can even attempt to fix his fuck-up, Claire laughs.

"You're kidding me," she says, looking between me and Lennon. "He didn't tell you?"

"Didn't tell me what?" Lennon says slowly, looking at me.

"Macon owns the rec center now," Claire says. "He bought it from the Billings because they had to move back to Massachusetts when James' dad got sick."

Lennon's face is one of complete surprise, and I almost want to laugh. The idea of me being anything other than a complete disaster is such a shock to her, and I fucking hate it.

She's always going to think I'm a loser. She's never going to trust me.

"See, Len?" I say. "Not quite a fuck-up all the time, yeah?"

For a minute, the whole house is in awkward silence, and then Mom's phone rings. She grabs it from the counter and gasps when she sees the Caller ID on the screen.

"It's the hospital," she says quickly, putting her phone to her ear.

The tension in the room switches to something entirely different as we watch my mom talk.

"Hello? Yes, this is she. Yes. Really? Okay, thank you. I'll be there right away."

She looks to us with tears in her eyes.

"He's awake," she says. "Trent's awake."

"They said that confusion is normal. Expect him to seem kind of disoriented and foggy," my mom explains to us in the waiting room. "The doctor said he might sound funny, too. Scratchy voice or slurred speech. Just act normal, okay? We don't want to upset him."

"Okay," Lennon says, her head nodding. "Okay. Can we see him now?"

"They said two at a time," Mom says, then fidgets with her hands glancing between us.

They won't let Eric in because he's not family, so he's staying in the lobby with Evie, which leaves me, Claire, Lennon, and Mom to pair off.

"Lennon can go first with you, Mom," I say softly, and I don't miss Lennon's grateful glance. Claire doesn't argue, thank god, and Lennon and Mom disappear behind the ICU doors.

"I'm scared," Claire whispers. Masters puts his hand on her shoulder, but she looks at me. "I don't know why, but I am."

Moments like this, where Claire lets herself be vulnerable and doesn't feel the need to hide behind her spikes, I'm reminded of how she used to be before everything went down with our dad.

She's tiny little Claire Bear again. My baby sister. She's hiding in my bedroom closet to make sure I'm okay after a fight with our dad. She's slipping me water and fruit snack packets when dear old dad sent me to bed without dinner. She's begging me to tell mom the truth about my broken wrist.

She used to love me. We used to get along. It fucking sucks that it takes a tragedy for us to be kind to each other.

I pull her in for a hug, and she hugs me back.

"He's okay, Claire," I say to her. "He's awake. That's huge. He'll be back home before you know it."

"I don't want Evie to grow up without a dad like we did," she whispers against me. "Trent's a good one."

"I know," I tell her. "She won't."

We spend the rest of the wait passing Evie between us, playing with her to avoid talking to each other. I feel lighter, though. For the first time since Trent's collapse, I feel like I can think positively. Like maybe my actions did some good. Maybe I did save his life.

When the ICU doors buzz open, I shoot to my feet. Mom walks out first, but my eyes are on Lennon. She looks terrible. Sad. She's staring at her feet as she walks. I rush to them.

"Hey. What's up? How is he?"

"He's good," Mom says softly. "A little disoriented, but the doctor said that's normal."

Lennon finally looks at me and my throat tightens. It's nothing but despair and guilt and loss in those hazel eyes.

"He doesn't know me," she whispers, her voice hollow. "He didn't know who I was. He asked about Evie and you. He asked about Claire. Even Eric. But it took prompting to get him to know me, and even then, I'm not..."

She shrugs.

"I think he might have been lying, you know, because he didn't want to upset me."

"He knows you, sweetie," my mom says, pulling Lennon into a side hug. "He's just confused. But he knows you."

Lennon nods.

"Okay," she whispers, and I want to pull her to me.

I want to wrap her in my arms and promise her I'll make it all better. But after last night, touching her is off-limits. So, I do the next best thing.

"Go paint," I tell her.

I pull my extra key out of my pocket, the one she left on my nightstand, and hold it out for her.

"My studio is yours, okay? I won't be back until this afternoon."

"Really?" she asks quickly, then her eyebrows scrunch up. She shakes her head. "No. It's fine."

"Lennon," I say firmly, "go paint. Don't be stubborn."

"I'm not being stubborn," she huffs, her mouth twitching slightly with the smile she's fighting. "I don't want to trouble you."

"It's not any more trouble than you've already given me," I say with a smirk, keeping my voice low.

Lennon flares her eyes and flicks them towards my mom, but I keep mine on her. She worries her lower lip with her teeth, and I shove my hands in my pockets to keep from reaching for her.

"You sure?" she asks, and I smile softly.

"Yeah, Len."

I reach out and take her hand to press my spare key into her palm. I don't let go right away. I feel everyone's eyes on us, but I hold on to her hand. I caress her wrist with my thumb. I *feel* her.

"Go paint," I insist again. "Clear your head."

"Thank you," she says on an exhale. I drop her hand, and she takes a step back. "Thank you."

I watch her leave.

I don't acknowledge the eyes that I know are on me. I don't feel like explaining myself or making excuses. Try as hard as I can, I'm never going to be able to act like she means nothing to me. I'll never be able to treat her like a stepsister. I don't want to deal with the inevitable disappointment and disgust.

"I'm going in," I say to the room, then turn and walk through the ICU doors.

I'm surprised when Claire doesn't follow, but I'm more relieved. I take a deep breath when I get to Trent's room, then I knock three times before stepping through the doorway.

He looks up at me, and seeing him awake is enough to make me weep with joy. He furrows his brow for a moment, probably searching his memory to place me, then his lips turn up into a smile.

"Macon," he says, and I smile back.

I ignore the way his voice rasps, hoarse as if he's gone days without water. Or days with a tube shoved down his throat.

"That's me," I joke, crossing the room to stand by his bed. I reach out and pat his shoulder. It feels smaller. "About time you woke up, old man."

He snorts a laugh.

"I was just catching up on sleep," he says wryly. "How's my munchkin? You been looking after her, I hear."

"She's good," I tell him. "She'll be stoked to see you."

"Thank you," he says. "Thank you for what you did. The doctors said I would be dead if it weren't for you."

My neck and cheeks heat, and I have to clear my throat before I can respond. I wave a hand at him, brushing off the compliment.

"It's nothing," I say. "Don't even mention it."

"It's something, Macon."

His voice cracks and his eyes fill with tears. Mine do the same.

I've seen Trent cry three times in all the years that I've known him.

Once when he married my mom, once at the hospital when Evelyn was born, and once on the day he took Lennon to the airport to send her to England.

Right now, in this hospital room, makes four.

"I can't imagine what I would do if I couldn't see Evie grow up," he says. A tear trails down his cheek. "If I couldn't hold your mom again. What you did...Thank you."

I sniff and wipe my eyes with my palms. All I can do is nod. If I try to talk, I'll lose it. Trent is quiet for a minute, his eyes distant as he runs something through his head.

"I didn't know who Lennon was at first," he says, breaking the silence. "She looks so different. I saw her and I just...nothing. I really upset her."

His expression is one of guilt. He feels terrible. I grip his shoulder again, this time giving it a reassuring squeeze.

"She'll be okay. She understands."

Trent looks at me. Studies my face for a moment, searching. My defenses start to rise and my shoulders tighten. I know what's coming.

"Have you talked to her?" he asks. I shake my head. "You should."

"It's not the right time," I say quickly.

"The timing will never be perfect," he says, "but life is too short. If your accident hasn't taught you that, then mine should. You should be proud. You're a good man, Macon."

I brush off the comment and take a step back.

Sure, I'm in a better place. But good? No.

I'll always be the addict. I'll always be the fuck-up. It doesn't matter how much I do; it doesn't change who I am at my core.

I fucked up so many times with her already. She doesn't trust me. She doesn't believe I can ever be worthy of praise or affection. And what if she's right? What if, even after everything I've accomplished, I still manage to let her down?

Last night proves that I haven't grown as much as I thought I had. Taunting her. Provoking her.

I want to squeeze my eyes shut in disgust at the way I let myself treat her. I played into every single one of her negative opinions of me.

"I'll think about it," I say to Trent, but I can tell from the way his lips purse that he doesn't believe me.

He opens his mouth to speak, but we're cut off by another knock at the door.

"Hello, sir," Claire calls playfully. "You an admiral yet?"

He laughs a raspy, painful laugh, and she winces at the sound.

"Not quite," Trent says, and Claire crosses the room and gives him a hug.

I hear her start to cry on his shoulder.

"Shh, shh," he whispers. "We're all okay now. It's all going to be okay."

NINETEEN

Macon

I LEAVE THE HOSPITAL SHORTLY AFTER CLAIRE ARRIVES.

The doctors told us not to overwhelm Trent, and not to stay too long. He needs his rest, and they still have to monitor him.

I head back to the rec center and get some work done. July 4th is next week, and we have a whole day of activities planned for the kids. My heart might be elsewhere, but my mind needs to make sure this shit runs smoothly.

At five, I check in on the evening classes, then make my way slowly up the stairs. I don't know for sure if she'll still be here, but I'm on edge anyway.

I twist the knob to find the door locked, so I take out my key and let myself in quietly. I stand by the door, holding my breath, until I can hear the music coming from the studio.

She's here.

I take my shoes off, walk into my room and change into my throwing clothes, then take a leap of faith. I walk slowly to the studio door and knock twice.

"Come in," Lennon calls, so I push open the door and step inside.

She's sitting at my drawing table, and the sight makes my throat go dry.

There's a large piece of watercolor paper covering the table, her paints and brushes are set up in the exact way I remember them from all those years ago, and Fleetwood Mac is playing on the speakers. She looks perfect here. She looks like she belongs here.

But what really gets me, what strikes me completely dumb, is that her hair is in a braid.

She catches me looking at it, and she winces. She reaches up and fingers the end of it.

"It's the best way to wear it when I'm painting," she says. "I hope it's okay that I'm still here. I lost track of time."

"Are you feeling better?" I ask, and she gives me a small smile.

"I am. Thank you for letting me use your studio."

God, this conversation is so stilted and awkward. It's torture. She can barely look at me.

"Commission?" I nod to the painting she's been working on.

"No," she says with a hollow laugh. "Therapy."

I nod because I get it. And for a split second, she flicks her eyes toward me, and we're both caught in the beam of the other's attention.

A freeze frame of this moment would suggest that everything was perfect. Nothing bad has ever happened in the reality that these smiles exist.

After a few breaths, just before it gets too intimate, she looks away, breaking eye contact and sitting up straighter in her chair.

"I should probably get going," she says, reaching for something on the floor.

"You don't have to," I say quickly. "I was going to throw. You can stay if you don't mind."

The pause is tense, charged, as she thinks it over. She almost declines twice, before opening her mouth and saying, "okay."

I move to my wheel and start my set-up. I try not to look at her. I try to give her some privacy, but my eyes have always been drawn to her. When I glance at her, I find her looking back, and I raise an eyebrow.

"What?" I ask, and she cocks her head to the side.

"Why didn't you tell me about the rec center?"

I sigh.

"I didn't think you'd care." It's a half-truth. "You already had your mind made up about me, and what I do with my life doesn't interest you. I figured it wouldn't matter."

Her eyebrows scrunch and her lips turn downward.

"The things I said to you that first day...You just let me say them? You didn't even try to correct me."

My lips quirk up into a small smile and I shrug.

"It's not too far off to believe I'd be dishonorably discharged for drugs," I say.

She doesn't smile back, and I sigh.

"Would it have mattered, Lennon? Would *Capri* have cared?"

"Macon," she says, pleading, and closes her eyes. "It's just...three and half years sober? Owning the rec center? You were in a god damn helicopter crash, and no one told me."

She opens her eyes and locks them with mine.

"Why did no one tell me any of this?"

"I also sell my pottery online," I add lightly, and her jaw drops in surprise. I blow out a harsh laugh before hitting her with honesty.

"Why would they tell you, Lennon? Last I knew, you vehemently refused to hear my name and had to be triple reassured I was out of the country before even thinking of setting foot back on American soil. You wouldn't have cared to know that your stepbrother was turning shit around. He was already dead to you."

The words burn coming off my tongue.

My feelings are hurt, yes. But it hurts even more because I did this to myself. Her eyes fall to the ground, staring hard at nothing. The worry lines between her eyebrows are prominent, and I want to smooth them away.

"I'm sorry," she whispers finally. "For assuming. I'm sorry, Macon."

I nod, but I don't speak.

I finish with my wheel, grab my clay, and sit down to throw. Within seconds, a sense of ease and rightness settles over me. Something I have only ever felt when working alongside Lennon.

She's the spark that sets my creativity ablaze. She's my artistic other half. I've never felt more whole than when I'm with her.

Every so often, I let my eyes wander to where she sits, perched on my chair with her paintbrush poised in her hand. She chews on her lip as she works. Sometimes she mouths along with the song playing through the speakers.

She's always done this thing, where she'll sit back to survey her work and hold her paintbrush lightly while rolling the wooden end of it across her lower lip. I used to wait for that movement in high school, and when she did it, it would take my breath away.

Fuck, how badly I wanted to be that paintbrush.

When she does it now, it has the exact same effect. I might as well be nineteen again. My dick hardens, my heart kicks up, and I can't tear my eyes away from that fucking paintbrush and her plush lower lip.

She stands up slowly and stretches, her shirt lifting just enough that I can see a sliver of pale skin. Skin that I had in my hands last night. That I felt and squeezed. Visions of her bent over my kitchen counter invade my mind, and I have to stop the wheel before I ruin my vase.

She glances at me over her shoulder and her breath hitches when she catches me staring. The same old zap of energy. The same need. When she sinks her teeth into her bottom lip, I have to clench my clay-covered hands into fists.

"What," she whispers. Her eyes bounce between mine, heating me up, then drop to my mouth before dragging back up. "What?"

"You've got a little," I say, flicking my eyes to her jaw, "paint."

"Oh."

Her brow furrows, and she swipes at the opposite cheek. Slowly, I rise to my feet. Her eyes never leave mine, beckoning me to her.

"No," I say, walking toward her, until I'm right in front of her. "You missed it."

I gesture to the right side of her jaw. A splotch of bright green right on her delicate jawbone. It reflects the green in her eyes.

I want to wipe it off myself, but my hands are covered with wet clay. I watch her throat contract with a hard swallow, her fingers trembling slightly as she raises them and wipes at her jaw, smearing the paint across her face.

My mouth twitches into a small smile, and her eyes fall to the movement. Her pupils dilate and her lips part on a shaky inhale.

My body makes the decision before my mind does, and I reach for her. She closes her eyes just as I cup her jaw, smearing cold clay over the paint mark before sliding to her neck and pulling her into me.

Her lips are needy and soft, opening for me immediately, and I want to consume all of her.

She moans into my mouth and her fingers fist into my shirt,

digging her nails into my abs. I reach behind her and take the ribbon from the end of her braid, then wrap the braid around my fist, pulling just enough to tilt her head back, to put her at my mercy.

I use my other hand to grab onto her waist, letting myself finally touch that expanse of skin that was tempting me minutes earlier and mark it with slick clay.

Our tongues tangle, hurried but not as rushed as last time. There's no clacking of teeth, no animalistic collision of bodies. No self-loathing. Just lust and desire and Macon and Lennon.

Just her and me.

Lennon pulls me with her as she walks backward until she's running into the drawing table. Water sloshes and a jar clanks. Something clatters to the floor.

She throws her hand back to catch herself just as I lift her up and sit her on the table. I slide my hands up her torso, groaning when I find that she's not wearing a bra under her shirt. She gasps, and I palm her breasts, my dick throbbing with the desire to see her naked body covered in the clay from my hands.

She claws at my back and at my hair, moaning softly as I kiss down her face and neck. She brings her hand to my head, sliding cool, slick fingers from my face into my hair, bringing the distinct scent of fresh watercolor paints.

She pushes my shirt up, and I lean back, just enough to pull it the rest of the way over my head. She slides her hands down my torso and up to my biceps, leaving cold streaks in her wake.

I tug her shirt over her head and kiss down her collarbone. She arches her back, pressing her chest into me, and I close my lips around one of her taut nipples, rolling my tongue around the metal piercing.

Fuck, this fucking piercing. So damn sexy.

She whimpers and drops her head back, and the sound drives me crazy.

I want to eat her pussy while she's laid out on my drawing desk.

I reach for the waistband of her shorts, and she widens her legs, but when she does that, her knee bumps into one of her water jars and it falls to the floor.

Water splashes our feet, and Lennon and I break apart.

We're both panting and shirtless, eyes wide with surprise, when we take in the mess we've created, and we both start laughing at the same time.

Paint is smeared all over the desk from where Lennon's hands must have landed to support herself. Brushes are scattered on the floor. And our bodies...

"You're covered in clay," I say with a grin, my voice rough. My eyes want to stay glued to her fucking perfect breasts, but I keep them on her face. She laughs at me, not even bothering to try and hide her nakedness.

"You're covered in paint," she counters.

I reach up and wipe at my face, and sure enough, my hand is covered in green and blue paint when I pull it back.

I glance down at my chest to see handprints smeared all over my skin. I can see exactly where Lennon's fingers were, where she grabbed and scratched in her need for me.

I look at her body to find the same, but with clay, where I touched her with my hands, and paint, where our bodies connected.

Sensual, sexy, erotic fucking art.

My cock aches, and I have to palm it over my joggers. Her breath hitches, and I glance up to find her eyes locked on my hand. I squeeze, and she whispers *yes*.

"I want to watch you," she says, and my heart stops. "I want to watch you touch yourself."

"Yeah?" I say, swallowing hard before giving my cock a pump over my joggers. "Like this?"

"No," she says, shaking her head. "Take it out."

I do as she wants, then run my fist over my hard cock, stroking it a few times before squeezing the head. I hiss at the feeling, at the way she's staring, pupils huge and mouth agape, watching me touch myself to thoughts of her.

"You want to watch me beat my cock, Lennon?"

"Yes," she says, eyes never leaving my hand. "What are you thinking about?"

She's breathless with her heightened arousal, and the question is laced with hope and nerves.

"You. I'm thinking of you," I tell her honestly, roughly running my hand up and down my shaft.

"I'm thinking of tongue-fucking your sweet cunt while you're laid out on my desk, covered in my clay handprints."

"Yeah?" She flicks her eyes to mine quickly before dropping them back to my cock.

"Yes," I say on a groan. "I'm thinking of having your cum dripping down my chin."

I tense at the visual, pumping faster, chasing the tingling feeling. I close my eyes and drop my head back.

"I'm thinking of your lips wrapping around my hard cock, so I can fuck your throat nice and deep. Until you're choking on me. Until I can come on your tongue."

I'm pushed back a step and my eyes fly open to find Lennon moving to her knees in front of me. I freeze, stunned, as she looks up at me through those long as fuck lashes and wraps her hands around mine, guiding my cock to her mouth.

"Oh fuck, Lennon," I breathe out.

She swirls her tongue around the tip of my cock, then closes her lips around it. I groan and drop my hands, letting her take over.

She licks up my shaft, pumps me a few times with her hand, and takes me into her mouth on her own, hollowing out her cheeks, then swallowing around me.

"Fuck, that talented mouth."

She pulls off me for a moment and looks up at me.

"Fuck my throat," she commands. "I want to taste you."

"Christ," I say, wasting no time.

I grip her jaw with one hand and rub it, the clay starting to dry and flake off. Then I use my other hand to glide the head of my cock back and forth over her tongue.

"You want this?"

She nods eagerly, so I push in slowly, giving her a chance to adjust. The moment I hit the back of her throat, she moans, and I can't hold back any longer.

"Yes, this fucking filthy mouth," I growl as I thrust in and out, hitting the back of her throat and making her gag.

I'm not going to last. Fuck, I want this to last.

"You want to taste my cum? Want me to dirty up your filthy little mouth?"

She moans in response, and the vibrations push me over the edge. I come with a long groan, spilling deep into her throat as she swallows around me.

When the last jolt of my climax fades, I pull out and step backwards, staring down at Lennon like the fucking goddess that she is.

"Remind me to thank the French," I rasp, offering her my hand to help her back up.

She barks out a laugh as she lets me pull her to her feet.

She reaches out and pulls my joggers back up, tucking my dick inside them. I inhale sharply when her fingers brush the sensitive underside of the head, and she smirks. Evil little thing.

I watch as she bends down and picks up her shirt, pulling it back over her head. I try to keep my face neutral, but the realization fucking stings.

She's leaving.

She's just choked on my dick and now she's leaving.

She glances again at the mess we've made, but I wave her off.

"I'll clean it," I tell her. "Sorry," I say, gesturing to her now ruined therapy painting.

She shrugs, and I can tell she's retreating back into her head.

"I'm going to head out," she says, walking quickly toward the door. "I want to get to the hospital early tomorrow."

I try like hell to ignore the feeling of being discarded, but it creeps up anyway, and my anger spikes.

I scoff just as her hand hits the knob.

"Have a great night, *Astraea*," I say slowly, taunting her.

She whips around and hits me with a glare.

"You know, Macon, it was clever in high school," she says. "Innocence and purity, ha ha, let's all make fun of Goody Two-shoes Lennon Washington. But maybe, given recent events, it's time to find a different way to *attempt* to insult me."

She turns and walks out, and I give her three seconds before I follow. I catch her just before she leaves the hallway.

"I think you're forgetting something," I call out, halting her steps. She turns and looks at me expectantly. "Innocence and purity, yeah. But you know what you're missing?"

She cocks her head to the side and raises a brow expectantly.

"*Astraea* is also the constellation Virgo," I tell her. I pause, just enough for it to sink in, then I tap the constellation tattoo on my chest. "Virgo."

I break eye contact and walk to my bedroom, opening the door and looking at Lennon one last time before I walk inside.

"Lock up on your way out, *Capri*."

Then I step into my room and shut the door behind me.

I walk quietly to my bed, sit down, and pull out my phone. I scroll to Jessica's contact and hit call.

I'm cracking. I can feel the fissures forming. My skin is starting to tighten, to itch.

Lennon Capri Washington is going to be my undoing all over again.

TWENTY

Macon

"Hey, Ma," I say into the phone. "What's up?"

I'm a little nervous she's calling me this early. I'm not supposed to be at her house for another few hours. I'm still wrapped in a towel from my shower.

"Change of plans," my mom says brightly. "We get to all go see him today. They've moved him out of the ICU, so I'm bringing Evie."

"That's great," I say with a smile. For the first time since Lennon's exit last night, I feel a little more relaxed. This is good news. "That means he must be one step closer to home, yeah?"

"Hopefully," Mom says. "I'm going to head over to the hospital in an hour. Can you make it?"

"I'll see you there," I tell her, then pause. "Um, you're going to have to call Lennon. She's back at the motel."

Saying it pisses me off. A flash of her back as she walked out last night runs through my head. *Find a new way to insult me*, she said. As if I'm the one doing the insulting.

"I'll call her now," Mom says. Her voice is tight, but neither of us acknowledge it. Instead, I tell her I love her and I'll see her soon, then I hang up as if I'm not a total fucking mess.

I keep replaying my conversation with Trent. He says to talk to Lennon. He says the time will never be perfect. Life is too short.

And he's right.

But it's not the right *time* I'm waiting for. It's the right *me*.

The strongest me. The worthiest version of me. And now that Lennon's back, I'm not sure that version of me will ever exist. I've talked to my therapist more in the last few days than I have since I started the program three years ago.

To be fair, Jessica knew this might happen. I just really hoped it wouldn't.

The problem is my craving for Lennon has always been more powerful than any of the others.

Drugs, liquor, sex, pain.

They've always been temporary fixes to curb my need for her. They're crutches to fall back on when I can't have the one thing my body desires.

And with her this close? Close enough to touch, to kiss, to fuck, but to never really have?

It's messing me up.

I've always been fucked-up, but having her here is making it worse.

But I can't stay away.

I dry off and dress, eat a quick breakfast, then head to the hospital to meet my mom. She texted me Trent's new room number, so I navigate my way through the hospital until I'm stepping off the elevator to find my mom and Lennon sitting in a waiting room with Evelyn.

"Macon," Mom calls, waving me over.

I smile quickly at Lennon then give Mom my attention.

"Ready?" I ask. "What are we waiting for?"

The elevator beeps behind me and I turn around to watch Claire step out of it, answering my question.

"Sorry, I'm late," Claire says with a wince, and I resist the urge to roll my eyes.

"It's okay," my mom says softly. "Are we all ready?"

She's practically bouncing with nervous energy. We've already been briefed on Trent's situation. His heart is weakened. He's going to tire easily. We don't want to overwhelm him.

Mom weighed the pros and cons of this group visit, but we decided it would be a good way to lift his spirits. Trent isn't taking too well to being confined to a hospital bed.

I can relate. After my accident and femur surgery, I was going stir crazy. I know exactly how Trent must feel being cooped up here with an ability level half of what it was just days ago.

"Ready," I say to Mom, then I boop Evie's nose. "Ready to see Dada?"

Evie squeals and claps.

"Dadadadada," she chants, and it brightens the mood immediately.

Lennon laughs lightly, and when I glance at her, she mouths *thank you*. I'm not really sure why she's thanking me, but I nod anyway.

We all follow Mom as she walks down the hall to Trent's room. She checks in with a nurse on the way, and then she's knocking on his door and stepping inside.

"Good morning," Mom says lightly, and I hear Trent's laugh before I step into his room.

"What a sight for sore eyes," Trent says, and Evie immediately loses her shit.

She starts chanting *Dada* and bouncing in Mom's arms, squirming like hell to get to her dad. Evie says something that sounds like *hug* and *down* and we all laugh.

"Hello, my munchkin." Trent chuckles, and he reaches his arms out to her so my mom can hand Evie over to him.

Her little hands close on his cheeks and she slobbers his face with a kiss before snuggling into his chest in the cutest way. He closes his eyes and hugs her tightly.

"Oh, I missed you too, baby girl."

My smile hurts my cheeks as I watch them embrace, my eyes stinging slightly. When I glance at Lennon, my heart sinks. Tears are steadily falling down her cheeks, and she looks so torn.

I can't even imagine how she must be feeling. Out of place? Like she doesn't belong? Is she happy or sad right now? Jealous? Guilty?

I sidestep to her without thinking and slide my arm over her shoulders. She doesn't flinch or move away. To my surprise, she actually melts into my side, and I let myself pull her tighter into me. I feel her tense briefly when Trent looks at us, but his immediate smile relaxes her.

"Pumpkin," he says softly, then stretches out the arm not holding on to Evie. "Come here."

She sniffles and rushes to him, sitting lightly on the side of the hospital bed and collapsing into his outstretched arm.

The whole room is quiet, just the sounds of soft crying coming from Lennon and my mom, and then Evie breaks the tension by climbing up and slobbering a kiss onto Lennon's cheek.

"There are my girls," Trent says with a laugh, beaming at Lennon and Evie, and for some reason, my eyes flick to Claire.

She's been mostly silent, standing in the corner of the room, and now I know why.

She's watching the whole interaction with a furrowed brow. Not anger. Maybe some jealousy, but mostly just...hurt. Loss. Longing.

I glance back at the hospital bed.

Trent smiles and laughs with his two blood daughters. They both resemble him in a way Claire never will. They belong to him in a way she and I can't, and I know that bothers her.

Since the day Trent married my mom, he's always called Claire and me his kids. No *step* involved.

It's always, *have you met my daughter, Claire?*

Or, *This is my son, Macon.*

It's never been, *these are my stepkids,* or *meet my wife's children.*

But all of Trent's affection doesn't change the fact that we weren't good enough for our biological father. I've come to terms with that in recent years, but it's something Claire is still struggling with it seems.

My therapist summed it up for me a while back.

Claire has abandonment issues. She wants to be someone's first choice, and her insecurities complicate everything. She bites first, so she doesn't get bitten.

Before therapy, I just thought Claire was a bitch.

After therapy, I still think she's a bitch, but I understand her better now.

My mom says something, pulling my thoughts away from Claire, and Trent laughs. When I look to him, his attention is already on me.

"Has my girl been giving you trouble?" he asks with a grin, and my eyes immediately flick to Lennon. "Since you've been *babysitting*," Trent clarifies, and my shoulders loosen.

"She's an absolute terror," I say jokingly, and Evelyn squeals as if she knows I'm talking about her.

"Actually," I say, flicking my eyes to Lennon before stepping up and holding out my hands for Evie, "the squirt has something she'd like to show you."

Lennon sits up straighter and a smile stretches across her face. I nod to the space on the floor a few feet from me, and Lennon moves to that spot without argument, immediately crouching down on her knees.

"Alright, Squirt," I say to Evie, "let's show Dada the surprise you've been saving for him."

I bend over and set Evie on her feet, and she immediately drops down to a sitting position with a giggle. Everyone laughs, and I pick her up, attempting again to set her on her feet while holding on to one of her hands.

She bounces a bit, babbles and waves at Lennon, and Lennon laughs.

"Come here, Evie," Lennon says with a smile, reaching her hands out wide. "Come here, sweet girl. C'mon."

Evie squeals happily, claps her hands, then falls back onto her butt.

I've spent the last week knocking her over, so she could save her first steps for Trent, and now here we are and all she wants to do is sit. I crouch down behind her and scoop her back up into my arms.

"You're very stubborn," I say to Evie, and my mom and Trent laugh.

"She's not a trick pony, Macon," Lennon says wryly, as she stands back up. "She'll do it on her terms."

"You were like that, too," my mom says with a grin, then she looks at Claire. "You both were. *Very* strong-willed."

"Is that a nice way of saying pain in the ass?" Claire asks with a laugh, and my mom shrugs, which is basically a confirmation.

My mother deserves sainthood for all she's gone through with me and Claire.

"Lennon was the opposite," Trent says warmly. "For better or worse, she was always very agreeable. A people pleaser."

I watch Lennon's jaw twitch and her brow furrow slightly before Trent continues.

"I'm glad to see she's gotten more strong-willed with age."

He's grinning at Lennon, when she rolls her eyes and waves him off, but I don't miss the tint of pink on her cheeks or the way she has to fight to keep her small smile from growing into a much larger one.

I have to tame my smile, too, because I know the truth.

Lennon hasn't gotten more strong-willed with age. She's gotten more honest. Because, even at nine years old, in a blue and white polka-dotted dress and a French braid tied off with a white ribbon, she was as strong-willed as they come.

She just didn't know it yet.

We only stay at the hospital for another thirty minutes before a nurse comes and shoos us out, but Trent asks Lennon to come back later in the afternoon.

She agrees, and we all walk out the door like one big, happy family.

"What are your plans for the rest of the day?" Mom asks as we walk as a group to the parking lot.

"I'm meeting back up with Eric for lunch, and then I'm going to try and get some work done," Claire says as she types something into her phone.

"And what do you do for work?" Lennon asks, sliding a pair of sunglasses over her eyes.

Claire looks up from her phone quickly, and I have to bite back a laugh at the look of shock on her face. Lennon doesn't bother, though. She nearly cackles.

"You don't have to answer if you don't want to," Lennon says, amused. "I was just making conversation."

Claire huffs out a small laugh and shrugs.

"I work for a small marketing firm," Claire says. "I do social media research, tracking trends and things. Then I develop individualized marketing strategies for clients. I'm the newest member on the team, and fresh out of school, so I get all the tiny jobs."

Claire shrugs again.

"It's not *famous artist in Paris*-glam, but I enjoy it."

"I think it sounds really cool, actually," Lennon says casually, and I don't miss the way Claire's mouth drops open before she snaps it shut again.

"You've always had a knack for social media stuff. An eye for what's trending. I bet you're good at your job."

"She's very good at it," Mom chimes in. "Tell her about the bookstore," she urges Claire.

"Mom, she doesn't care about that," Claire mumbles.

"Tell me about the bookstore, Claire," Lennon insists, and my smile grows.

She's genuinely interested, but she's also taking a bit of pleasure in Claire's discomfort. I absolutely love it.

"Well," Claire says, trying and failing to act nonchalant, "one of my clients was this independent bookstore in Richmond, right? And I helped them increase their online sales by seventy percent and their in-store traffic has more than doubled."

"Wow," Lennon says as we reach the parking lot. "That's amazing, Claire. You'll be earning a promotion in no time."

Lennon takes out her key fob and unlocks her rental, then turns to me.

"Is it okay with you if I paint for a bit?" she asks, and I'm nodding before she finishes her question.

"I'll be working in the rec center, so just text or come down if you need anything."

"I don't have your phone number," she says quickly, and I smirk.

"It's the same it's always been," I tell her, and her eyebrows scrunch.

"Mine's different," she says, almost absently.

She's got dark sunglasses shading her eyes, but I'm willing to bet they're unfocused and staring at nothing while she's lost in thought.

"I've got the international app," I confess. "Text me on there. I'll save it."

I don't tell her that I already know her French phone number by heart.

"Okay."

She turns her head toward Mom and Claire who are both watching us with interest. Mom looks amused, and Claire looks concerned.

"See you guys later," Lennon calls out, then climbs into her car and drives off.

Ten minutes later, I get a message on the app.

My number, is all it says, and I can't help but smile at my phone.

Saved it under Lennon Astraea Washington, I send back.

She doesn't reply, but she doesn't have to. I already know I'm under her skin.

I MAKE THE ROUNDS AT THE REC CENTER, ANSWERING EMAILS, paying bills, and checking in on the volunteers and staff.

The place runs like a well-oiled machine. I owe that to James. When I bought the center a year and a half ago, the business was so well-organized that I was able to rely on Trent to help run things while I was enlisted. Then, after the accident, once I was able to walk good enough, I took back over.

Buying the rec center was a gamble. When James and Hank told me they had to move, there was talk of selling the center to some commercial group for a fast sale, which meant it would likely get bulldozed for some random strip mall.

I couldn't let the rec center get turned into a TJ Maxx, Staples, and a hair salon.

I talked it over with Trent and Mom, then decided to make James an offer. He accepted, even though it was nowhere near as good as the commercial group offer, and now I make payments directly to him once a month.

It's a little early to tell, but I think the gamble paid off.

I get a break around lunchtime, so I choose to spend it hitting a bag in the gym. My favorite bag had to be retired because it was more duct tape than anything else, so I have to beat on one of the new ones, but I still love it.

I change into some shorts and a tank top, slip in some earbuds, and box. Stationary moves, so Nicolette doesn't murder me, but I get a good workout in, even with my feet planted.

About halfway through my workout, my skin starts to prickle. I turn to the side and, sure enough, Lennon is leaning on the wall watching me.

Her face is blank, but I know her eyes have been all over my body. I can feel them, and the minute our gazes connect, I see her on her knees for me, just like last night.

I turn to face her, but I resist the urge to walk closer. Instead, I pull out my earbuds and wait for her to speak.

"I'm heading out. I just wanted to let you know," she says slowly after a few breaths, "and to ask if it's okay that I come back tonight."

She doesn't say *come back to paint*, but I don't ask. I feel like there's more.

All I want to do is hold her, kiss her, but both times we've hooked up, she took off right after.

It burrows into my brain, and I replay it over and over, her walking away. It reignites every insecurity and fear. It threatens to push me over the edge.

I need to stay away from her. It's better for both of us. I can't have her the way I want her—the way I *need* her—so I should let her go.

But fuck me, I don't think I can.

So, despite my better interest, I nod.

"It's fine. Just keep the key."

I don't point out that she could have just texted me. Her eyes fall to my thigh, then, and my scar burns.

"Does it hurt?" she asks quietly, and I tell her the truth.

"Yeah. Sometimes more than others, but it's not nearly as bad as it was, so I don't complain."

"How does that work?" she asks, brow raised. I raise a brow back, and she bites her lip. "Since you're sober, how do you deal with the pain?"

Ah, yes. Pain pills. Because I will always be a druggie.

"Extra strength ibuprofen and a lot of distraction," I tell her with a wry grin. She flicks her eyes from me to the bag and back.

"And if your distraction causes pain?"

I shrug and walk toward her, grabbing my water bottle off the bench beside her and taking a swig before answering.

"It's a catch-22, but at least it's a pain I choose willingly."

My answer doesn't surprise her. It shouldn't. It's always how I've felt about pain. I've just gotten less self-destructive about it.

"Do you mind telling me how it happened?"

Her eyes lock on mine, and I know I'll tell her anything when she looks at me like that.

"I was a crew chief on a Huey," I tell her. "That's the guy who—"

"Oversees operations on a helicopter. The second-most important person on the aircraft," she interrupts with a smirk. "Did you forget who my dad is?"

I grin back and shake my head.

"*And* I was the door gunner," I say with a waggle of my brows.

"How sexy." There's no denying the flirty tone in her voice.

The hair on my arms stands and my heart kicks up, but I manage a tiny smirk. I hold her gaze for a few breaths longer than I would have four years ago. She gives back as good as she's getting. We're both a little unsettled when I start to speak again.

"We were running a night flight. Resupply support," I say, avoiding going into detail. "It was enemy action. The pilot managed to get us far enough out before we went down, but there was cargo that came unstrapped. I pushed one of our guys out of the way, but it got me good. Pinned me, and the force from the crash snapped my femur."

I take a deep breath through my nose as pain ricochets up and down my leg.

"I was lucky, though. It was mostly a clean break, and it didn't puncture the skin."

Lennon doesn't say anything for a while. She just locks her eyes with mine while I wait for her to speak. I'm always waiting on Lennon, but I don't mind. I've been waiting on her since we were teenagers. What's a little longer?

"You saved that guy's life?" she asks finally, and I shrug.

"Saved him from a busted leg, a discharge, and six-plus-months of rehab," I say after some thought. "If that qualifies as his life, I guess it's a matter of perception."

She's quiet again, eyes scanning my face, lips pursed. She tilts her head to the side and pulls her lower lip between her teeth.

For a few breaths, she just studies me. Long enough that my heart is beating loudly in my head and goosebumps erupt on the back of my neck.

"Is it weird," she says slowly, "if I say I'm not surprised? That you'd hurt yourself protecting someone else?"

I tilt my head to match hers, hold her gaze, then say honestly, "that makes one of us."

TWENTY-ONE

Lennon

The only thing I can think as I drive to the hospital is how *Macon* that whole story was.

He's always put others before his own well-being. It's what fueled his demons in high school. He's always felt others' pain more strongly than his own.

And, selfishly, I wonder, why couldn't he have done that for me? I would have done it for him. I tried to. Hell, once upon a time, I did.

I would've loved him with everything in me.

Why couldn't he have loved me the same?

It would have been nice not to shoulder all the pain by myself.

Sam tried. She was wonderful.

But at the heart of it all, I needed Macon.

I've slipped twice now since I've been back, and I hate myself for it. I can feel myself falling back into old, unhealthy patterns.

Being here is weakening me.

Being around him is forcing me into a mindset I thought I'd outgrown. I thought I was smarter, stronger, but I'm not. I let my body override my good sense, and then I was overcome with shame.

Shame and fear.

I can tell it's going to hurt more this time. I need to get back to Paris. I need to get out of this town. I need to get away from Macon and Claire.

I can't be awash in nostalgia for much longer.

I'll drown this time. I know it.

"Hey, Pumpkin," Daddy says when I step through the door.

I walk to his bedside and give him a long hug.

"Did you get some rest?" I ask.

"As much as I could hooked up to all this," he says, gesturing to the monitors. I give him a sympathetic smile.

"You'll be out of here soon. Have they given you a date, yet?"

"Not yet. They still want to monitor me. My heart's not as strong as they'd like."

"That doesn't make sense," I say, shaking my head. "You're, like, the healthiest person I know. It's almost annoying."

He barks out a raspy laugh, then smiles.

"I've missed you, Lennon," he says, then winces. "I'm sorry. *Capri*."

My heart cracks a little, and I'm surprised at how disappointed I feel at hearing my middle name from him. It's never bothered me before. Ever since I decided to drop Lennon, I've felt empowered when anyone said it. Emboldened. Stronger.

But now, in this hospital room, hearing it from my father's hoarse voice?

I just feel sad.

"You can call me Lennon, Dad," I say softly. "Sam does."

He chuckles.

"That doesn't surprise me," he says, and I laugh.

Dad's liked Sam ever since he heard how she flew out to England and stayed with me at Aunt Becca's for the summer. I think it assuaged some of his guilt.

"I'm sorry I haven't come to visit more," I tell him honestly.

He sighs.

"I could have come to see you too, Len," he says. "It works both ways."

I shake my head slowly. That's a lie.

"No, Dad," I say. "You and I both know that I wouldn't let you come. You tried, and I denied you." I sigh and shrug. "Pretty sure I never even gave you my address."

He doesn't respond for a bit, and when he speaks, his voice is stronger than it's been.

"You're here now. That's what matters most."

I stay with Dad for an hour, filling him in on all the stuff he's missed. We laugh and we cry, and when I finally get up to leave, I feel like part of my heart has healed.

I hope his has as well, even if just a bit. Even if just in the emotional sense.

"Lennon," he says, halting me at the door. I turn to him and brace myself for something serious. "I know this will be a big ask. I know it might even seem unfair. But...I think you should talk to Macon."

My lips purse and my head jerks back.

"What?"

"I think there's a lot you don't understand. Maybe you weren't ready. I don't know. But now that you're home, and you two are in the same space, I think you should talk to him."

I don't even bother pointing out that Virginia isn't home anymore. *Paris* is home. *Paris* is where I belong.

But what he's saying...

He sent me away to keep me from Macon, and now he wants me to talk to him?

"That doesn't make sense, Dad," I say. "I know you want a happy family with happy siblings, but that's just—"

"It's not about you being siblings, Lennon," he says clearly. "It never was."

My confusion makes my defenses rise and my anger spikes. This doesn't make sense.

How can he say that when he sent me away because Macon was my stepbrother? How can he say this now, after four years? After everything that I've had to deal with, after all the pain and loss and self-doubt and self-harm?

Is it an attempt to assuage his guilt? To atone for things because he almost died?

My heart was shattered...

By him, by Macon, even by Claire. My confidence, my self-worth, all of it was damaged by what they did to me.

I had to erase myself just to survive it.

And now, he thinks he can just gloss over everything? He thinks it can be forgiven and forgotten with a simple conversation, by blaming me and saying I *wasn't ready* before?

Instead of breaking again, it just makes me angry.

"Maybe it's too late for that, Dad," I say firmly. "Maybe that bridge was burned four years ago. Maybe Claire poured the gasoline, you tossed the match, and Macon danced on the ashes. I won't be forced back into a box that I outgrew. I'm not going to forgive him just to make it easier on you."

He's quiet for a minute, anguish clear on his face. Guilt. Pain. It's more emotion than I'm used to seeing from him. He's usually stone. Maybe his health has softened him.

"I'm not asking you to do that, Lennon. Just...talk to him. Please. And please know that I love you. With everything in me. I love you."

My eyes start to sting, and I breathe through my nose slowly, trying to keep the tears from falling. I know this is important to him, but I'm not going to put myself in a situation that will make me backslide.

Every interaction with Macon—every conversation, every touch, every kiss—has threatened to pull me back in.

Even his smirk makes me feel things I haven't felt since I was seventeen, and I hate it.

I hate how he's the only one who can spark that fire inside of me. I hate it even more, because he's the only one who can ruin me so thoroughly.

I've always had a soft spot for the boy that can break me. I thought I strengthened it. I thought it was gone. But the closer I get to him, I can feel it weakening, and it's terrifying.

Loving Macon Davis destroyed me once. I won't let it happen again.

"I love you, too, Daddy," I tell him honestly. "I never stopped. But patching things up with Macon isn't something I'm willing to do. I'll be cordial while I'm here, but that's the best I can give you. When I go back home, to *Paris*, things will go back to how they've been. I hope you can understand."

I inhale slowly as I watch his face for confirmation. I let him see that I'm serious. I'm determined. His lips tighten and worry lines appear on his forehead, but I don't waver.

"Okay, Lennon," he says finally, and I give him a small nod.

"Thank you. I'll see you later, okay?"

I leave the hospital and head to Andrea's house.

If Franco mailed my painting like he said he would, it should arrive any day now. It might even already be here if he sent it express like I asked. I sent him the money for shipping, even though he said he'd cover it. He knows me better than that. I don't take handouts.

I park at the curb and sneer at the car sitting in the driveway.

Claire is here.

It's fine. I can be in and out. I tried to be civil with her at the hospital, but that doesn't mean I want to strike up a friendship. Claire and I will never be friends.

I knock on the front door and wait, shifting back and forth on my feet until it opens and reveals Claire.

"Oh," she says, glancing quickly over her shoulder and back at me. "What's up?"

It takes every ounce of restraint in my body to keep from rolling my eyes.

"Just coming back to see if a package was delivered for me."

When she doesn't budge, I gesture behind her, and she steps out of the way, letting me in the house.

"I haven't seen anything," she says as she trails me into the kitchen. I don't acknowledge her comment.

"Where's Andrea?" I glance at the stack of mail on the counter, but there's nothing that looks like it could be my piece. "Maybe she put it somewhere."

"She had to pop into work," Eric says, pulling my attention to where he's standing between the kitchen and the living room. I didn't even realize he was here, though I should have. It's his car in the driveway. "She had to do something about payroll. She took Evelyn with her."

I nod a thank you, then pull out my phone and send Andrea a text. I should have just done this to begin with. I don't even know why I didn't. But I'm here now, so I turn to head up the stairs.

"Where are you going?" Claire calls, trailing me once more.

I whirl on her, stopping her in her tracks in the middle of the stairwell.

"I'm checking my dad's office. Maybe Andrea put it in there." I turn back around and walk toward the office. Claire follows, but I ignore her. I sift through some things on the desk and check the bookshelf. Nothing. Then my phone buzzes with a text from Andrea.

Sorry! I had to run into work. I haven't seen anything come for you, but I will let you know if it shows up. You're always welcome to come back and stay at the house. Then you'll know right away.

Despite my immediate irritation with Franco, I can't help but smile. Andrea is trying to make me feel welcome, but there's no way in hell I'm staying here. I send back a simple *thanks*, then turn to Claire.

"Not here," I say simply, then push past her.

"I told you it wasn't."

Her voice is sharp, like she wants to provoke me, so I ignore her. I bypass the kitchen and head straight for the front door.

"Where are you going now?"

I sigh and turn around, keeping my hand on the doorknob.

"To go paint."

"At Macon's?"

"Yes, at Macon's," I say flatly, then raise an eyebrow. Are we really doing this again? Are we not past it? I swear her eye twitches as she watches me. "What, Claire?"

"You're just spending a lot of time with him, is all."

"It's really none of your business who I'm spending time with."

I turn again to leave, and her voice stops me in my tracks.

"Are you sleeping with him again?"

The agitation and barely restrained anger in her voice set my teeth on edge. When I spin around to face her again, she can tell. Her eyes flare, and her jaw tightens. I take one step forward.

"It's none of your business who I'm sleeping with, either."

Her jaw drops, her eyebrows slant, and she jerks her head.

"He's your *brother*," she hisses.

I can't help it. I scoff and roll my eyes. She's fucking unbelievable.

"Let's get one thing straight, Claire." I speak slowly and annunciate my words. "Macon is no more my brother than you are my sister. And you will *never* be my sister." I drag my eyes down her body and sneer. "Now fuck off."

She sputters something else at me, but I don't turn back around. I walk calmly to my car and shut the door with less force than I feel vibrating through me.

Because I'm pissed, I send Franco an angry message telling him to mail my fucking painting, and then I call Sam.

The moment she answers, my chest loosens. She's my reminder that not every person on Earth is unreliable or a trash heap.

"Babe," she says brightly, "how's your dad doin'?"

The very topic of my dad knocks the encounter with Claire out of my head. If I told Sam about it, she'd probably order a hit, and I'm not there yet. It's better that I keep it to myself for now.

"Better. He knows me, at least."

"I told you he would," she says with a smile. "He'd never forget his pumpkin."

Sam has been filled in on every aspect of my dad's recovery via daily texts and nightly calls. I've told her about Evie and Claire and Eric, but only a little about Macon.

The bickering. The painting. The strange revelation about the rec center and the surgery.

But not the intimacy.

Not the spark of electricity that I resent. Not the pull that I can't seem to deny. Not how much I hate myself for still loving him, no matter how hard I try not to.

I haven't told her because none of that stuff matters.

Despite my love for him, I can never forgive him, and I can't have real love without forgiveness. No matter how much I wish I could.

Or maybe, I haven't told her because it matters too much.

"Well, I'll be there in a few days, and I can keep you company," she says gleefully. "These politicians drive me bonkers. It's hard pretending I don't hate everything they stand for."

I snort out a laugh. I don't think she realizes how badly she pretends. They probably all know how much she hates them. They just choose to ignore it because her dad is Senator Thom Harper.

His name is as pretentious as his soul is black.

"I have bad news though," she says slowly, and my stomach drops. "It's why I called. I just found out that my dear old dad is coming home, too, so he'll be at the house."

"It's okay. I can just stay in the motel."

"I hate that you're in that ratty, old place." She grimaces. "At least let me put you up some place better. I'll use the campaign credit card," she says with a bounce of her eyebrows, and I laugh again.

"The hotel is too far away. Since Dad's awake, I want to be close."

"I know," she says with a sigh. "I can't even be mad about it."

"When you get back, though, we're getting together." Relief shoots through me. "Early birthday present to me."

"Deal, bitch," she says. "Fucking deal."

TWENTY-TWO

Lennon

I HANG UP WITH SAM AND DRIVE BACK TO THE REC CENTER.

I have a few hours of daylight left, and I'm almost finished with one of my commissions, which means I will be able to free paint until the piece Franco shipped me gets here.

That's the one downfall of commissions.

My time to free paint isn't as frequent, and god, do I miss it.

I let myself into Macon's apartment, relieved to find it empty, and grab a soda from the fridge before heading to the studio.

This is all so fucked up.

Being around Macon is messing with me, but the only way to clear my head is to paint, and to paint, I have to be around Macon. I have to be in his space, surrounded by his energy and his scent.

It's intoxicating in the most debilitating of ways.

It's like I need him so that I won't need him, but it's going to blow up in my face.

I force the thoughts out of my head as I lay out my brushes and fill my jars with water. I start to mix my paints, but then remember that I'm out of white. I was going to run to the art store to get more, but I forgot after the conversation with my dad.

A conversation that I'm still trying to process.

I don't have time to drive to Norfolk now, so I decide to head down to the art room to see if there are paints in there. Back in high school, I had it stocked with my favorites. It's probably not anymore, but it's worth a shot.

I head out the door, locking it behind me, and make the walk to the art room. It's weird how comfortable I feel here. Even in Macon's apartment, I've adapted quickly.

I choose not to analyze it.

In the art room, I dig through the boxes in the back storage closet. They're not labeled anymore, which irks me, but I find the tote with paints and about squeal with joy when I see exactly what I need.

"Bingo," I say, sorting through the paints. I take a white and a blue, then decide to take a black as well. I'll replace them tomorrow.

A large board canvas in the corner catches my eye. It's propped backwards against the wall, but I can see speckles of color along the outer edges. It looks like it might be someone's finished painting, and I walk toward it on instinct, curious.

Something inside me is both thrilled and scared to flip it over. I don't even know why. I like surveying other people's work, but this one, tucked away and backward in the storage closet, makes me feel like I've stumbled upon a secret.

I take two deep breaths when I reach it, and then I turn it around.

It takes a minute to process what I see, and when I do, my heart pounds so fast in my chest that I feel like I'm going to pass out. The light is dim, just filtering in from the classroom outside, but even in the semi-darkness, I can make it out perfectly.

It's me.

It's me on prom night, laughing in my dress. It's a watercolor painting, and it's rough, but it's me right down to the freckles. Even the navy-blue dress is exactly as I remember it.

The background of the painting appears to still be in progress, which makes me think this project is unfinished. Then why was it hidden back here? Who is it being hidden from?

Me.

I scan the painting for the name of the artist. I don't find one, but I don't need one.

I've seen those eyes drawn over and over in Macon's sketchbooks. It's his style. I've seen my lips and my nose. My ears. My hands.

But I've never seen them together.

Then I notice another painting, this one in a frame, leaned behind a shelf with the front covered with a sheet.

My hand is trembling as I slide it out of its hiding place. I hold my breath as I turn it around.

I know what it's going to be even before I let the sheet drop to the floor, but I still start to cry the moment I see it, my hand shooting to my mouth to stifle my gasp.

It's my painting.

The one I sold for twelve-thousand dollars.

The one I painted during the darkest point in my life.

The one that pulled me from the bottom and revived my love for painting.

And within the painting, almost camouflaged into the background, is the Carson McCullers quote. The one I fell in love with after reading everything I could get my hands on by her.

"The heart is a lonely hunter with only one desire! To find some lasting comfort in the arms of another's fire."

I'm staring at the painting when someone steps through the storeroom door behind me. I turn around slowly.

"What is this?" I whisper to Macon. His face is full of sorrow.

"Lennon," he says, then he closes his eyes.

"What is this, Macon?" I ask again.

"You weren't supposed to see that," he says, his voice strained. "Not yet."

"Why would you have these?" I push my hands through my hair and pull. "This doesn't make sense, Macon." I raise my voice because I need to hear myself over the pounding in my head. "You abandoned me. You didn't care. You left me alone because you didn't care."

He shakes his head, and my tears fall faster.

"This doesn't make sense," I yell again, and fling my hand backward, pointing at the paintings. "*What is this?*"

"I never abandoned you. I couldn't. You have to know that, Lennon."

He walks toward me, and I back up, bumping into the paintings. He stops.

"You're mine," he says, his voice full of conviction. "You've *always* been mine, and I've always been yours. That hasn't changed. You belong with me."

"No. No! You and I are nothing. I belong in Paris."

"That's bullshit," he spits, and I cut him off.

"Why are you doing this?" I yell. "Why are you messing with my head again?"

I start to pace, my fingers pressed to my temples. Everything is so confusing, so muddled. None of this is right.

I belong in Paris.

I'm a successful painter.

I don't belong here. I don't belong with Macon. He shouldn't have my painting. He shouldn't have painted me.

Macon *does not* care about me. He never has.

"I'm not messing with your head, Lennon," he growls. "*You're* the one who refused to come back. *You're* the one who decided to stay in England and go to art school without telling anyone."

"I did what I had to do!"

"That's bullshit! You got stubborn. You threw a temper tantrum for being sent to England early, and you cut *everyone* off. You were supposed to come back, and you didn't."

"Don't you dare put this on me," I sneer. "You don't know anything."

"Yeah, well whose fault is that?" he snaps back, and my mouth drops open in shock.

He's really trying to say this is my fault? That I chose this?

"You *abandoned* me," I say. "You *ignored* me. You ignored me when I needed you. You don't get to shame me for finally making my own decisions."

"I went to *rehab*, Lennon!" he shouts, angry and desperate. "What fucking universe are you living in? I was in *rehab*. I was getting clean so I could be good enough for you. But I got out and you hadn't come back. *You* left *me*."

"No," I say, shaking my head. "*No.* That's wrong. You're lying."

"Why the fuck would I lie about that?"

He stops and squeezes his eyes shut, the only sound in the small room is our rapid breathing.

"I fucking went to rehab for *us*," he says, his voice shaking. "So I could love you right."

Love.

So I could love you.

The words echo inside my head, slamming from side to side until my ears ring.

No. No. This is wrong.

No one told me. No one. He can't say he did this for me. He can't buy my painting and think that one act forgives everything. He hasn't cared for four years. Maybe he never did. I can't second-guess this again. I can't let him pull me in like this again. I can't do this with him again.

My heart aches.

So many memories cycle through my head, both good and bad. His overdose. His strange relationship with Sam. The rec center. The Marines. The way he is with Evie. What my dad said.

But four fucking years.

I endured so much bullshit, and for what? Four fucking years of silence, just for him to imply it was my fault? To say *I* was the one who left *him*?

"Why," I say, and the pain in my voice makes me angry.

Why does this hurt so much? I was done hurting over him. I'm supposed to be stronger than this now.

"Why now, after four years? I was doing *fine*! I was doing *good*, and you have to come and derail me again? I was doing fine without you!"

"Fine?" he spits, his face twisted and his eyes ablaze. "You don't want *fine*, Lennon. You want *madness*. You want fire. Anything less is a waste of time."

"You don't know what I want!"

"Yes, I do!"

He takes a step closer and flings his finger at the paintings behind me.

"Unforgiving. Difficult to master. You don't want *easy*. You don't want to erase your mistakes. You want to build on them and transform them into something beautiful. You've never wanted *fine*, Lennon. You want *watercolors*."

His words hit me right in the chest, tears I can't stop flood my cheeks. I can taste them. The collar of my shirt is wet from them.

That night in the rec center art room floods my mind and I can almost see it playing out in front of me. He's leaning on the doorframe, staring at me with his blue flame eyes. I'm wiping down tables, and already falling desperately for him.

So, you like watercolors because they're beautiful, difficult to master, and unforgiving?

Yeah. It's my love medium.

Rehab. My paintings. Four fucking years.

"I explained," he says, shaking his head.

His voice is laced with confusion and desperation. He's begging me to understand, and I just can't.

"I asked you to wait for me. I asked you not to give up."

My eyes pop open, and I shake my head in disbelief. He can't possibly mean...

"The note?" I say on a gasp.

A crumpled sticky note? He thinks that will make up for everything?

The memory of hurling a ceramic mug at his back, note shoved inside, plays out in front of me. Then finding it on the pillowcase after prom.

Then everything that came after.

"How the *fuck* do you expect me to wait for you based on something that meant *nothing* to you in the past?" I ask. My voice is a low growl. "Radio silence, Macon. The worst fucking time of my entire life and you gave me *nothing*—"

"I came for you!" he yells, his hands gripping his head. "I came back for you, Lennon. When I got out of rehab, I came back," he repeats. He slams his eyes shut.

"And you know where I found you? In an alley behind a pub with your mouth on some English fuck and his hand down your fucking pants."

My mouth drops open and my eyes widen. I search my memory and find it immediately.

I know exactly what night he's talking about. The beginning of my spiral. The start of my self-destruction. My stomach swirls with the need to vomit.

I know, but I still ask, because I'm teetering, and I deserve to fall.

"When?" I force out.

"Right after you didn't come back for school. You practically disappeared, and no one could get ahold of you."

I choke on a sob. I fist my hands to calm the trembling and breathe through the intense pain ravaging my body.

My chest hurts. My head hurts. My heart...

"But you didn't answer my emails," I whisper, grasping for something, anything, to make this make sense.

"I didn't exactly have access to my email while being treated for drug addiction, Lennon," he says softly. "And when I got out, my school email was locked. I never thought to try and get back in it."

When I finally look back at him, his eyes are pleading and glassy with unshed tears.

"I came back for you," he chokes out, "and I found you in that alley, and I relapsed. I went on a bender, and when I finally came out of it, I had your dad pull some strings, so I could enlist in the Marines."

He walks toward me, and this time, I don't back away. I let him cup my face gently, his blue flame eyes boring into mine.

"I enlisted because, after my relapse, I knew I still wasn't good enough for you. I enlisted because it was my last-ditch effort to make something of myself."

He leans forward and presses his forehead to mine.

"I never gave up on us," he breathes out. "Even after you did, I didn't. Because you belong with me, Lennon Capri. You always have and you always will."

I close my eyes, let his words wash over me, and when he kisses me, I let him. I feel my heart shatter, my eyes burn.

And then I feel seventeen, and I cannot be that girl. I swore to myself I would never be that girl again.

Macon has always been so good at deceiving me in the past. Climbing through my window and whispering promises only to break them later. Calling me pathetic after saving his life. Kissing me and holding me only after breaking me down so gloriously.

He lies and I listen because I want so desperately to believe him.

I can't think straight around him. I never could. I cling to him when I should push him away. I say yes when I should say no. I forgive him and forgive him and forgive him, when all I should really do is forget him.

"I can't do this with you right now," I choke out, turning my head and dropping my hands to my side. "I need to think."

I push past him and leave the storeroom. I hear his footsteps behind me.

"Don't," I beg. "You'll only make it worse."

I take two more steps, then against my better interest I turn back to him.

"I'll be back, okay? I just need to think this through first."

He nods slowly, and when I walk away again, he doesn't try to follow.

TWENTY-THREE

Macon

London, 4 Years Earlier

My legs bounce as I wait to exit the plane.

My neck aches, and I have to piss. I pop another stick of gum in my mouth and chew furiously. For the hundredth time, I pull up the address on my phone.

I found Lennon's address by calling her new art school and pretending to be Trent. It was easy to track her down, considering how seamlessly she cut us all off.

Mom and Trent think Lennon needs space.

I think they're both idiots.

I didn't just spend months in that fucking rehab getting clean to come home and find that Lennon has just fucked off to London without even an explanation. I didn't get out just to find that all my plans have been shot to hell. She was supposed to come home, so I'm going to bring her back.

When I'm finally off the jet bridge, I practically sprint through Heathrow. I stop to piss and grab a coffee, then I jump in a taxi.

Fifty-fucking-pounds to get from the airport to Lennon's

apartment. I haven't worked for months, but I haven't spent money, either. Not much to buy in a drug treatment facility.

It's almost 10 p.m. by the time the taxi drops me off. I check the address one more time, take a few deep breaths, then take the stairs two at a time.

I find the door easily and knock twice. I wait thirty seconds, then knock again.

Silence.

I knock a third time, louder and faster, and still no one comes, so I turn around and take a seat by the door. I'll wait here all night if I have to.

An hour passes and my stomach starts to ache. I haven't eaten all day. I'm agitated as fuck, overtired, and now I'm hungry. None of these things are good for sobriety.

Fucking hell.

I take out another piece of gum and pop it in my mouth, but it doesn't do shit, so I do the next best thing. I stand up and head out the door to find some cigarettes. I was a fucking idiot to think quitting now, after quitting everything else, was a good idea.

If I can't rely on pills and booze, I need something. This nicotine gum isn't cutting it.

I leave the apartment complex and choose a random direction based on lights and noise. Where there are people, there are cigarettes. Especially in Europe.

A few blocks down, I find a small pub and a crowd of people spilling out into the street. I stop by the first smoking person I see.

"Hey," I say, forcing a charming grin, "can I bum one?"

The woman looks me over from head to toe, blowing out a cloud of smoke before taking a pack of cigarettes from her purse and holding it out to me.

"Thanks."

I take the pack, shake out a cig, and before I even have it

between my lips, she's holding a lighter up for me. I lean toward her and light my cigarette, inhaling deeply as the end glows red. I let the smoke settle in my lungs, my body already going loose, then blow it out into the night air.

"I've got something a little stronger if you want," she says to me. Her voice is raspy, sexy even, and the promise of something stronger sends chills over my skin.

"Nah. I'm good, but thanks."

She shrugs and takes another drag, blowing the smoke out of her nose.

"Have a good night," I say to her and turn to leave, when laughter stops me in my tracks.

I freeze and tilt my head to the side. I don't even breathe as I listen. The crowd is loud, the music from the pub is spilling out the street, but I know what I heard.

A few seconds later, I hear it again.

It's Lennon. I know it is.

I head in the direction I heard her laugh, an alleyway between the pub and the building beside it. As I push through the crowd, she laughs again, and if there weren't so many people out here, I'd be sprinting.

I push through a few more people, and then I see her leaning up against the wall of the pub. Her hair is shorter, and she's wearing more makeup than usual, but it's her.

I walk toward her, but stop again when her face disappears. Someone stepped in the way.

No.

Someone's covering her.

I shake my head and look again. No.

Someone is *kissing* her.

And she's kissing him back.

My gut churns and my vision sparks red. My hands fist and my nostrils flare. I shove toward them. I'm going to beat the shit out of this guy.

What the fuck is she doing?

I'm footsteps away when I hear Lennon gasp, and the guy pulls back enough for me to see her face, tipped to the sky with her eyes closed.

No.

I've seen that face before. I've heard that gasp.

I scan them, and suddenly I want to throw up.

He's touching her. His hand is down her pants. He's touching her, and she's going to...

I stand, frozen in place, and watch. I watch his arm moving, her hips thrusting, the way her pants mold around his hand. Then I hear her gasp again, and I snap my eyes to her face.

I know the minute she comes.

I know that sound by heart. I know her expression. It's stored in my memory.

I thought it was only mine.

I run to the other side of the alley, brace myself against the wall, and throw up. It's nothing but water and bile, but my body tries again, until I'm sweating and dizzy.

I turn around again, because I'm a fucking idiot, and my eyes fall back to her and that douche. He's still plastered to her. I can see her hands gripping his sides.

I want to kill him.

I would kill him. I know I would. I have just enough presence of mind to stop myself before committing murder, then I turn around and throw a punch to the brick wall.

One. Two. Three. My skin splits and my knuckles crack, and I envision beating that fuck's face in until someone yanks me off the wall.

"You gotta stop, mate," some English prick drawls. "You're gonna fuck yourself up good."

I look from him, back to Lennon, then down at my decimated, bloodied knuckles.

I shrug off my coat and wrap it around my hand.

"You gonna be alright, mate?"

I look up at the face and it's burry. I blink, and it becomes clearer. My cheeks are wet. I'm crying.

"No," I tell him clearly, then I push past him and into the pub.

I slap my card down on the bar when the bartender looks at me.

"Shot of whiskey. Cheap shit. And keep them coming."

I throw back five shots before my head spins, then I push back out onto the street, my eyes zeroing in on the woman from earlier.

"You still got that something stronger?" I slur, and her lips curl into a grin.

"Yes."

"Wanna leave?"

"Yes." She scrapes her nails down my chest, but I stop her before she reaches my waistband. "For a fix, not a fuck."

She eyes me again, one brow raised, and I don't have time for this bullshit.

"I'll stop by an ATM," I say, and she smiles.

"Follow me."

I WAKE UP ON THE SIDEWALK NEXT TO THE THAMES.

My head pounds and my hand aches. My knuckles are covered in dried blood and swollen to twice their size. I groan and roll onto my back.

Everything about the night before comes back to me, hitting me all at once, and I roll back over and vomit on the pavement.

I push myself up, scooting away from the mess I just made, and prop myself beside a bench. I take inventory of my pockets. My jacket is gone. My wallet is gone. My passport is gone. My phone, miraculously, is in my front pocket, but the screen is cracked to fuck.

I relapsed. I didn't even last a month out of rehab.

I smoked, I drank, and I took some bullshit someone handed me. I might have snorted something. After a while it all blends together.

But fuck, what the fuck have I done?

I squeeze my eyes shut, but the disappointment hits me hard, and tears slip past my lashes. All those months. All that therapy. And I just fucked it all up.

And Lennon...

Lennon and that guy.

I thought she was mine. I thought she felt the way I felt.

I thought she'd wait for me.

I drop my head into my right hand, my left cradled in my lap as I try to breathe through all the pain. Fuck.

After a moment, I reach into my pocket and pull out my phone. I hold my breath as I attempt to power it on, and heave a sigh of relief when it blinks to life.

For the second time now, I dial Trent.

"Macon," he answers. "Did you find her?"

"Yeah," I rasp.

"Is she okay? Is she coming back?"

I swallow hard. I try like hell to keep from crying again. I must look ridiculous busted to shit and bawling on the sidewalk.

"Macon? You still there?"

I clear my throat.

"You were right. She needs space." I take a deep breath. "And I need your help."

TWENTY-FOUR

Macon

I watch her walk out.

My body screams to follow her. To make her see the truth. But I don't.

You'll only make it worse, she said. I don't know how it could be worse than this. It already hurts more than anything ever has.

I cover her painting back up, turn the other one back around, and slide them both back into their hiding spot.

Lennon's painting usually hangs on the wall in the rec center art room.

My painting of her usually stays in my studio, so I can work on it.

I hid them both from her.

I knew it would be too much at first, but I didn't expect this. I thought it would be embarrassing to explain. I thought I'd scare her away.

But this anger? The pain?

Fuck. What have I done? I thought I was making the right choice. I thought I was doing the right thing.

I don't register the walk back to my apartment.

I'm in a daze when I sit down at my wheel, not even bothering to change.

I don't even turn on music. I just throw.

I work the clay into nothing, smashing it and forming vases only to collapse them on purpose. I do this until the sun goes down. I do it until the sun rises again. If I have to, I will do it until my skin doesn't itch and my nerves aren't frayed.

Throwing clay, sketching, and boxing. Those are my outlets now.

They have to be enough.

I take a break to check on Mom, to go through the motions at the center. I don't neglect my responsibilities. If I do, everything will fall like dominoes. Too many people rely on me. I can't let them down. I can't let myself down.

The moment I'm finished, I go back to the wheel, and I do it all over again. Throwing in silence. Forming and collapsing clay into nothing until the light disappears from my studio.

I don't stop until my phone rings. I miss the call when I get up to wash the clay off my hands. I'm drying them when my phone starts ringing again.

"Hello."

"Macon," my mom says, her voice strangled, "you have to come to the hospital."

I hear muffled crying on the other end, and my first thought is Lennon. She did something. Something happened and I lost her, and I have to grip the sink for balance.

"What is it?" I force out.

"It's Trent," she sobs, and my shoulders loosen just to shoot back to my ears. "They had to rush him into surgery."

I'm already putting on my shoes and locking up my apartment.

"Does Lennon know?" I ask as I run to my car.

"She's here," she says, her voice cracking again. "She was with him..."

No.

I crank my engine and peel out of the lot, turning toward the hospital.

This shit can't happen to her again. She's already been through too much. Her mom. Me. She can't do this with her dad too.

"I'm on my way."

I drive as fast as I can. Luckily, the roads are clear. I don't know what I would do if I got pulled over. I park in emergency parking and sprint into the hospital. I don't stop running until I'm pushing through the door of the OR waiting room and screeching to a halt in front of my mom.

I fall to my knees and pull her into a hug, then my eyes scan the room. Claire is sitting next to Mom, her hand on her shoulder, and Lennon is standing alone in the corner. Her face is pale like a ghost, her eyes are red. Her lip is bruised and swollen, like she's been biting it.

There is no Evie, and I wonder if she's at the house with Masters.

"What happened?" I ask my mom, holding her tight as she cries into my shoulder.

"Ventricular aneurysm," Claire answers. Her voice is a quiet scratch, and her face is splotchy and red from crying. She sniffles as tears start to fall again. "They took him for open heart surgery."

She holds my gaze, then flicks her eyes to Lennon and back.

"She was in there with him when it happened," Claire whispers. Her tears start to fall again. "I've never seen her like that, Macon. She was so..." She shakes her head and squeezes her eyes shut. "I'm really worried about her."

I look at Lennon. She's leaning on the wall and staring at the floor, her hands fisted together in front of her. God, she looks so small. Like a nine-year-old who just found her mom's lifeless body.

Like a seventeen-year-old who just had to perform CPR to save her boyfriend from an overdose.

I kiss Mom's cheek and push myself to standing. Lennon's eyes drag slowly to mine. I take slow, measured steps toward her. She doesn't look away. I don't know what I'll do when I reach her, but I need to be next to her.

The door to the waiting room flies open, and we break eye contact, looking toward the noise.

"Len," Sam breathes out, then rushes to her side. They immediately embrace, a tight, clingy type of hug, and Lennon starts to cry.

"I know," Sam whispers into Lennon's hair. "I know. I'm here."

Sam turns her head and acknowledges me with a small nod. I return it, then step away. I don't know what happened when Sam went to England to be with Lennon, but I didn't realize how close they'd become. This hug is practiced. Sam's gesture of comfort, the way Lennon clings like she's a lifeline, isn't new.

They've been here before, and something tells me that it was my fault.

For six hours, we wait.

Sam bullies the nurse into letting us eat in the waiting room and then orders food to be delivered. She makes small talk with me and my mom, and she pointedly ignores Claire. Lennon barely speaks, but she and Sam don't leave each other's sides.

It makes me want to hug Sam. I want to thank her, despite my jealousy and guilt. If I can't be the one to comfort Lennon, I'm glad she has Sam.

When the doctor comes out, we all shoot to our feet. It was

a successful surgery, he tells us, but there will be a long road to recovery. Trent is still under anesthesia and probably won't wake for another few hours. After that, he needs rest. We can see him in the morning.

The nurse tells Mom she can stay in the room, so I tell her I'll take Evie for the night. Claire leaves to go back to the house. I'll follow behind soon to pack Evelyn's things.

I try to hang back to talk to Lennon. I need to check on her, but she's attached to Sam's hip, and Sam keeps giving me the side-eye.

Just before we head out to the parking lot, Lennon breaks from the group to use the bathroom, and I corner Sam.

"How is she?" I ask, and she gives me a warning glare.

"She's definitely been better," Sam says, then adds cryptically, "but she's been worse."

I know it's a dig at me.

"What do you mean?" I push, and she shakes her head.

"Nope," she says quickly. "Don't even try to pump me for information."

Irritation flares with my need to know more about Lennon, to make sure she'll be alright. I know this is hard for her. Being in the room with her dad when this happened, monitors going off and Trent going unconscious, had to have terrified her.

All I can think of is the story about her mom, and my chest aches for Lennon.

"Come on, Sam," I say. "Give me something, here. I just want to make sure she's okay. We used to be friends, right?"

Sam barks out a laugh and raises her eyebrow.

"Loyalty has an expiration date, Macon. My loyalty is to her now, and you're not going to get shit out of me."

She looks away from me to dig some Chapstick out of her bag, then applies it. She smacks her lips together, then looks back at me.

"You care so much," she says, "you'll ask her on your

own." Sam's eyes flick behind my shoulder, then she flashes me a half smile. "See ya later, Davis."

She walks past me and says something to Lennon. Lennon nods, then leaves with Sam. She doesn't so much as look at me, and my stomach falls to my feet.

Ask her on your own, Sam said.

But how? And more importantly, do I even deserve to know?

TWENTY-FIVE

Macon

On the drive to Mom's, it starts to rain, the water coming down in hard sheets and coating my windshield. My wipers can barely keep up.

I run into the house, getting drenched in the process, and kick off my shoes at the door.

"She's asleep," Claire says when I walk into the kitchen. She's sitting next to Masters drinking a cup of hot tea.

"It's okay," I say. "I know how to move her without waking her."

Claire chews on her lip a moment, flicks her eyes to Eric, then back to me.

"You can leave her, you know," Claire says. "I can watch her. I don't mind."

I try not to look shocked. Claire has never showed much interest in babysitting Evie. I volunteered once a few months ago so Mom and Trent could go out on a date, and then it just kind of became my job. I enjoy doing it, though. I like having the squirt around.

"That's okay, Claire," I say. "I'll take her."

I start to walk toward the stairs, but Claire stops me. When I turn back around, her brow is furrowed, and her eyes are sad.

"Please leave her, Macon," Claire says softly. "I want to watch her. I want to help." She twists her hands in front of her and shifts from foot to foot. "I know I haven't exactly been...*present*...but I'd like to change that. I just...I guess I didn't feel like I was needed?"

She shrugs then takes a deep breath before hitting me with a sincere, determined gaze.

"I would really like it if you would let me watch Evelyn tonight, Macon," she says clearly, as if she'd rehearsed it. "I promise I will call you if I need anything."

I look over Claire's shoulder to Masters. He's watching us intently, but when he catches me looking, he shoots his gaze away. I have to stifle a laugh.

I consider Claire. She sounds sincere as she waits for my decision. It's weird holding so much power over her right now. I could say no. It would hurt her, because this opportunity to watch Evie seems important to her.

I could give her a taste of everything she's given me—given *Lennon*—in the past.

But I'm not that person. I never have been.

"Okay," I say with a nod. "Let me walk you through bottles and morning routine. I can write it down for you, and then you can just call if you need help with anything."

Claire's smile is huge as she glances between me and Masters.

"Okay, yes," she says, nodding eagerly. "Of course. And I promise I'll call. Thank you."

I manage not to show my amusement.

I write down a crash course on watching Evelyn, the same way Mom did for me that first time I babysat. I show Claire how to warm up the bottles, and then I say my goodbyes.

As I'm putting my shoes back on at the front door, I can

hear Claire and Eric talking. Their voices are hushed, but their conversation still carries.

"I'm so proud of you," Eric tells her. His voice is encouraging and soothing. "You did so good."

"I'm so happy he's letting me do this," Claire says. "That's a good sign, right?"

"I think it is."

I'm smiling when I run back to my car. Maybe Masters is good for Claire. Maybe their relationship is more than just Claire being a bitter bitch. I guess I'll have to wait and see.

I have to drive slowly because of the rain, and I'm soaked when I push my way into my apartment. The summer storm is likely to go all night.

I strip out of my clothes and throw on some gym shorts, then head to the kitchen to warm up something to eat. I'm pulling leftover pizza out of the microwave when there's a knock on my door.

A chill shoots through me and my heartbeat speeds up.

Before I even open the door, I know.

On the other side is Lennon. She's soaked from head to toe, standing in a small puddle of rainwater. Her clothes stuck to her body and her hair plastered to the sides of her face. Her skin is pale, her eyes rimmed red.

I don't say anything. I just hold her eyes as she peers into mine. She opens her mouth twice before finally speaking, and her voice is a cracked whisper.

"Make me feel something else," she says, and I don't hesitate.

I know exactly what she wants, what she needs.

I slide my hand to her neck, brushing my thumb on her pulse point, and pull her to me, covering her mouth with mine. She whimpers, then paws at my bare chest as I walk us back into my apartment, kick the door shut before pushing her back up against it.

This kiss feels different.

It's needy. Vulnerable and honest. It's my Lennon. My *Astraea*.

Lennon slides her hands up my chest roughly, dragging her nails to my shoulders then back down to my abs. Her tongue tangles with mine and she slides her hands lower, gripping onto the waistband of my shorts. My cock hardens, and she wastes no time dipping into my shorts and wrapping her hand around it. I groan at the contact, thrusting once. I tug her shirt up over her head and drop it. It lands on the floor with a thwack, and goosebumps erupt over her wet skin.

"God, you're beautiful," I whisper. I palm her lace-covered breast then tug the cup of her bra down so I can dip my head low and suck her nipple into my mouth, pulling the metal piercing past my teeth and biting behind it. She gasps, and I massage it with my tongue, making her moan.

Make me feel something else.

"Yes, more," she rasps, and I unhook her bra and drag it down her arms, dropping it next to her shirt. I move to her other breast and lick around that nipple and bite down. Her grip on my dick tightens and she starts to pump.

"Fuck, Lennon," I groan. I'm so hard I'm aching for her.

"Macon," she breathes out, and a thrill dances down my spine.

"Say it again," I command. I need to hear my name on her lips, her voice sexy and turned on.

"Macon," she repeats. "Macon. Yes."

I move down her body, dragging my lips and teeth over her naked torso, leaving red marks behind.

I'm not making the same mistake I made in my kitchen and in my studio, fucking her in a frenzy fully-clothed, or letting her make me come without giving her what she deserves.

I'm worshiping her.

I'm doing everything I should have been doing every day for the last four years. I'm making her feel something else.

I drop to my knees and tug her shorts over her ass and down her thighs, taking her panties with them, until she's standing completely naked above me.

She shivers, and I wonder if it's from the air conditioning hitting her damp skin, or from my touch.

I rub my palms over her silken skin, digging my fingers into the flesh of her thighs and ass, before letting myself look at her naked pussy, glistening with arousal beneath a thatch of dark curls.

"Fucking gorgeous," I say. "You're already so wet for me, Len."

I glance up at her and find her watching me, her pupils blown wide and her chest rising and falling rapidly.

"You know how long I've waited to taste you again?" I drop my forehead to her pelvis and inhale, breathing her in. "I'm going to suck and lick your clit until you're screaming."

"Please," she says, and I drag my tongue over her pussy, groaning when I finally taste her.

She whimpers, pressing her hips closer to my face. I chuckle against her.

"So needy," I say. I swirl my tongue around her clit, then back away. "So eager for me to tongue-fuck you."

I bite her inner thigh, and she growls.

"Quit teasing," she pants out, and the thick desire in her voice pushes me over the edge.

I close my mouth over her, sucking and licking in earnest. When she starts to quiver, I stop just long enough to press my forearm against her pelvis and lift her leg over my shoulder. Then I bury my face back between her legs. I suck her clit and slip two fingers inside her, her wet pussy sucking them in and pulsing around them.

"Fucking hell," I say. "I want you to come all over my face."

I bite her thigh again and suck hard before moving back to her core

"Soak my lips with your cum. And then I'm going to shove my cock into this sweet pussy and fuck you," I say on a growl. "You want that?"

"Please," she moans, and that's all I need.

I finger-fuck her while licking her, sucking her. I crook my fingers the way I know she likes, massaging her inner walls while I flick my tongue over her swollen bundle of nerves.

She thrusts her hips, rubbing her herself back and forth over my mouth, and I groan against her. My cock is leaking precum, drenching my shorts, and I'm so hard that it hurts.

"Oh yes, Macon," Lennon says. "Like that, like that."

I keep pace until she tightens around me, until she explodes with a breathless cry, and then I rise to my feet.

She pushes my shorts down and grabs hold of me, squeezing again, and my moan is strangled, guttural. She hitches her leg around my hip, I grab onto her thigh, and she guides me to her pussy, rubbing me up and down over her slickness.

Fuck, I could come right now, but I'm not fucking her against this door.

I take a step back and kick my shorts off, then lift her. She wraps her legs around my waist, and I capture her lips again as I walk us to my bedroom. When I get to the bed, I lie her down gently before climbing over her. I kiss her lips, her jaw, her neck. Every part of her that I've dreamed of, I savor and taste.

When she reaches between us and grips me again, I groan. I'll never get tired of her hands on me. She pushes my cock against her pussy and moves on me. Both of us are panting. We're both desperate for this.

But then I halt and squeeze my eyes shut.

"What," she says against my mouth. "What's wrong?"

"I don't have a condom," I say, remembering how upset she was the last time, and the silence stretches.

"Not in your nightstand?" she pants out. "In your wallet?"

I release a strained laugh.

"None there either," I tell her, and she stiffens.

I know what she's thinking, that I've been fucking women bare, and I kiss her quickly before easing her worries.

"I haven't been with anyone since prom," I confess. "Only you."

Her mouth drops open, and she pulls her head back. She stares at me, bounces her hazel eyes between mine, and I can tell she's at war with herself.

I stay quiet. I let her think it through. I wait for her words.

"I'm on birth control," she whispers finally, her voice quaking with something I don't quite understand.

There's so much damage between us. So many secrets and broken promises. I should tell her we can wait. I should reassure her and prove to her I'm a better man now.

But in moments like this, I'm not sure I am.

I'm always going to be an addict, and she's always going to be my greatest temptation. The only addiction worth ruining myself for.

"Are you sure?" I ask, trying like hell to mask the desire in my voice.

She nods and slowly guides my hard cock back to her center.

"I'm so sure," she says earnestly, rubbing me over her once more before positioning me at her entrance.

She holds eye contact as she pulses her hips upward.

"More sure than I've been of anything in years."

The thread holding my restraint snaps, and I give in. I lean in and kiss her, long and deep, and I push into her slowly, savoring every single inch that we connect. We sigh together, and I hold for a moment, breathing her in. Telling myself that this is real. That we can do this.

And I fall harder.

I move slowly at first, letting us adjust to each other. To breathe in the euphoria. My lips never leave her body. Her hands never leave mine. With every whimper and moan she releases, it gets harder to contain myself.

She starts to move with me, meeting my thrusts, and we speed up. Her breath collides and tangles with mine, our sweat mixes, making our skin slick where our bodies connect.

Her breasts press against my chest. Her hands in my hair. Her legs around my waist.

"You're perfect," I rasp against her lips. "You're so fucking perfect."

I love you, I want to say.

I love you. I love you.

But I don't.

I break away from her and rise on my knees, lifting her ass off the bed and digging my hands into her hips.

"Yes," she cries, and I pound faster. "Macon, please."

I use my thumb to rub her clit as I fuck her, until she's quivering and shaking on the edge.

"Come for me," I say, my voice strained. "Come on my cock. Give me what's mine."

She moans and her thighs clamp around me. She slides her hands to her chest and twists her nipples, the silver bars catching the light with a flicker. I rub her clit in circles, and she starts to spasm, coming around me with a breathless hum, then I follow behind her, pulling out just in time to come on her stomach.

Her legs drop to the bed and her eyes are closed as she works to catch her breath. All you can hear is our heavy breathing and the rain pounding the windows outside.

I look her over, memorizing every detail right down to the

wet strands of hair on her shoulders and fanned on my pillow. I'll never be able to sketch anything else. I already know I'll have entire books dedicated to this Lennon. My Lennon.

"Thank you," she says quietly after a moment. My stomach churns. My chest tightens.

Thank you, as if this was doing her a favor.

I don't answer. I get up and grab a washcloth, then wipe down Lennon's stomach before going to the kitchen to grab us some water. My nerves are shot when I walk back to the bedroom, half expecting to see her ready to leave, but I heave a sigh of relief when I find her fast asleep. Her breathing is deep and even, her face is soft without a trace of worry.

She's been through a lot today.

I should leave her here. I should sleep on the couch. I should give her space.

Instead, I set the water glasses on the nightstand and climb into bed next to her. Just as I start to drift off, she rolls over and puts her head on my chest, her arm wrapping across my middle.

For the first time in years, I feel complete.

And in the morning, I wake to an empty bed.

TWENTY-SIX

Lennon

Dad is back in the ICU and only allowed one visitor at a time.

He's pale and tired and in pain, and I hate it.

But he's alive.

I don't let myself think about the monitors going crazy after Dad started gasping, or how the color was leeched from his face when he lost consciousness. The nurses rushed in and pushed me out of the way, transporting me to that basement bedroom with Macon.

I might as well have been wearing a ruined bridesmaid dress for how lost and terrified I felt.

It feels like I'm haunted by death. It's always hovering just around the corner, and I'm so damn tired of it.

The doctors say Dad could go home in five days, which seems ridiculous to me. He just had his chest cut wide open. How can he go home in five days? It doesn't seem right, but I'll be glad to see him eventually looking more like himself.

His cheeks are growing gaunt and sallow, and dark circles are always shadowing his eyes. Even smiling seems to wear him out, so I try to smile enough for the both of us.

I spend about an hour with him before he starts to drift off to sleep, so I kiss him on the forehead and tell him I love him, then walk slowly to my car.

I thought I would be back in Paris by now. A few days ago, I was itching to be back, but now? Now, I'm not so sure.

Being here hurts, and I feel it in my bones. They ache with all the weight this month brings, and it just doesn't end. Now my father is sick on top of everything, and I know I should stay longer while Dad recovers. At least until he's out of the hospital and doing better. I can spend more time with Andrea and Evie. Sam and I can suffer through my birthday here.

And Macon.

I tell myself he has no influence over my decision, and then I tell myself it's not a lie.

But last night...

When I think about it, my whole body burns. When I think about his hands, his mouth. The way he made me feel. I fist the steering wheel and try to push the flashbacks out of my head, but I can't. They're on a constant loop.

Make me feel something else.

Him pinning me to the door. Carrying me to his bed. The slow, sensual sex. I didn't know sex could feel like that.

I give my head a shake. I can't think about this right now.

I'll deal with it later, or not at all.

I've made the mistake of letting my guard down with him too many times in the past. For all I know, this is just another game for him. Using me to feel better about himself.

In high school, I was the only one who tried to see past his troubled exterior. I always tried to find the good in him, and it always backfired.

But...I don't know.

It *feels* different this time. He says he hasn't been with anyone else. Could that be true? Or could he be trying to manipulate me? He told me I wasn't special that night in his kitchen. Which one is the lie?

I think, deep down, I know the truth. I don't know what it says about me that I wish I didn't. It would be easier if he were a monster.

I turn my radio louder to drown out the rest of my thoughts as I drive.

I'm heading to the art supply store in Norfolk to buy replacement paints when my radio cuts off with an incoming call from Franco on the Bluetooth. I've been avoiding him, and I don't even fully understand why.

I click accept and answer.

"*Cou cou, mon cher,*" I sing-song, forcing brightness into my tone. "I'm driving, so I can't video chat. What are you up to?"

"*Cou cou,*" he says back. "I just wanted to talk. I haven't heard from you, and I wanted to check in. Do you still need your painting, or will you be home soon?"

Home. Paris. Right.

"Actually, Franco..."

"Nooooo," he whines. "You must come back. I am going through withdrawal."

"I'm sorry," I say, laughing at his dramatic tone. "It's just that my dad got worse. He had to have emergency heart surgery and now he's back in the ICU."

"*Ah non,*" he gasps. "What happened?"

"He had a ventricular aneurism," I tell him. "So he's going to be in the hospital for another five days...and then he'll be undergoing intensive therapy..."

"*Je suis vraiment désolé,*" he says softly. "I know this must be difficult. So, you will be there another five days?"

I swallow hard then nod, even though he can't see me.

"Yeah, at least," I say. Then I think of Evie and Andrea. And Macon. "Perhaps longer."

Franco assures me he will send the painting this week, and

I make sure he knows I'm annoyed that it's not on the way yet. He apologizes in his French *c'est la vie* way, then expresses his sympathy twenty more times, and hangs up with, *à bientôt.*

When I get to the art store, it's practically empty. I make my way to the paints and snag the ones that I need, then walk to the registers.

"The store is dead today," I say to the cashier, a teenage boy with shaggy blond hair and a bored look on his face.

"Yeah, good thing we're closing early," he mumbles, without looking at me.

"Yeah," I say, and he hands me my bag. "Have a good day."

"Yep, you too," he says, but he's already gone back to his phone.

When I get to my car, I close my eyes and take a few deep breaths. I need to go to the rec center and drop off these paints, but I don't know if I want to run into Macon or not.

I snuck out on him this morning. No note. No warning. He was sleeping soundly, looking absolutely beautiful, and I left him. I was feeling too much. I was thinking too much.

I just needed space.

No one has ever made me *feel* the way he does, in every possible way. It's like he lights a fire inside me. He winds me up until I'm so full of energy, I could burst. And yet...I've never felt contentment with anyone else. I've never felt safe with anyone but him, and that's what is so confusing.

Because no one has ever broken me quite like he has.

He's the star in some of my best memories, but he's also caused some of my worst.

I don't like feeling vulnerable with him again. I hate it. I feel exposed, and there is still so much that hasn't been said.

I want him. I will *always* want him, but I don't know if there will ever be a right time for us.

I roll that thought over and over in my mind as I drive to the rec center.

Maybe Macon and Lennon can only ever exist in memories and fantasy.

I PULL INTO THE REC CENTER PARKING LOT AND AM SURPRISED to see it's filled with cars. Way more than usual. I'm curious, so instead of slipping through the side door, I walk through the front.

It's a bustle of energy. Everyone is running around like mad, carrying boxes and chairs and something that looks like tents. One volunteer has a plastic tub filled with water balloons.

"Lennon," a voice chirps, and I turn to find Payton grinning at me with her arms full of reusable shopping bags. "*Bonjour,*" she says, and her accent isn't half bad. I smile back.

"*Bonjour*, Payton."

"Are you here to help?" she asks, and I tilt my head to the side.

"Help with what?"

"The Fourth of July event." Payton laughs lightly. "It's tomorrow."

My jaw drops. It's already the fourth? How did that happen? Before I can answer, another voice interrupts, and Payton and I both turn to the speaker.

"She's here to help, P," Casper says with a mischievous grin. "She's with me."

He turns to me and raises a brow in challenge. He looks over my outfit—it's chic and fashionable. Very French.

"Ready, *Capri*? Or have you been in Paris so long that you've forgotten where you come from?"

I squint at him in disbelief and purse my lips, but I can't fight the tiny smile from breaking through.

"Do your worst, *Christopher*," I say in my best French accent, and his grin is so big that I laugh and roll my eyes.

Casper leads me through the center and puts me to work. I hang decorations and sort through the pieces of three different pop-up canopies.

The event tomorrow will be half inside and half outside. The parking lot will be roped off and Macon has okayed it with the grocery store to let everyone park there.

Outside, they'll have water games, a slushie stand, and a cookout. Inside, they're doing basketball scrimmages, a relay race, some crafting stations, and a few other things. Then, at dusk, everyone will walk to the park together to watch the fireworks.

It's all so very *small-town America*. Charming and wholesome family fun, and not a single place to get wine or cheese.

"Macon planned this whole thing?" I ask Casper as we work together to lay out the crafting supplies in one of the art rooms. He glances at me quickly then back to the table.

"Yep," he says with a smile. "He's done a lot of cool shit with the place, Len. He's become quite the community staple."

I nod, but I don't say anything else. It's a lot to process. It's difficult to reconcile this Macon with the Macon I once knew. I've always known the man he could be, but I never thought I would see it happen.

I did exactly what he asked me not to. I gave up on him.

I get lost in my thoughts, moving on autopilot to set up the craft stations. They're meant to be activities that require little to no guidance, and Macon did a good job selecting them. One of the volunteers will be in here tomorrow to oversee, but it's mostly a hands-off job.

Someone steps through the door and my eyes shoot to the person. His attention is on a clipboard, and he's got a pencil in his hand, marking something off. He's wearing a pair of athletic shorts and a tattered Franklin Youth Rec Center t-shirt that I recognize from high school.

I notice his hair curling slightly out the sides of his black backwards ball cap, and my heart kicks up a beat. I had my hands in his hair last night. It's getting longer, and I hate how much that turns me on.

"Hey, Casper," Macon calls after stepping inside the room. "I thought you w—"

His sentence cuts off short when he looks up from the clipboard and sees me. His eyes bounce from me to Casper and back.

"Hi," is all I can say.

The last time I saw him was this morning while he was sleeping soundly in his bed. Just before I snuck out on him without so much as a goodbye.

"Hi," he says slowly, then shakes his head. "What are you doing here?"

"She's helping," Casper answers for me, and I show him the ball of yarn I'm currently cutting foot long strips from. "I think she'd be good at face painting tomorrow."

I shoot my eyes to Casper and find him giving me a trouble-making smile.

"C'mon, Len," he goads. "You'd be way better at it than Jaxon. He'd much rather be manning the grill."

Casper looks from me to Macon.

"You know Jaxon is gonna suck at face painting. Emoji smiles and hippie flowers."

I laugh and look at Macon. His eyes are already on me.

"I can do face painting," I say before overthinking. "It'll be fun."

"Are you sure?"

His voice echoing the same words to me last night replays in my ears. The way his gaze heats, I think he's thinking it too. I nod slowly.

"I'm sure."

Macon tells me the plan for tomorrow and leaves me to continue setting up with Casper. When we finish, Casper moves us to the kitchen and instructs me to take final inventory on all of the freeze pops and juice boxes we've got.

When Casper leaves, I pull out my phone and call Sam.

"Hey," she says when she answers. "Where've you been? I thought we were getting lunch."

"Oh shit, sorry." I totally forgot about my plans with her. "I kind of got distracted at the rec center..."

"Distracted doing what?" she asks, then adds, "or doing *who?*"

"Setting up for tomorrow's Fourth of July event," I tell her, choosing to ignore her last comment. "And I kind of volunteered to volunteer tomorrow."

"Hmmm."

"What?"

I can practically hear her shoulder shrug.

"You're an adult and I trust you to make your own decisions," she says slowly, and I roll my eyes.

"But...?"

"*Buuuut,*" she takes a deep breath and delivers the blow, "you're fucking dumb if you think you and Macon can ever just be friends. You know you guys are like sodium and potassium just waiting for a rainstorm."

I snort a laugh at her chemistry pun.

"You're such a nerd." I hear her laugh followed by a harsh sigh.

"You know what I mean, though, Len," she says softly. "I've seen you together since you've been back. I can tell. That much sexual tension will shoot any shot of platonic friendship straight to hell."

I bite my tongue, something like shame or embarrassment washing over me. I hear Sam gasp in the silence.

"Oh my god, you've already hooked up," she says, and I don't answer. "Oh my god, when? Why didn't you tell me? When did it happen?"

I squeeze my eyes shut. "Which time?"

"OH MY GOD," Sam screeches from the other end, and I have to pull the phone away from my ear. "I can't believe you didn't tell me."

"I'm sorry. I'm still processing."

"Well, was it at least good?" she asks, and I can't help but smile. My face heats and a spark of desire shoots through me.

"Yeah," I whisper, and Sam goes quiet. I wait a few breaths before prodding. "What?"

She sighs, and I brace myself.

"It's just...be careful, okay? You might be trying to forget everything, and I respect that. But *I* remember. *I* was there. I saw what his carelessness did to you. Something like that...it shouldn't just be forgiven. God, someone who makes you feel like that? That deserves bloodshed."

I bite my lip and squeeze my eyes shut.

She's right.

I know she is. I can't just push everything that's happened to the back of my mind and pretend it didn't.

But Sam's always been a fire first, hold grudges after kind of person. It takes a vengeful act as harsh as the one that hurt her to move her forward. I don't fault her for it. The shit she's been through would harden anyone's heart.

But...

I'm not sure I can do that with Macon.

Maybe I'm not as strong as I thought I was. I've always been pulled to him. I probably always will be. Especially right now, when my body is seeking comfort.

I need to go back to Paris.

"I'm not telling you what to do," she continues when I don't speak.

Her voice is softer this time, and it reminds me of England Sam. London Sam. The Sam who spent an entire summer with me just so she could hold me at three in the morning when I thought my world was ending.

I trust her. I trust her more than anyone else in the entire world.

"I respect any decision you make," she says clearly, "and if you decide you can forgive and forget, I'll support you. *I* won't forgive and forget, but I'll play nice. But please just think it through, okay? Don't let your pussy play with your head."

I snort a laugh, and I hear her sigh. I can picture her smiling on the other end, but she's not stupid. She knows it's my heart that's causing the trouble. It always has when it comes to Macon.

"Okay," I say quietly. "I promise I'll think it all through."

"Good." She hesitates just long enough to send my defenses up again, then she drops a bomb. "Have you told him?"

My stomach twists with her question, and I have to take two deep breaths before I can answer.

"No."

"Are you going to?"

I shrug, even though she can't see me. I run my options over in my mind, and I feel sick.

I swallow hard, and my head is spinning when I finally say, "I don't know."

TWENTY-SEVEN

Lennon

SAM SHOWS UP AT MY MOTEL ROOM EARLY THE NEXT MORNING with to-go coffees and croissants.

"They're not French, but they don't suck," she says as she hands me one.

I take a bite and chew.

"Parisians definitely know how to do pastries," I say after I swallow, and she hums her agreement.

"I'm going to eat my weight in *pain au chocolat* next time I visit you," she says. I don't respond, and I don't even know why. I can feel her side-eyeing me on the walk to her car.

"Though, I suppose I could try my hand at making them. Then I could have them whenever I want."

My lips twitch with the need to smile. Sam always knows what to say.

She drives us to the rec center and parks at the grocery store, then we walk slowly to the familiar double doors. The parking lot is roped off, just like Casper said it would be, and music is pumping from a small DJ stand set up on the far end.

When we walk into the building, we run smack into Macon.

"Hey," he says to me with a smile. "I'm glad you made it."

"Of course. Looking forward to painting some faces."

He holds my gaze for a brief moment, just enough to give me goosebumps, then flicks his eyes to Sam. He raises a brow.

"Harper."

"Davis."

"You here to work?" he asks, and she gives him a cheeky grin. I have to bite my lip to keep from laughing.

"Don't you know?" she says sweetly. "I was born to work."

I lose my control after that and bark out a laugh. Macon rolls his eyes with a grin, then gestures over his shoulder.

"C'mon," he says. "You can face paint with Lennon."

We're set up under a tent outside with a flash sheet of face painting options. They're pretty basic and bland. *Emoji smiles and hippie flowers,* as Casper said.

I hand the flash sheet to Sam and pull up some pictures on my phone. Last night I researched face painting and found some really cool things I'd like to try. I saved the images to my phone for reference.

There's no way I'm going to paint something from a flash sheet on these kids. I'm not pretentious, but I am an artist, and my work should reflect my abilities.

A FEW HOURS LATER, I'M SURPRISED AT HOW MUCH FUN I'M having.

These kids are a blast. So far, I've transformed them into every superhero you can think of, some absolutely gorgeous butterflies, a few tigers, and one very interesting interpretation of "a plate of spaghetti." Because yes, I take all requests.

At one point, my line was twenty kids and parents deep, and my smile was so big, my cheeks hurt.

Sam ended up giving up trying to paint faces and started working as my assistant, filling my paints and switching my brushes as I needed them. She also started taking pictures of my designs, and I cannot wait to look at them later.

When there's a break in the line, I feel eyes on me, and I glance over to find Macon walking in my direction. His smirk heats my blood, and I can't look away from him until he's stepping right in front of me and setting two glasses of lemonade on the table.

"Brought you something to drink," he says, flicking his eyes to Sam briefly and then back to me. "How's it going? The kids look great."

"Thank you," I say, smiling. "We're having a lot of fun."

I grab one of the glasses of lemonade and bring it to my lips, taking a sip slowly. I don't mean for it to be sensual, but the way Macon watches, eyes zeroed in on my throat as I swallow, turns me on in a way I didn't expect.

"Okay, well, I gotta pee," Sam says quickly, standing up and leaving without waiting for a response.

Macon and I both nod, but we don't break eye contact. Sparks fly between us, and all I can think is sodium and potassium.

I've always loved a rainstorm.

"Thank you for doing this," Macon says, and my lips hitch up at the corners.

"I'm having a great time," I tell him honestly. "It's amazing that you put this all together."

"I had help." He shrugs, playing it off like I knew he would. "But it seems to be going well, yeah?"

"It definitely does."

"Well…" he says slowly, "I need to run a scrimmage and a relay race before these kids turn feral."

"Okay," I whisper.

He nods his head toward the grill.

"Make sure you eat something, okay?" He smiles playfully. "We don't want leftovers."

I watch him walk away until he disappears into the building, and I swear, every mom here had their eyes on him, too. They all see that he's gorgeous.

A community staple, Casper said.

Damn it. Why can't he be a little less attractive?

A little while later, Andrea shows up with Evie, Claire, and Eric. Claire and Eric break off before they get to my table, and I'm grateful for that. I smile at Andrea when she plops herself down in my chair with Evie on her lap.

"I think we'd like our faces painted," Andrea says, then looks to Evelyn. "What do you think, Evie?"

Evelyn claps and giggles, reaching out her chubby little baby fingers for me. I boop her on the nose and she squeals, making me and Andrea both laugh.

"Okay, Drea, what would you like?" I ask, then look up to find her eyes wide with surprise. "What? Is everything okay?"

She nods quickly and smiles.

"Yeah, of course," she forces out with a laugh. "Sorry. It's just...you haven't called me that in a long time."

My brow furrows as I think it over. I called her Drea. And she's right. I haven't said that since...before I left. I don't know how I feel about that, so I simply nod and change the subject.

"I'm thinking matching hearts," I say, "for Dad."

"That sounds wonderful."

I paint red hearts on Andrea and Evie's cheeks.

Andrea's is a little more detailed, with dimension and glitter. Evie couldn't sit still, so hers is small, glitter-free, and kind of smudged. She giggles the whole time I paint, and I have to dodge her grabby hands more than once.

When they leave my tent to explore the rest of the event, my smile is huge, and my chest feels full.

"Well, that was adorable," Sam says, and I look up to find her eating a red, white, and blue popsicle shaped like a rocket. "Look at you being all *Lennon Washington Golden Girl*."

She wiggles her brows at me, and I roll my eyes.

"Where have you been?" I ask, and she waves her popsicle in the air.

"I got sidetracked. You know Macon has a freezer full of these things? I've already had three."

I do know, because I had to count them yesterday.

"You went snooping in the kitchen?"

She winks. "I was looking for some alcohol." She rolls her eyes and shrugs. "No luck."

I laugh out loud, and her smile returns, almost masking the concern on her face. She won't bring it up again, but I know she's worried about me.

"I think you've painted the face of every single kid here," she says, gesturing to our nonexistent line. "Let's go grab some food."

Sam and I walk around, surveying all the activities and making small talk with people we used to know. I keep my eyes in a constant dance, jumping from person to person, scanning for a backwards ballcap and a blue tank top, khaki shorts and an arm covered in tattoos.

I see Macon three times.

Each time, our eyes lock and hold. Each time, my throat gets tight and my fingers itch to reach for him. Each time, someone pulls him away, and I'm left staring at his retreating back.

When it turns dusk, we start the walk to the park for the fireworks. The glimpse I catch of Macon fills me with something I don't want to acknowledge.

He's got a young girl on his shoulders, maybe six or seven, and her little hands are resting on his baseball cap. She's got a purple butterfly painted on her face, and her smile is huge. They're walking with an older couple, possibly the girl's grandparents, and he's chatting with them about something.

The group is all smiles and laughter, and despite trying not to, I feel left out. Sam instinctively throws her arm around my waist, and I lean into her the rest of the walk.

We reach the park and find a place to lay out the blanket we brought. Then, Casper plops down beside Sam and they start talking. I listen until my neck heats and my skin prickles.

I know who it is without having to look, and when Macon sits next to me, I have to count to ten before I glance at him.

"Hey," he says with a small smile. "Cool if I sit here?"

I shrug and give him a half grin, then gesture to the American flags posted up all around the park.

"It's a free country," I joke, and his smile grows.

I don't know what to say to him, so I say nothing. I just look him over, and he does the same to me. His blue eyes are fire on my skin, and I have to dig my fingers into the blanket beneath me to keep from shivering.

Macon is beautiful.

He always has been, but now, with his features sculpted and matured, the stubble on his strong jaw and the depth of his eyes? He's almost breathtaking. It's hard not to touch him. God, I want to.

I want to feel him above me again. I want my hands on his chest and in his hair.

"Lennon," he whispers, leaning in close.

"Hmmm?"

I lean closer, until I can feel his breath tickling my cheeks. We stay in that position, mere inches from one another, for what feels like a lifetime. Until I can taste him and feel him from memory. Then, just as he starts to close the distance, a loud explosion sounds around us, and we jolt apart.

Everyone cheers and claps, and it takes me a few moments before I register what happened. I look up to see sparkling bursts of color. I haven't celebrated the Fourth of July in years. It almost makes it possible to ignore the permanent sinking feeling in my gut.

"Fireworks," Macon whispers.

I laugh, looking back at him, his body awash in the red and blue lights from the sky. His smile is so big, showing straight, white teeth framed by soft, full lips. I can't stop giggling as I take in his face, the glittering lights making it even more beautiful.

"Fireworks," I repeat, and even in the din of the crowd, my breathless voice rings loud.

SAM DRIVES US BACK TO MY MOTEL AFTER THE FIREWORKS display. We listen to music and chat about the day, but she thankfully doesn't bring up Macon.

"You sure you don't want me to come in?" Sam asks as she idles in the parking lot. "We can drink wine and watch shitty TV."

"Tempting," I tell her, "but I'm exhausted. I'll see you tomorrow, though?"

"Of course," she says, then her face grows serious. "You know I got you, right? No matter what."

I smile. "I know. And I got you, too."

"I know." She leans over and pulls me into a tight hug. "Love you, Len."

"Love you too."

She waits in the parking lot until I am safely inside my room, then I strip and get into the shower. It was hot today, so my body is covered in dried sweat and firework smoke.

After my shower, I dress in pajamas, and then I pace.

Up and down, back and forth, wearing a trail into my cheap motel room carpet.

I try to talk myself out of it a hundred times. I mentally list all the reasons why it's a bad idea. But then my mind rebels, and I start considering all the positives.

Maybe we can handle this now. Maybe us being different is

a good thing. Maybe that means we won't make the same mistakes again.

Maybe this is something that can last.

I make up my mind and grab my keys. I don't even bother changing out of my pajamas. I just lock my room door and hustle to my car. I don't listen to music the whole drive. I don't try to talk myself out of it anymore, either. I just hum a Fleetwood Mac song and try to stay calm.

When I pull into the parking lot, it's almost midnight. The lights in the center are off, but I know he's awake. I use the key he leant me to let myself into the building, then make my way up the stairs with slow, measured steps. When I reach his door, I close my eyes and count backwards from ten before knocking.

Macon opens the door moments later. Shirtless and in gym shorts, just like the other night. But this time, I'm not trying to erase something. This time, I'm not close to drowning and in desperate need of a life preserver.

He doesn't say anything as I step closer to him; he just watches me with wide eyes.

When I place my palms on his chest, he sucks in a harsh breath, but he doesn't make a move to remove them. I slide my hands up to his shoulders, brush my fingers over his jaw, then lift myself on my tiptoes, until my lips are centimeters from his.

I hold there, waiting, trying to tame the wild beating of my heart.

"I was hoping you'd come," he whispers against me, his lips ghosting over mine.

I close my eyes and lick my lips.

"I'm here."

Then I kiss him, and this time, I let myself feel it.

TWENTY-EIGHT

Macon

Lennon lies with her head on my bicep, sleepily trailing her fingers over the tattoos on my chest. My skin is covered in goosebumps from her gentle touch.

"Tell me about the paint brushes." Her voice is hushed as she circles her finger around the clock on my pec, and I hold my breath for a moment.

I've been spilling all my secrets to her lately.

What's one more?

I settle my hand over hers and squeeze lightly before running my thumb back and forth over her soft skin.

"It's for you," I confess, and she stills. "Because I was homesick for you. Because the only decision I've ever made in this life that I'm sure of was being selfish for you."

She's quiet, motionless, as my confession settles around us. Then she pushes herself up to sitting, clutching the bedsheet over her chest. I search her eyes. She's warring with something.

I know this is a lot. Fuck, *I'm* a lot. But I'm done trying to keep things from her. I'm laying myself bare.

"Macon," she says finally, her voice cracking, "I don't think

I... You don't know that I'm worth all of this. So much has happened. So much has changed."

She stops and shuts her eyes, breathing deeply.

Memories cycle, emotions claw at my throat.

I know what she's thinking. We're not those kids anymore. We can't be naïve enough to think that we can work. But... Why can't we?

I sit up and reach for her hand. I just want to touch her, to keep that connection, but I give her time to collect her thoughts. I wait for her to speak.

"You've built me up so much in your head," she says after a moment. When she looks at me, her eyes shine with unshed tears. "I'm just... I'm not going to live up to it."

I give her a small smile. She doesn't get it.

"Lennon, there is nothing you could possibly do to fall short of how I see you, because I see you just as you are."

"But the tattoos... the paintings... all of it," she chokes out. "It's just... it's a lot, Macon. It's *intense*."

I smirk, then, and raise an eyebrow.

"I'm an addict, *Astraea*. I don't know how to do anything small. I *feel* intensely. I *want* intensely. I *crave* intensely. For me, if it's not a healthy obsession, it's not love."

There's that word again. *Love*.

It heats my blood and sparks anxious swirls in my stomach. I wait for her to acknowledge it, but she doesn't, and I feel the need to break the tension.

"Or, at least, that's what my therapist tells me."

She blinks at me, speechless, then furrows her brow as her eyes scan my face. If I were a painting, she'd be rolling her paintbrush over her lip right now. She's studying me. Trying to understand me. She's unsettled, and so am I.

I reach out and tuck a strand of hair behind her ear, then drag my knuckles over her jaw.

"My turn," I say, and she raises her eyebrow in question.

"You've gotten a lot out of me. I want to know something, now."

She swallows hard and blinks a few times.

"Okay."

Her response is tight and forced, but I move forward. This is too important to ignore.

Slowly, I reach for the bedsheet draped over her legs and drag it off her, exposing her naked thighs. She stops breathing and pulls her lower lip between her teeth, biting hard.

With one hand, I reach up and free her lip, rubbing gently over the bite mark she left. With the other, I rest my palm on her thigh, right over the small, raised scars. She shuts her eyes and sucks in a harsh breath. My heart fucking aches for her.

I noticed them briefly in my bedroom the other night, but it didn't register right away. Not until tonight, in slightly better lighting, when she let me have her again.

"What are these, *Astraea?*"

She shakes her head slightly but opens her mouth to speak. Then she closes it again.

I slide my hand to her neck, running my thumb over her pulse point, and she leans into me. I wait. A lifetime stretches in the silence.

Finally, she opens her eyes and locks her gaze with mine. She shrugs, giving me a tiny, sad smile.

"It was a grasp for control when I thought I had nothing else," she whispers, and my chest cracks wide open.

I want to rage. I want to break things. I want to pull her into my arms and never let her go. To fix everything I broke. To undo every mistake I've made.

She's experienced so much pain, and I worry I've only scratched the surface of the damage. I worry I'm the cause of it.

I pull her to me and press our foreheads together.

"Never again," I force out on a rough breath. "I promise. I swear it. Never again."

When I wake, it's late morning.

I can tell from the way the sun is shining through the window, even before opening my eyes. Blindly, I reach for Lennon, needing to pull her back to me.

I stretch my arm out and grasp only air.

My hearts stops, and I fist the sheet. I keep my eyes closed and listen for any sign of movement in the apartment. Music from the studio, or dishes in the kitchen.

Silence.

I open my eyes and stare at the ceiling.

I breathe in once, grit my teeth, then turn to the empty side of the bed. I sit up slowly and work through my thoughts, and before I completely lose my shit, assuming the worst, a piece of paper on the nightstand catches my eye.

I practically throw myself at it, snatching it off the table and reading it in a single breath. Then my shoulders relax.

Went to Dad + Drea's to pick up a package.
Be back soon.
xx

Jesus, the anxiety I just felt was unreal, and all I can think about is how shitty Lennon must have felt waking up after prom. I press my hands to my eyes and rub, then stand and get dressed. I skip a shower. I don't want to wash her off of me just yet.

I go to the kitchen and make some coffee, then grab a protein bar from my cabinet. I've got a few things to do at the rec center today, and then I'm going to lay all my cards on the table.

Lennon belongs with me. We're meant to be together, and we've waited long enough.

I'm stepping into the rec center office when my phone buzzes in my pocket. I take it out and check the screen. A text from Mom. I open it and read it, and it takes a moment to process what she's saying.

I tried to call Capri but she didn't answer. If you see her, can you tell her that her French friend is at the house with Claire? I won't be home for a while. Thanks! Love you.

I want to laugh first. My mom sends texts like she's sending an email or leaving a voicemail.

Then I get angry.

Her French friend.

That can only mean one person, and I see red.

This is not happening again. I turn around and head straight to my car. Work can wait.

TWENTY-NINE

Lennon

My brain is running a mile a second as I drive to Andrea's.

I woke up at 10:15 to a message from Franco, saying my newest painting should arrive this morning at ten. It's a welcomed distraction.

Everything from yesterday is such a blur. It's making me question everything I thought I knew. Everything I believed for the last four years is crumbling.

And what about us now?

Macon and I have changed, yes. But maybe we could still work. Being with him...it still feels right. Better than before, even.

Once again, I replay what he told me in the storage room.

He says he didn't abandon me on purpose. He says he expected me to come back. He says he never gave up on us.

But something just isn't adding up, and I can't pinpoint what.

What does all of this mean? Did I build a life based off misconceptions? Am I to blame for everything?

No.

Someone could have told me where Macon was. Someone could have told me the truth.

Andrea could have told me at any time during our fleeting check-in calls for the first few weeks I was at Aunt Becca's. Claire could have told me when she emailed me back instead of telling me Macon was "better without me."

Hell, even Macon could have told me instead of leaving me naked and alone in that hotel bed with nothing but a crumpled sticky note and a broken heart.

Why did he leave me there? Where did he go? What happened that night that made him disappear before I woke up?

Did he freak out? Did he regret what we'd done? Did he run scared?

God, we have so much left to talk about. It's scary. What if we can't handle all that's happened between now and then?

But Macon did come back for me. I know he's telling the truth. He was there the night I self-destructed. Three days after Sam had to leave me for Georgetown. A week after I moved to London for art school and started going by Capri. One year before I dropped out and moved to Paris.

He came for me, and then he just...left me there.

I fight the urge to close my eyes.

I want to be angry that he didn't show himself, but at that point, would it have changed anything? The damage was probably already done.

You don't want to erase your mistakes.
You want to transform them into something beautiful.

Maybe Sam is right. I can't forgive Macon for what he did. I shouldn't. But maybe that Macon is different from this Macon. I feel different from that girl four years ago. Why can't it be the same for him?

All I know is, for the first time in a long time, I'm excited to crawl back into bed with someone. I'm looking forward to another conversation. Another kiss. I want someone next to me when I paint. I want someone next to me always.

And that someone is Macon.

Not Macon from high school. Macon from today. Marine Macon. Community Staple Macon. Amazing Big Brother and Son Macon.

Maybe, finally, he can be my Macon too.

I pull up to the curb at Drea's house, noting that there are no cars in the driveway. Drea must be at the hospital, but where are Claire and Eric? When I twist the doorknob, I find it unlocked, which is strange, and when I step inside, I hear laughter.

Claire's...and...

"Franco?" I say as I walk into the kitchen, shocked to find him sitting at the kitchen island with Claire.

I look between their smiling faces.

"What are you doing here?"

"*Mon bijou,*" Franco croons, standing from his seat and wrapping me in his arms.

I return the hug, resting my head on his familiar chest. He smells of Cuiron by Helmut Lang, and I breathe him in.

"I was worried about you," he whispers into my hair as he rubs his hand up and my down my back. "How is your father? Your stepsister says he's doing better."

I pull back and look him in the eyes.

"He's doing as well as can be expected right now. I haven't seen him yet today, but when I saw him yesterday, he was in good spirits."

"That is good, *oui?*"

"*Oui,*" I say with a laugh, then pull him back in for another hug. "It's so good to see you. I wish you would have told me you were coming, though."

"I wanted to surprise you."

His smile is comforting, but something about his presence

makes me feel a little uneasy. Is this something we would normally do? Is this the kind of relationship we have?

"Well, it's good to have a friend."

I emphasize the word *friend* and watch his face. He doesn't wince or flinch. He doesn't look disappointed.

Maybe I'm overreacting. I wouldn't think twice if Sam just showed up somewhere to surprise me. Why should Franco's appearance concern me?

No. It's nothing worth worrying about.

"You should have called when you landed, though. I'd have been here sooner."

I step away from Franco and flick my eyes to Claire.

"Your sister has been keeping me company."

He smiles and gestures to Claire, and I raise a brow.

"*Step.*"

Claire rolls her eyes but keeps her mouth shut, and my anger flares.

I sent her dozens of frantic emails after being shipped off to England. Dozens.

Apologizing. Begging. *Pleading* for her help to get me in touch with Macon. Sure, we'd been in a fight, but we'd also been best friends for most of our lives. I thought maybe that would afford me a little bit of sympathy.

Or, at the very least, honesty.

But what did she do?

He doesn't want to talk to you. Take the hint.

He's doing better now that you're gone.

She could have told me he was in rehab, but instead, she said what she knew would hurt me.

You're being pathetic. It's embarrassing.

The series of events that email triggered flash quickly through my head, each one making me more emotional than the last. Blocking everyone. Changing universities. Moving to London. The depression spiral. The cuts on my thighs. The inability to paint. The fear and the pain. The drugs and alcohol and sex.

The irony is almost too much.

Macon was in rehab getting help, while I was self-destructing.

While I was flunking out of college because I was getting drunk and high and sleeping around, he was getting clean.

And it all could have been avoided if she would have just told me the fucking truth.

I turn slowly and face Claire.

I stare at her until she looks at me. When she finally does, her nostrils flare and her eyebrows pull together.

"What?" she asks, and the pitch of her voice is enough to make me wince.

I don't look away from her, but I speak to Franco.

"I'm surprised she didn't try to talk shit about me while she was keeping you company." I tilt my head to the side and rest my hand on my chin as I watch Claire's face turn red. "Or did she?"

"Jesus Christ, Capri," Claire spits. "Of course, I didn't talk shit about you."

"No?" I keep my voice calm, almost sweet. "But ruining the things I love brings you so much joy."

Claire's jaw drops and she puts her hands on her hips.

"If this is about Eric—"

I laugh loudly, shutting her up. She knows damn well I don't care about Eric. I didn't in high school. I don't now.

"Capri." Franco places his hand on my arm. "Perhaps we should go get some coffee?"

I don't acknowledge his comment.

"Lennon," I say clearly, reciting from memory, "please stop emailing Macon. He doesn't want to talk to you."

Claire's eyes grow wide, and the color drains from her face

as I speak. I can feel Franco's attention on me, but I stay locked on Claire.

"Take the hint. You're being pathetic and embarrassing."

I take three steps, so I'm directly in front of her across the kitchen island. She flinches, but she doesn't step away.

"He's doing better now that you're gone."

My voice booms on the last word.

"Remember that, Claire? Remember? Remember how Macon was *in fucking rehab*, but you chose to make me think he didn't care about me anymore?"

Her mouth drops open, her lips quiver. So many unexplained emotions dance over her face before settling on defensive. She preps for a fight, and I'm ready to give her one.

"You were supposed to come back," Claire says. "You weren't supposed to stay in England. You were supposed to be back when he got out."

Bullshit.

"So you, what, just wanted to hurt me a little bit more? Just wanted to cause me pain for the summer?"

"No! No. I was just...I was mad," she says. "You weren't supposed to stay gone."

"I was never supposed to leave," I shout. "Were you so fucking jealous that you had to orchestrate the whole thing?"

"What? No!"

"You're such a miserable bitch, Claire. Couldn't stand that you weren't the center of my attention? You were so fucking petty that you had to split us up?"

"No, Lennon, Jesus," Claire shouts. "I didn't know you'd go AWOL after that email, okay? I thought you would come home at the end of the summer and then—"

"—And then what? And then fucking what, Claire?"

"And then you'd know! And then it would be fine and fixed, and we'd go back to normal! I thought you just needed to cool off. To get Macon out of your system. This wasn't supposed to happen!"

This is un-fucking-believable.

Everyone else was making the moves in my life, and I was left with nothing. I was a pawn.

"So, you got me sent away? Do you know how fucked up that was, Claire? Do you even know what a mess you caused?"

"I didn't get you sent away!" She fists her hands at her sides, and she narrows her eyes. "I shouldn't have said those things in that email, but I didn't send you away."

I laugh sardonically, loud and ominous.

"You might as well have. You told my dad—"

"I didn't tell your dad shit, Lennon. It was Macon."

My head jerks back and my mouth snaps shut as I stare at Claire.

"*Macon* told your dad that you'd slept together on prom night. He asked your dad to send you. *Macon* is the reason you were sent away early. Quit blaming me for everything."

What? No. Macon wouldn't do that.

"You're lying," I spit out. "That's what you do. You're fucking lying."

"I'm not! I swear to god, I'm not."

Tears are starting to trickle down her cheeks, and she brushes them away hastily.

"And you know what else? Macon was here. That day you were crying and begging to say goodbye? He was here, upstairs, beat to shit and bloody, and he hid from you."

I take a step backward, tripping over my foot and falling backward into Franco's arms. I search Claire's face frantically, looking for malice or lies, but all I find is sorrow and shame.

"I'm not the reason you were sent away early," she says again. "I've done a lot of petty shit I'm not proud of, but that's not one of them."

I can't speak as I run what she's said through my mind.

Macon ratted us out? Macon hid from me as I frantically called for him downstairs? He was *beat to shit and bloody?*

"*Chérie,*" Franco says, rubbing his hand up and down my arm.

He speaks, but I don't hear him. I turn toward the front door and walk.

"Lennon, wait," Claire calls, but I ignore her.

I walk to the front door and push out into the sun. I take three steps toward my car when a hand wraps around my wrist, halting me and spinning me around, then pulling me into a hug.

"Talk to me, *chérie*. Tell me what I can do."

I start to cry into his shirt. He takes my chin between his thumb and forefinger and tilts my head up, so he's looking into my eyes.

"Tell me what I can do, Capri. Let me help."

Franco rubs his thumb over my jaw, and I close my eyes, trying to calm my breathing. Then I'm suddenly yanked forward and Franco is ripped from my arms.

My eyes snap open just in time to see Macon throw Franco to the ground. Franco grunts in pain, and I throw my hands to my face.

Not again.

Visions of Macon attacking Eric, attacking his father, flood my head, and my heart starts to race with fear.

"Stop it, Macon," I shout.

Franco tries to get back up, but Macon shoves him back down, harder this time, and Franco shouts something in Italian.

"Stay down," Macon warns, his voice shaking. "Stay down, or I swear to god, I'll snap."

"Macon, don't," I say again, expecting Macon to launch himself onto Franco and start throwing punches, but instead he whirls on me.

"Are you fucking kidding me with this?" Macon yells, flinging his finger backward at Franco. "After everything, after last night, you're going to pull this?"

I jerk my head back in shock before my anger spikes.

"You don't know what you're talking about!"

"Is this your fucking Frenchman? Did he just come to America for you? You're just going to go back to your fucking Frenchman?"

"He's not *my* Frenchman, Macon," I yell. "I was coming back to you!"

Macon barks out a humorless laugh and tugs on his hair.

"Fuck, it's like fucking Masters all over again," he shouts at the sky, before flinging a finger at me. "You're never going to choose me, are you? It doesn't matter what I do or what I change, I'll *never* be good enough for you."

I choke on my anger, my vision blurring with tears.

"I *did* choose you! I chose you. I made you *everything*, and it blew up in my fucking face!"

I swipe at my tears, my hands trembling, the words bursting from me on a sob.

"I just found out that you're the reason I was sent to England early."

Macon freezes.

His eyes bounce between mine as he tries to piece together what I'm saying. Is he surprised that I know? Is he wondering how I found out? Was he *ever* going to tell me?

God, I was hoping it was another one of Claire's lies.

"Is it true?"

He doesn't answer, just stares at me.

"Is it true?" I shout. "Did you tell him? Did you ask him to send me early?"

Macon closes his eyes briefly, but he doesn't deny it.

"It wasn't like that," he says. "Lennon, I—"

"No," I cut him off, "that day, when I was sobbing and

calling for you, begging to say goodbye, you were upstairs the whole time."

I take a step backward.

"I thought I was being punished by my father for my relationship with you, but this whole time, it was your fault. I was sent away because of you? Do you have any idea what you did? What I went through because of you?"

"Lennon, I told you," Macon chokes out, and I laugh. "I'm sorry. I'm so sorry, but I told you. I explained—"

"I was pregnant, Macon."

The statement is quiet, spoken plainly, but it leaves my mouth like a bullet from a gun, and the color drains from Macon's face as if he's been shot.

"What?"

"You sent me away, cut me off for months, and I was pregnant."

I clamp my eyes shut. I haven't said those words out loud in years. Not since I confessed to Sam. Not to anyone else since.

I can feel everyone's attention on me.

Macon. Franco. Probably Claire. Hell, maybe even the neighbors.

For four years, only two other people knew my secret, and I just shouted it for anyone close enough to hear. The realization makes me sway on my feet.

I open my eyes when Macon speaks, the pain in his jagged voice slices right through me, and I can empathize. I've felt it before.

"Lennon, do we...Do we have a baby?"

His flame blue eyes burn me alive as I shake my head slowly, and my tears fall faster down my cheeks.

"No," I whisper. "That decision was taken from me, too."

The memory plays out in front of me like a movie, bright and loud in technicolor.

The pain shoots through my body all over again. I can hear

Sam trying to soothe me on the way to the hospital. Can feel Aunt Becca's hand squeezing mine. The fear and devastation choke my windpipe. My heart shatters. All I can feel is pain. All I can see is darkness.

It's okay, Lennon. It's going to be okay. We'll get through this.

It hurts. It hurts so much.

I know. I know. I'm here. Just hold on to me, okay? It's going to be alright.

I'd been going back and forth on what to do about the pregnancy.

I'd given up on Macon. I'd cut ties with my family. Sam and Aunt Becca said they would support me no matter what.

I thought I'd made up my mind. I was almost out of the first trimester.

But, in the end, the choice was made for me.

And deep down, I still don't know how I feel about that.

"When," Macon asks, and I laugh. It's painful and haunted. The moment our eyes connect, his face reflects how I feel.

"On my birthday."

God, I hate this month.

Four years ago, I spent the first part of July anxious and terrified.

I spent the last half drowning in grief so thick, I didn't recognize it until years later. I've spent every July since trying my best to ignore it and make it to August.

When Macon found me in that alley behind the pub in London, I'd finally decided to say fuck it all. Sam had just left for school, and I had assured her I was fine, but I lied.

I wanted to forget everything. Erase everything.

Things got worse before they got better, but I'll always hate July.

I watch as Macon runs through everything in his head, as

he wars with himself. Then I watch as he shuts down. He takes a slow step toward me, then another.

"Lennon," he whispers, but I put up a palm, halting him.

"Don't. It's over."

"I'm so sorry you had to go through that alone."

His voice is soft and shaking, and it hits me in the chest. I close my eyes and breathe through my nose.

"I wasn't alone," I force out. "I had Sam. I had Aunt Becca."

"You should have had me," he says, and I open my eyes and lock them with his.

"Yeah, I should have. But I didn't. And nothing is going to change that now."

His eyes flutter shut; his face full of anguish.

"Lennon," he says again, and his voice is a shaky whisper.

I wait to see if he'll say anything else. I give him one breath, then two, then three, before my heart falls to my feet.

"Just go, Macon. Just go."

He stays quiet, and I keep my eyes shut until I hear his car drive off down the street. Once he's gone, I collapse to the ground in tears.

Franco's arms wrap around me, his familiar scent calming my nerves, and he rocks back and forth, whispering soothing words in Italian and French.

This isn't how I wanted to tell Macon.

I don't know if I ever wanted to tell him, but I definitely didn't want him to learn about it like this.

Two hours ago, I was thinking about all the ways we could maybe make it work between us. But now? Now I know it's impossible.

There's too much damage. I can never forgive him for sending me away, for leaving me with nothing, and from the look on his face when he left, he knows it, too.

"Lennon."

I look up from my spot on the ground, cradled in Franco's arms, into Claire's tear-soaked face. She looks absolutely stricken, and I can't bring myself to care.

"Not now, Claire."

"I just..."

She squeezes her eyes shut and releases another small sob.

"God, I'm so fucking sorry, Lennon. I didn't know. I didn't know. I was just angry and jealous...I was going to give it back in the fall, but then you didn't come back. Jesus, I'm so sorry."

I'm confused, watching her stand above me spewing tear-filled apologies. I don't grasp what it is she's saying—Give me what? Sorry for what?—until I notice an envelope in her hands, and an eerie chill runs down my spine.

I explained.

I told you.

I asked you to wait for me.

"Claire," I say shakily. "What is that?"

She whimpers and holds the envelope out to me with trembling hands. The handwriting on it takes my breath away.

Astraea.

"Claire," I say again, staring at the envelope like it's a bomb. "*What* is that?"

"He put it in your suitcase," Claire says. "I...I took it out. I was going to give it back when you came home after the summer. I never read it. I just——"

I stand quickly and snatch the envelope then walk to the far side of the yard. My breath is coming hard, my heart pounding wildly in my chest. My hands are shaking so badly that I'm terrified I'll rip something important as I tear open the seal of the envelope.

I hold one piece of paper as a second flutters to the ground. When I crouch down to pick it up, I start to cry all over again.

It's a sketch of me.

Of my naked back, sitting on the bed on prom night. Macon's initials aren't in the corner, but I know it's his work. I trail my fingertips lightly over the paper, tracing his pencil lines and shading.

I've never been more scared than I am right now. I know that the grudge I've been holding, the way I've been punishing Macon in my head for four years, is about to go up in flames.

And what will I do after?

Slowly, I unfold the second piece of paper from the envelope. It's also torn from a sketchbook, but there are no drawings or doodles on this one. Only words.

I run my eyes over the familiar handwriting, sentences scrawled in a messy, hurried script, and my hand shoots to my mouth as I read. My head starts to spin and my heart cracks wide open as my tears land in fat drops on the paper.

His handwriting is jumbled and chaotic. The words are rushed, but the sentiment is clear.

This note, the one he put in my suitcase four years ago, changes everything.

My Astraea,

I'm sorry. If you're reading this, that means your luggage got to your aunt's house and you're an ocean away from me. Fuck, I miss you already. Prom was the best night of my life. That memory is going to fuel my recovery, Astraea, I promise. I have to go to rehab. I'm leaving today after Trent drops you at the airport. I'm sorry I couldn't tell you sooner. Please don't be mad at your dad. I asked him to send you early. I promise I'll explain in detail when I get out and you come home in the fall. Enjoy England. I know it's been your dream since you were little. Take lots of pictures because I want to hear all about it. Don't give up on me, Astraea. Just wait for me a little while longer. Then when I get out, it's you and me. For real. Out loud. Forever. I love you, Lennon Capri Washington.

See you soon,

-M

I fold the papers carefully and stick them back into the envelope, then I stand slowly and turn around.

Claire and Franco are watching me. Claire is sobbing.

I take even steps until I'm standing just a few feet in front of them. My eyes stay on Claire.

"Do you have any idea what you've done?"

"I'm so sorry, Lennon," she chokes out. "I'm so, so sorry."

I feel nothing for her but disgust.

"You know, Claire...In high school, I never would have believed you'd be the villain in my story. But now? Now I'm just disappointed I didn't figure it out sooner."

I reach out and squeeze Franco's hand.

"I'll be back later, okay?"

He nods and squeezes my hand back, but he doesn't speak. I give Claire one last glance, and then I turn around and walk to my car.

Only one thing matters now.

I have to find Macon.

I keep myself from speeding through town. A familiar fear courses through my body with every turn, and I have to remind myself that this isn't the same.

I'm not that naïve seventeen-year-old girl in a battered bridesmaid dress, and Macon isn't the same lost, broken boy with demons to keep at bay.

So much has happened. So much has changed.

I tell myself this over and over as I drive through town, but I still nearly faint with relief when I find Macon's car in the parking lot of the rec center.

I turn off my car and walk calmly through the side door, then up the stairs that lead to Macon's apartment. He could be in the office or the gym, but something tells me he's up here.

I get to his door and contemplate my options, then decide to knock.

When no one comes to the door after a minute, I knock again.

It's fine.

He's probably just listening to music in his studio. I repeat that over and over as I wait.

It's fine. He's fine. We're fine.

I knock again and wait.

When another minute passes, I take out the key and let myself in. The moment I step into the apartment, I'm hit with an overwhelming smell of alcohol, and my fear spikes.

"Macon?"

I try to fight the wobble in my limbs as I walk through the hallway, but when I step into the kitchen, my legs almost give out from underneath me.

There is shattered glass and spilled liquor all over the floor, as if a bottle had been thrown. The way the glass shards are scattered all over the room, and the liquid splashes on all the walls, there's no way this was from an accidental drop.

The realization makes me breathe easier.

The irony.

A full liquor bottle hurled at the wall, shattered on the floor, is so much better than an empty bottle completely intact.

If the booze is on the floor and walls, then it couldn't be consumed.

But god, the emotions that must have caused this...

Slowly, I walk back into the hallway. I peek into the bedroom, but I know I won't find him inside. It's empty, so I continue toward the studio.

I start to worry when I realize there is no music playing. I've never known Macon to create without music. When I get to the door, my fingers are trembling as I wrap them around the knob and push it open.

My breath comes out in a whoosh when I see Macon behind his pottery wheel, shirtless and clay-covered with the front of his hair pulled back by a pink butterfly clip.

His eyes shoot to mine before I can speak, and he turns off his wheel immediately.

For a few moments, we just stare at each other. I look him over, his eyes and face and body. He's sober, I'm certain. I don't know what happened in the kitchen, but I know he didn't relapse. He didn't give in to his addiction, but he definitely went through *something* here in the last hour, and I think I can guess what it was.

I pull the envelope out of my back pocket and hold it up.

He looks at it, then back at me.

"My note?"

"Claire just gave it to me."

I take slow steps toward him and stop when I'm just out of arm's reach.

"She *just* gave it to you?"

Macon's eyes search mine as he tries to piece it together, and it makes me want to rage at Claire all over again.

He's spent the last four years thinking I had this note.

Thinking I had it and chose to stay in England anyway.

He's spent the last four years thinking I willingly gave up on him, and yet he still held on.

"She took it out of my luggage," I tell him clearly, and his face drops with shock. "Today was the first time I saw it. Before today, I didn't even know it existed."

He doesn't say anything for a long time. He stares at the envelope in my hand with a furrowed brow and sad eyes. It takes all of my strength not to rush to him, but I wait for him to speak. Finally, he brings his eyes from the envelope back to my face.

"Did you read it?"

I nod.

"You said you'd explain in detail," I tell him. "If you don't mind, I'd like to hear that now."

THIRTY
Macon

Prom Night

Gently, I run the strand of Lennon's hair between my fingers, twirling it around and letting it drop before doing it all again.

She's been asleep for an hour now, but I can't stop staring at her.

Fuck, she's beautiful.

When I started the night, I didn't think I'd end up here. I still can't believe it. I'm afraid if I fall asleep, she'll disappear. It will all be a fucking dream.

This is it for me, though. We're coming clean in the morning. Our parents are going to have to be okay with this because this is happening.

Me and Lennon, for real and out loud.

I'm not going to love her in secret any longer. I'm not hiding this from anyone. Not anymore.

Lennon stirs when my fingertips brush her naked shoulder blade, and she hums, a sound that resonates deep in my stomach. Goosebumps raise on her skin, and I tug the comforter a little higher over her body. I don't want her to be cold, and I don't want to wake her.

My phone vibrates on the table beside the bed, and I roll my eyes when I see the Caller ID before hitting ignore.

Like I'm going to fucking answer for Chase Harper.

I told that dick last time he was in town to fuck off for good. I'm not running drugs for him anymore. I'm not playing candy man at parties. Not after the last time. He can find someone else. I'm out.

He rings through again, and I ignore him, again.

Then he sends a text. It's a picture of Claire, Josh, and Eric. They're in the clothes they wore to the dance, but they're at some party by a bonfire. I scan the faces around them. Must be a high school party at Josh's. The fuck is Chase doing there?

Then another text comes through.

Bet I can find your bitch before you do.

He's talking about Lennon. A not-so-thinly veiled threat. Fuck, Chase is such a fucking dirtbag. He must not know I'm with her. I move to turn my phone off when another text buzzes through.

This one is a picture of Claire. Just Claire. No Eric or Josh. Just Claire standing by the bed of a truck, holding a can of beer and scrolling on her phone.

This one will work.

A chill creeps down my spine and I squeeze my eyes shut, then I turn my head and glance at Lennon.

I can be back before she wakes up.

I roll over and press a kiss to her forehead.

"Macon," she mumbles, and I kiss her again.

"Shhh, baby. Sleep. I'll be back soon."

I stand and shoot Chase a text, telling him I'm on the way, and then I throw my clothes back on. I'm not afraid of this prick. It's time I show him that.

I go to put my phone in my pocket when my fingers brush over something. I pull out the crumbled sticky note and smile, then set it down on my pillow. Just in case she wakes before I get back.

I park at the end of the gravel road, about a mile from Josh's house. Chase is already leaning on the hood of his car when I turn off my engine. I leave my lights shining on him, though, because I don't trust his pretentious ass.

"Harper," I say as I take a seat on my own hood. "I told you I'm not runnin' for you anymore."

Chase smiles, looking just like his father, then shrugs.

"I know. Not why I called."

I tilt my head to the side and cross my arms over my chest. I'll give him a minute. He thinks he's running the show, but I've got a warm bed to get back to, so my patience is wearing thin.

The back door of his car opens, and two more guys climb out. I tense. For the first time, I feel a little uneasy. I wasn't expecting two more idiots, but I guess that was a rookie fucking mistake.

Casually, I slide my phone into my pocket and wrap my hand around it, just in case.

"You remember my friends, right, Davis?"

The two guys lean next to Chase, and I almost laugh at how back-alley mobster this feels. Chase Harper is a pretentious, spoiled, rich boy, not some mafia underboss. He probably still has a nanny to manicure his fingernails.

"Can't say I do," I say slowly. I don't ask. He's gonna tell me anyway.

"You met them at the party in Birchwood in December."

The hairs on the back of my neck rise at the mention of that party. That's the one where I overdosed while playin' candy man. *A favor*, Chase said. He failed to mention I'd have to sample the product, too. I stay quiet. I know Chase wants to talk, so I'm going to let him.

"Well, you might not remember them, but you should definitely remember Fuller's girlfriend."

Chase nods to the big guy on his left. I look him over, but he doesn't jog my memory.

"I didn't hook up with anyone at that party, Chase," I drawl, bored. "What are you getting at?"

"You gave her that shit," the guy, Fuller, speaks, and I sit up straighter. "You gave her that fucked-up shit that killed her."

My stomach starts to swirl, and I shake my head.

"I was slinging Chase's drugs, and as far as I know, I'm the only one who got a bad dose."

I try to keep the bitterness out of my voice, but I fail. I was there to peddle the pills, not pop them. Fucking Chase.

"You were too busy dying," Chase says, and I sneer at him. "But Fuller's girlfriend was right there with ya. She took what you gave her, and even though you walked away, she fell into a coma and died a month later."

Every ounce of chill I had moments earlier disappears.

This isn't a favor shake down. Chase isn't looking for someone to sell his shit.

He's looking for blood.

"Those were your drugs, Chase," I say clearly. "I didn't dose them."

Chase doesn't acknowledge my words as he stands from the car, and the other two dicks follow. Then it dawns on me.

He's passing this on me.

He brought these fucks here, to me, to get them off his back.

"Those were Chase's drugs, Fuller. You too afraid to fuck with a senator's son, though?

You'd rather come after the runner? You want justice for

your girlfriend, then go after the source. I was just doing what he told me to, and I almost died in the process."

I try to spin it in my favor. For a minute I think it worked. I see Chase's shoulders tighten. Watch Fuller and the other guy give Chase a sidelong glance. Then Chase smirks.

"I'm a *Harper*, Davis. I'd never be responsible for something like that. My dad wouldn't allow it."

Fuck it.

The fucking threat in his words is obvious, and the goons he's with hear it loud and clear. If they want blood, I'm the best they're gonna get.

"Where's that little stepsister of yours, Davis?" Chase says casually. "I think Fuller would like to meet her."

I shoot to standing and clench my hands into fists. I breathe through my nose. Don't do anything impulsive. This could go bad fast.

Fuck, it's already bad.

"Don't go there, Chase," I say calmly.

"You think it's a fair trade if we just fuck her, or should we kill her too?"

"You stay the fuck away from her."

I force the words through my teeth as the visual of what Chase is capable of invades my brain. If he touches her, I will kill him.

"Bet we could make her scream," the other guy starts to say, and I snap.

I see red, and I launch myself at him. It's the way it was heading anyway. I might as well get the jump. A jab to the nose, a knee to the gut. I swing twice at the prick's jaw and land both before I'm pulled off of him.

Then it fully hits me how fucked I am. Three against me, and I'm wearing a suit and dress shoes.

I try. I swing and swing and kick, but I'm out numbered, and they've got size on me, too.

I do as much damage as I can, and then it's just a lot of pain.

I feel my lips bust open. Sharp hooks and jabs to my cheekbones and nose. I feel someone's knuckles cut on my teeth, and the metallic flavor of blood in my mouth could be mine or theirs. I spit it out in between blows.

I bite my own tongue to keep from crying out as a kick to the stomach nearly splits me in half. It'll have me coughing up blood if I survive this.

God, I have to survive this.

I can't fucking die here on this back road in a pool of my own blood.

I'm in a fetal position on the ground in front of my car. There's sticky blood in my eyes and mouth. I might have broken a tooth. Something is probably ruptured inside me. The pain engulfs my body. It's hard to breathe.

They don't stop.

They won't stop until I'm dead, and the only thing I can think of is Lennon.

I left her there without an explanation. I haven't even told her I love her. I fling out another punch, land a kick on someone, but I can't get up.

I try, but I fall back into the dirt, and one of the dicks laughs. Someone hovers above me, but my eyes are swollen and bleeding. I can't tell who it is.

"Tell her I said hello," the guy says with a growl, and then something gets shoved in my mouth.

I can't taste anything with all the blood, but I know what it was. He just slipped me the same shit that was in those capsules the night I OD'd.

They're trying to fucking kill me.

"Why now?"

I don't even know how I say it. I don't know where the question came from, only that I have to know.

Winter break was months ago. Why now? Why now, after I finally make up my mind with Lennon and see a light at the end of the fucking tunnel?

I hear one of the guys laugh, but it's a sad laugh. A painful laugh, and I feel a twinge of sympathy for the dick who just beat me near to death.

"Had to grieve," the guy says. "Your girlfriend will understand soon enough."

Fuck. Lennon. This is going to crush her.

I hear car doors slam and then Chase's voice.

"You can watch me fuck your stepsister from hell."

The car peels out and leaves me lying on the gravel in the light of my high beams.

Everything hurts. All I want to do is close my eyes, but Chase's threat gives me just enough adrenaline. I pull my phone out of my pocket, try my best to find the contact through my less swollen, bloody eye, and hit dial.

It only rings three times before the call is answered.

"Macon? Everything okay?"

"Trent," I cough out, "I need your help."

I WAKE TO THE SOUND OF ARGUING.

Trent and Mom's voices.

My head pounds. My body aches. Everything is spinning.

"You can't just ship her off tomorrow, Trent," my mom yells. "She deserves to know what's going on and to make her own decisions. She's not a child."

"She is *my* child, Andrea," Trent yells back. "You heard what Macon said. You saw what those people can do. It was *my* mistake that killed her mother. My inaction. My indecision. That won't happen again. She's going. That's final."

I hear something banging and turn my head in time to see my mom snatch a small pink suitcase from Trent.

"Let me do this," my mom snaps. "You wouldn't have any idea what to pack for her."

My mom disappears up the stairs with the suitcase, and I watch Trent hang his head. I think he might actually cry, and this is all my fucking fault.

"Trent," I grunt out, and he stands straight and walks to where I'm laid out on the couch.

"Macon."

He drops to his knees next to me and looks me over.

"Not high," I joke, "but in a lot of pain."

Well, I'm a little high.

But whatever that dick gave me wasn't strong enough to knock me on my ass this time. Just enough to take a bit of the edge off the hurt.

"You're sending her?" I ask, and Trent nods.

"I'm deploying for six months. And until I can get some intel on that family, it's safer for her to be in England."

I give my head the smallest possible nod. I agree.

"She can't see me like this. She can't know yet. She won't go if she does. You know that."

Trent is quiet for a minute, looking me over with stoic eyes.

"I can't keep this from her," he says finally. "I'm already taking her choice away by sending her early. I can't send her and keep the truth from her, too."

I close my eyes and take shallow breaths. Deep breaths hurt.

"If she sees me beat to hell like this, she won't get on the plane. You know she won't, I can't be the reason she doesn't go to England."

She's wanted this for so long. As long as I've known her. I refuse to be the reason she passes up this opportunity. And then there's...

"And I...I don't know if I'm strong enough to stay at the facility if I know she's here unprotected, while you're off hunting down terrorists or whatever the fuck it is that you do."

Trent huffs out a laugh, and I manage a small smirk before my lip resplits and I taste blood.

"I don't know, Macon." Trent hesitates, so I pivot.

"Get her on that plane tomorrow, but don't tell her about me. Not yet. I'll tell her once she's landed."

Trent raises an eyebrow in question.

"I'll write her a note."

"You can barely breathe. How are you going to write?"

I lift up my hand and wiggle my fingers, and he gives me a small smile. I put my arm down and open my mouth to thank him when the doorbell rings.

My whole body tenses, but Trent lays a calming hand on my thigh.

"That's my buddy," he says softly. "The one who's going to check you out."

THE SOUNDS OF LENNON CRYING AND CALLING FOR ME PLAY IN my head on repeat.

All I could do was sit on my bed with my bandaged head in my bandaged hands. It took every single ounce of restraint to keep from going after her, and the only reason I held back was because I knew it would be bad for her if I did.

I tell myself she'll be okay by tomorrow.

As soon as she opens her luggage and sees my note, we'll be okay.

"You alright over there?" Trent asks from the driver's seat.

"Yeah. Just thinking."

"She'll be okay," he tells me. "She won't stay mad long."

He's so full of shit with his optimistic nonchalance. I saw him crying this morning. He's just as torn up about this as I am. I open my mouth to call him out, but then I shut it again.

What's the point? We've only got two hours until we reach the drug treatment facility. I'm not going to waste that time ribbing him. Instead, I cut to important shit.

"I'm in love with your daughter, Trent."

I freeze and watch him. His body stays loose, his hands resting on the wheel. He doesn't even scowl. But he's a Navy SEAL. He's probably going to snap my already weakened neck.

"I know," he says finally, and my jaw drops. He glances at me and then gives me one of those *dad* laughs. "You kids aren't very subtle."

I roll my eyes.

"Well, I just thought you should know, you know, since we're technically stepsiblings or whatever. I don't want you to be caught off guard when I start dating her."

"What makes you think I'm going to give you permission to date my daughter, Macon Davis?"

"Because I'm *a good kid who's going to be a good man*," I say, throwing his words from the night of his bachelor party back at him. His lips twitch up at the corners. "And because no one will ever love Lennon the way I do. I love all of her. Even the parts that she doesn't show the world."

"But she shows you?"

"Yes, sir, she does."

I say it without sarcasm or snark, and it rolls off my tongue easily. Because it's true. Trent doesn't answer right away, so I wait him out. I give him space, just like I always do with Lennon.

He needs time to think it over. That's fine. I'm not going anywhere. At least not for the next ninety days, or however long they've got me in this treatment facility. But not after that, either. Lennon Capri Washington belongs with me. She knows it. I know it. Everyone else will figure it out soon enough.

I don't mind waiting.

Present Day

"Everyone thought I knew," Lennon says quietly, staring at the envelope in her hand.

She looks over at me.

"You and Dad and Drea...You all thought I knew you had gone to rehab and I just...What?... Hated you anyway?"

I shrug.

"We all thought you knew, yeah, but I think everyone just figured you had your reasons, and your reasons weren't necessarily ours to know."

I close my eyes against the memory of her crying out my name.

"I think everyone still felt guilty for that day, too."

"Did Sam know?" she asks, and I can hear the fear in her voice, and I answer quickly.

"I don't think so. I doubt it. Trent dealt with the senator when he got home from deployment. I'm not sure what went down, but Chase disappeared for a while. I never saw the other two guys again."

I shake my head and hold eye contact.

"You know how that family is, Lennon. There's no way they would have told Sam, and there's no way she would have kept it from you."

She blows out a harsh breath, relieved.

I still don't understand the friendship Sam and Lennon have. It happened sometime after my overdose, but I was so far in my own head that I didn't ask about it.

Maybe they bonded over the trauma.

Maybe they both felt like they had no one else, so they gravitated toward each other.

Whatever caused it, I'm so fucking grateful for it.

I think Sam and Lennon needed each other. It hurts to say, but neither of them had any real friends before that. Claire was fucking terrible to Lennon, and I wasn't much better to Sam.

I tried. God, I tried, but I failed her. I was too selfish to be a good friend to anyone. I guess Claire and I had that in common. It nauseates me to think about.

"God, Lennon," I breathe out, hanging my head in my hands. "You deserved so much better than we gave you."

"No," she says quickly. "No, you did what you thought you had to. You didn't know Claire would take the letter, or that I would end up pregnant."

She whispers the last part, and pain jolts inside my chest. My throat is so tight, my stomach so uneasy. I want to throw up.

She was pregnant.

With our baby.

"I'm so fucking sorry, Lennon. You have no idea how fucking sorry I am."

Her eyes flutter shut, and she inhales deeply, then exhales. She speaks without opening her eyes.

"Maybe I should have just told Drea... But I didn't want to tell her before you. And nothing would have changed the outcome, anyway. You still would have been in rehab. I still would have lost the pregnancy."

"But you would have known that I didn't abandon you. You would have come home."

If Claire hadn't taken that note, so many emotions and resentments could have been avoided. And why'd she do it? Some petty, immature stunt?

One small fucking decision that had a giant fucking impact on my life. On Lennon's life.

"She responded to my email," Lennon says, her head tipped to the ceiling.

She sounds defeated. Completely emotionally depleted.

"After you weren't responding, I emailed Claire. I asked her where you were. I told her I needed to talk to you. God, Macon, I begged her for answers. I was so desperate."

My stomach sinks. My heart crumbling further in my chest. I tried to make excuses for my sister. I tried so hard to understand her. And now this?

"What did she say?" I ask.

I know it'll change everything.

Lennon takes a deep breath before speaking.

"She told me to stop emailing you. That I was being pathetic. That you didn't want to talk to me, and you were doing better without me."

She shakes her head. She looks exhausted, her words full of grief.

"I've spent so much time being angry with you," Lennon breathes out. "I don't regret Paris. I like what I've done with my life. I like who I've become. But everything I've done, everything I've accomplished, has been tainted by this bone-deep need to recover from being betrayed by you, and come to find out, it was all a lie."

She hits me with the saddest eyes I've seen from her in a long time. Heartbroken and pleading. Lost.

Are we too far gone to fix?

I should have pulled that guy off her in that alley. I should have showed myself to her, instead of running away and drowning myself in cheap liquor and street pills.

I never should have let her go a second time.

This whole time, I thought she knew.

My chest cracks when the first tear trickles down her face, and the sounds in my head start to echo. It's too late. We missed our chance. Too much has happened. Too much has changed.

When she speaks again, her voice is a hushed confession,

trembling with need and fear. The last words on the lips of your lover. A death bed declaration.

"I'm so tired, Macon. I'm tired of hiding. I'm tired of fighting this. I'm tired of pretending it hasn't always been you."

We move at the same time, my hands sliding to the back of her neck and hers gripping onto my biceps. I kiss her hard, insistent. The first honest kiss between us in four years.

An *I'm sorry* kiss. An *I missed you* kiss.

A *you've always been mine* kiss.

Then I lift her in my arms and carry her to my bedroom, where I plan to make up for lost time.

THIRTY-ONE

Lennon

His tongue snakes into my mouth, toying with mine. He nibbles on my lips, then pulls his mouth from mine to kiss my jaw and neck.

"I could taste you forever," he rumbles over my skin before setting me gently on my feet. When he takes a step backward, I reach for the hem of my shirt and pull it over my head, then unhook my bra, dropping both pieces of clothing onto the floor.

His eyes scan me from head to toe, setting ablaze to every inch of my skin. We're smoldering. Just having him look at me is turning me molten.

His eyes, his touch.

He's the only person who can set me on fire and coax me to dance while I burn.

He reaches out and cups my breast with his big, tattooed hand, and brushes his thumb over my nipple, making me hiss. Then he lifts his other hand and does the same.

"Beautiful."

He slides his palms down my sides, hooks his fingers into the waistband of my pants, and drags them down my legs.

Then he drops to his knees and kisses my stomach with a reverence and softness that make my throat tight.

What was. What could have been.

He'll never forgive himself for not being there. I've had years to mourn that pregnancy. He's only just begun.

I cup my hands on the side of his face, tilting it up to look at me.

"It's not your fault," I whisper.

Macon's eyes flutter shut, but he doesn't speak, so I bend down and kneel in front of him.

"It's no one's fault," I tell him.

It's something I struggled with for a long time, but I'm certain of it now.

"It would have happened no matter what."

He searches my eyes, seeking the truth. Seeking sincerity. When he finds it, he kisses me. It's gentle. A promise, one that I know deep down he'll never break. I know now that he never has.

I wrap my arms around him, pulling him closer, kissing him deeper. Four years without him and now I can't get enough. I don't understand it. I'm vibrating with need for him, a soul-deep longing, yet he's right here in my arms.

"What is this?" I whisper. "What is this feeling? I feel like I'm drowning. Like I'm suffocating and you're my oxygen."

He presses his forehead to mine, lips ghosting over my lips as he speaks.

"I think it's love." I feel him smirk. "You get used to it."

Love.

I think it's love.

"I love you, Macon Davis." I press a single kiss to his lips. "I've loved you since I was seventeen. I never stopped."

He laughs lightly.

"I know."

I smile and roll my eyes. This man. He kisses me again, and

it's the kind of kiss that heats my already boiling blood and makes my nipples hard. I drag my hands up his arms and down his chest. I trace my fingers over the waistband of his shorts, and he moves his mouth from my lips to my ear.

"Hey, Len," he whispers.

His breath tickles, and I tilt my head to the side to expose my neck to him.

"Hmm?"

He kisses my neck, then bites just hard enough to make me gasp.

"I love you, too," he rumbles against my tender skin.

I smile, my eyes stinging and my heart racing.

"I know."

Macon stands up and takes my hand, pulling me to my feet, then walks me backward until my thighs hit his mattress. He smirks, then gives me a light shove, so I'm falling back onto his bed.

He's so fucking beautiful, standing above me.

His sculpted chest, rising and falling rapidly with his quickened breaths, is decorated in the most intricate tattoos. The Virgo constellation and the clock with the paintbrush hands just over his heart.

I scan my eyes over his strong shoulder, down his defined bicep and forearm to the watercolor rose on the back of his hand. Every inch of skin is inked with beautiful art—images of his own creation—and someday soon, I'm going to memorize every single one of them.

But not today.

I drag my eyes from his arm to his abs, following the deep lines of his pelvis to the low-slung waistband of his shorts. His erection is perfectly outlined down his left thigh, and it makes my mouth water and my thighs sticky with arousal.

"Take your shorts off," I rasp.

He does it slowly, an infuriating smirk on his full lips,

revealing himself to me, inch by inch, before his erection springs free of his shorts and they drop to his feet.

His thighs are solid muscle. Even the left one, which now sports an angry red surgical scar, looks sculpted from stone.

It's almost too much.

"You finished?" Macon rumbles, his hand snaking into my vision and gripping his erection.

I bite my lip as he squeezes himself, then pumps once slowly.

"If you're done eye-fucking me, I'd really like to fuck you for real."

My mouth drops open with a surprised laugh as my attention shoots to face. He's smiling, his blue eyes dancing with mirth, and I find that just as much of a turn-on as his naked body.

The spirit of the boy I fell for in the body of the man I love.

"I'm finished."

I scoot farther back on the bed and drop my legs open, exposing myself to him fully. He groans, his eyes glued to the apex of my thighs as he strokes himself.

"Look at you, *Astraea*," he rasps, taking two steps forward then climbing on the bed. "Just fucking look at you."

He lowers himself between my legs and presses kisses down my inner thigh. He bites the soft area just above my clit, teasing me, before moving to my other thigh and covering it with kisses.

I feel myself growing wetter, can feel it dripping down my inner thighs, and just as I'm about to reach down and rub my clit, Macon moves to my pussy and licks it with the flat of his tongue before circling around my clit and sucking.

"Yes," I whimper, raising my hips off the bed. "Yes."

He hums against me, swirling around my clit before dropping back to my opening and shoving his tongue inside me. He rubs at my clit with his thumb as his tongue thrusts in and out of my pussy.

Fuck, it feels so good, and I pulse my hips up and down off the bed. I grab my breasts and squeeze, before pinching my own nipples, toying with the metal piercings.

"More, Macon," I say, and he slips two fingers into me, making me cry out. "Macon. Macon, yes."

He plays with my body like he owns it, and I suppose he does, curling his fingers inside me and sucking on my clit until I see stars. When I come, I clamp my thighs around his head, but he forces them back open and holds his forearm down on my pelvis.

"I'm not done yet," he says, growling against me.

His tongue flicks faster, his fingers thrust harder.

"Oh god, oh god," I cry out. "Macon. I can't...I'm going to..."

My legs are quaking with the need to close around him. My hips are bucking against his strong arm. Tears are leaking from my eyes from the overwhelming sensations, the heightened sensitivity of my clit and his unrelenting, wicked mouth.

He grazes his teeth over me, and I moan and shake.

"Come for me again, *Astraea*." He bites down and I jerk upward with a gasp. "Come on my face, so I can taste you for weeks."

He flicks his tongue fast, and I come a second time with a strangled cry.

"Good girl," he says, his words vibrating over my swollen pussy, and I'm aching for him all over again.

Good girl. Good girl. Good girl.

That praise on Macon's tongue, falling from his lips.

I thought I was done being the good girl, but lying naked underneath Macon, reeling and tingling from my orgasm, I'm dying to be her again.

He presses one last kiss to my clit before trailing his lips up my torso, biting once on my nipple, before taking my mouth.

He's wet with me, his lips and tongue tasting of my orgasm. I claw at his back, scraping my nails down to his waist, then gripping the firm globes of his ass. Fuck, every part of him is sexy.

I thrust my hips, rubbing my swollen, wet core over his hardness, and he groans.

"Fucking hell, Lennon."

He props himself up on one arm and reaches between us, pressing his dick against my pussy, then thrusts, running his erection through my pussy lips and over my clit.

I can feel the rigidness of his cock as he moves himself back and forth over me. It's erotic, and I need more. I whimper and twist my nipples again before thrusting with him.

"There we go, baby," Macon says as I move on him. He halts his movements, so I'm dragging my pussy over his erection. "Yeah, move just like that."

He's watching our bodies move with eyes almost black. He licks his full lips then bites his teeth into the lower one, his nostrils flaring with his fast breaths.

"Say it again," I ask, and he flicks his eyes to mine.

He searches my eyes for an answer, then his lips curl up into a sinful smirk.

"Be a *good girl* for me, Lennon Capri," he says slowly, and my pussy pulses with need.

I whimper, thrusting harder, rubbing the head of his cock over my clit.

"Fuck my cock until you come again."

As he finishes his sentence, my body tenses with another orgasm, and he thrusts his cock into me before it's over. He pounds fast, riding out the quaking of my release with a guttural groan.

"Fuck, you squeeze me so tight, baby," he says.

He pushes in again, grinding his pelvis against me, then pulls all the way out, slapping the head of his dick on my swollen clit. I gasp, and he does it all over again.

"Macon, that feels so good. You feel so good."

He does it twice more before pulling out and falling next to me on his back, then maneuvering me so I'm straddling his waist. We grab his cock together as I lift onto my knees, positioning him at my entrance before I slide down over him with a deep moan.

I lean back and put my hands behind me on Macon's thighs, then I pulse on him, lifting myself up then falling back down. Slowly at first, then faster.

"Fuck, you fuck me so good," he says, his voice strangled and breathless. He watches like he's in awe of me, and I relish the power I have over him.

He grabs onto my hips as I ride him, and I watch him watch me. His eyes caress every inch of my exposed flesh, but they keep falling back to our connection, where he's sliding in and out of me, as I move up and down on top of him.

I bring my hands up and lace them behind my head, and he groans, palming one of my breasts as I swivel my hips on his pelvis. He tweaks one of my nipples, and I gasp, riding him harder.

"There's my good girl," he says.

He brings his thumb to my clit and presses hard before rubbing me in circles. My pussy clenches and he groans.

"Fuck, my good girl is such a slut for me."

"Yes," I say, quivering around him, "for you."

"Only for me," he says with a growl, and suddenly, I'm being flipped onto my back, my legs are shoved together, and they're thrown up over one of Macon's shoulders.

When he slams back into me, it's so deep that I gasp.

"You're a fucking slut for me, Lennon Capri. You're *my* good girl. You're *my* slut."

"Yours."

My words are a breathless whisper. Macon's pumping into me so fast that I'm rocketing to my orgasm. I dig my fingers into his biceps, holding on tight as he brings me to the edge, closer and closer until...

"Come," he growls, and I explode around him with a guttural moan.

Tears stream down my face from the force of my orgasm as I ride it out. He doesn't stop fucking me. Doesn't stop hitting me so deep.

"Atta girl, atta girl," he says breathlessly, chasing his own release.

"Inside me," I beg.

His eyes snap open, his thrusts faltering for a second but not stopping.

"Come inside me," I repeat. "I want to feel it."

"Yeah?"

He's barely hanging on. I can tell, and I pulse around him, just to make him groan. I want him to lose it. I want him to feel just as euphoric as I do.

"Fill me with your cum."

"Oh, fuck." He moans. He speeds up, bucking into me, and then his body jerks with another moan. "Oh, fuck, Lennon."

His thrusts slow, and I can feel his release dripping out of me, mixing with my arousal and sliding down my skin, pooling on the bed underneath me.

Macon leans back, taking my legs by the knees and pushing them closer to my chest. His eyes stay on my pussy, and he pulls out slowly, watching with wide eyes and parted lips.

"Fucking hell," he says as his head slides out of me.

I clench my inner walls and can feel more of him drip from me, and he groans again.

Whatever he sees, it's almost too much for him. He's so aroused that it's turning me on again.

He grabs his dick and rubs it over my pussy once more, slick with our cum, then drags it up and circles my clit before pushing back inside me one last time.

He moves my legs, so they're back around his waist, then lowers himself over me.

"Lennon," he whispers, kissing my lips as he thrusts slowly.

I feel him start to soften, but he tangles his tongue with mine and keeps thrusting slowly. I dig my fingers into the sides of his hair, careful not to knock out the butterfly clip, and I moan into his mouth.

I pulse my hips in time with his, and soon, his cock starts to grow thicker, hardening once more.

He starts to thrust faster, and I meet his speed.

"Again?" I ask, hopeful yet surprised.

He pulls back just enough so I can see him smirk.

"Forever."

THIRTY-TWO

Lennon

I hold Macon's hand tightly as we walk through the hospital hall toward the elevator bank.

I made sure to shower, then blow-dry my hair fully before we came here. I'm not even sure why I needed to do it, but I did. Macon found it amusing.

Even now, as I strangle his hand with mine and fidget with the hem of my shirt with the other, he watches me playfully from the corner of his eye. No nerves. No anxiety. Not an ounce of uneasiness in his whole body.

"Why aren't you even a little nervous?" I ask, my voice a whisper. "They're all going to know we're banging now."

He snorts a laugh and presses the button for the elevator.

"We're *banging*? Is that what this is?"

I roll my eyes as he lifts my hand and presses a kiss to my knuckles.

"Look... I'm pretty sure they've all known, for the last four years, that I would gladly *bang you* in a heartbeat. Fuck, I'd probably have *banged you* on the kitchen table in front of everyone if you'd let me. I was that hard up for you."

I gasp, then swat his chest with my free hand, and shoot my eyes around the hospital.

"People are going to hear you!"

"Don't care."

He shrugs and yanks me into his chest, pressing a kiss to my lips before walking me backward into the elevator. The doors close and he pushes me against the wall, lifting my hands and pinning them at the wrists above my head.

He leans back and surveys me.

"I think I need to draw you like this. Pinned up for me, unable to run."

"I'm not running," I tell him, and he leans back into me, kissing my jaw.

"No?"

"No."

Macon's mouth covers mine, and my lips part immediately, welcoming his tongue. He releases my wrists and moves his hands to my hips, just as mine thread through his hair. I hum, pressing my body as close as possible to his, kissing him deeply.

A throat clears, and we spring apart, whipping our eyes to the open elevator doors. I didn't realize we'd stopped. I didn't even hear the door open. An older man stands at the door with his brow raised. He doesn't look offended, just annoyed.

"Sorry," I say to the man, and I grab Macon's hand and pull him behind me off the elevator.

"I'm not sorry," Macon says as he pushes past the man, and I have to stifle a giggle.

"You're terrible."

"You love me anyway."

I don't answer, but it's true.

As we approach Dad's hospital room, I can hear talking filtering out the door and into the hall. My footsteps slow to a stop. Claire is in there.

"We can leave," Macon whispers, glancing from the door to me. "I don't really want to see her, either."

I actually *do* want to see Claire, but I don't want to upset my father. I've got a few choice words to say to her and my dad is supposed to be in a low-stress environment right now. I think it over, then make up my mind. I can keep a lid on it while we're here.

"No. Let's go in."

Macon doesn't argue, and he follows me through the room.

The moment we step through the door, I can feel everyone's eyes on us. Claire, Drea, Dad. Even Eric is here, and Evie is sleeping in Drea's arms. I squeeze Macon's hand and I don't let go.

"Hey, guys," I say brightly.

My dad's attention drags from our hands to my face. He's stoic at first, and then his lips curve into a sad smile.

"You've talked?"

"We have," Macon answers. "I think we covered everything."

My dad nods, then glances to where Claire is sitting. I keep my attention on Dad.

"Claire told us what she did," Dad says, and my jaw drops. "Everything."

I whip my eyes to Claire and find her staring at her feet with her hands fisted in front of her. She looks like she's been crying, but I can't bring myself to care.

"You never should have had to go through what you did, Lennon," my dad says. "I should have forced the issue when I heard you hadn't come home. I knew something wasn't right, but I—"

"No." I cut my dad off. "You believed I had the whole story and trusted me to make my own decisions. You gave me the space I thought I needed. It's not your fault Claire did what she did."

I bite my tongue, halting more words from spilling out. I take a deep breath, then turn to Claire.

"I'd really appreciate it if you left right now," I say calmly. "I'd like to talk to my dad and Drea alone."

"Okay," Claire says timidly. She stands and grabs her bag, looks over her shoulder, and walks toward the door with Eric trailing her. Just before she steps out into the hall, she turns around to face me.

"Lennon, I'm—"

"I don't want to hear it right now, Claire," I say, cutting her off. I don't even turn to look at her. "Go to the house. I'll be there in a bit."

I hear her whisper *okay*, then she and Eric disappear into the hallway.

The room is quiet, and I wait, dreading the moment someone brings up Claire. But instead, Andrea brings up a different topic.

"So, are you a couple, then?"

When I look at her, she's smiling softly. When I glance at my dad, he's doing the same. I look up at Macon to find he's already looking at me, and I smile too.

"Yeah. We are."

"What's the plan, then?" my dad asks. "For the distance. Are you coming home, or is Macon moving to Paris?"

My throat goes tight.

We haven't talked about this. I don't even know what to say. I know what I want, but I haven't broached the topic with Macon yet.

"We haven't talk about it," Macon says, speaking my thoughts out loud. "But I imagine Lennon has to go back to Paris for some stuff. Pack her things, take care of business, say goodbye to her friends. And then she's going to move in with me."

I can't stop my smile. It stretches so wide my cheeks hurt.

"Really?"

He rolls his eyes and shakes his head, then hits me with that stupidly sexy smirk.

"Yeah, Len, really. We've got four years to make up for. Can't do that living separately."

The giddy giggle that slips from my lips makes his smile grow, and then I hear Andrea laugh. I look to find her and Dad watching us with smiles matching Macon's, and for the first time in a long time, almost everything feels right.

MACON AND I DRIVE BACK TO DAD AND DREA'S HOUSE IN Macon's car.

He hasn't stopped touching me. One hand on the wheel, one on my thigh. Or threaded through my fingers. Or cupping the back of my neck. I never want his hands to leave my body.

"What are you going to tell the Frenchman?" Macon asks randomly, and I gasp.

"Shit. I forgot about Franco." I look at the clock. "You think he's still here?"

"That man isn't leaving you willingly," Macon says, his words laced with jealousy, and I shake my head.

I'm not going to argue with him. He'll see soon enough.

The moment we pull up to the house, my skin prickles with adrenaline. It takes all my strength not to jump out of the car, run into the house, and land a jab right on Claire's nose. Instead, I take a deep breath and walk calmly to the house holding Macon's hand.

Franco is the first person I see when we walk through the front door. He stands from the kitchen stool where he was sitting, and his eyes search mine. He's no doubt able to tell I've been crying, and his face falls.

"Told ya." Macon lets go of my hand and presses a kiss to

my head. "Go easy on him." He pushes past Franco. "Sorry, Frankie, but you never stood a chance."

I stare, jaw dropped at Macon's back as he retreats into the living room.

"What's he talking about?"

I roll my eyes.

"He thinks you're in love with me."

Franco raises an eyebrow. "*Would* I have stood a chance?"

I scoff playfully, then glance at him incredulously.

"Not in any way other than friendship," I say, though he already knows. "My heart has always belonged to Macon."

Franco's brow furrows, then his lips turn up on one side.

"That's what I thought." He reaches out and takes my hand. "We will always be fri—"

"Nope!" Macon shouts from the living room, cutting off Franco's sentence. I scowl in his direction, then look back at Franco.

"I'm going to be moving back here, but I would love to keep in touch. I'm going back to pack up my apartment and sell the things I don't want to bring back. I've got a few people to talk to and a gallery show to figure out, but then I'm coming here."

Franco nods.

"Your friendship means a lot to me," I tell him honestly. "You helped me in more ways than you know, and I'm grateful for that. But I need to focus on Macon and me right now. We've got a lot of shit to figure out."

"I understand," he says. "It was impulsive of me to come here without telling you first, but I was worried. I wanted to make sure you were alright. I thought you would need a friend." He chuckles and raises an eyebrow. "And I was bored."

I laugh.

"I thought the French didn't get bored? I thought doing nothing was kind of your schtick?"

"Perhaps the American was rubbing off on me." He shudders. "It's good you're leaving now."

I roll my eyes, but the banter feels good. It feels like we're going to be okay. I knew there wasn't anything deep between us. We kept each other company. We masked each other's pain for a while, but I have to own up to my shit now.

No more running. No more hiding from the truth.

I don't know what he's running from, we've never talked about anything that personal, but I hope he deals with it soon. He won't have me to distract him anymore.

Franco and I chat for a few more minutes. He tells me he's going to go back to his hotel. He gives me a long hug and tells me to text him when I get back into Paris, then he leaves me standing in the kitchen.

"How old is that twat, anyway?" Macon asks from the doorway.

"He's not a twat, you twat." I roll my eyes at Macon's smirking face. "He's thirty-five."

"Jesus Christ," Macon chokes out. "I was gonna guess like twenty-five at the oldest. He doesn't look thirty-five at all."

I nod. I get it. It doesn't make sense. Franco's been smoking and drinking since his teens. How is his skin so youthful?

"Weird, right? It's probably the pastries. I swear, they're magic." I sigh and glance toward the stairs. "Well, I should probably get this over with. You cool to stay here?"

"If here is where you want me, here is where I'll stay."

"Hm. Good boy," I say with a smirk, and he winks.

I walk up the stairs slowly and head toward the guest room. I take two deep breaths, then knock on the door.

"Come in," Claire calls quietly from the other side.

I turn the knob and push open the door to find her sitting with her legs crossed in the middle of the bed. She's hunched over and her face is red from crying. I feel nothing.

"Where is Eric?"

Claire whimpers, and I notice her rubbing her empty ring finger.

"He left. He, um, he said he needs to think about things." She clamps her eyes shut and her face twists up in pain. "He said he can't be sure if I really love him or if I just hate you."

My eyes widen.

Wow.

Go Eric. I'm surprised, and strangely proud, of him for standing up for himself. That was one thing Eric and I always had in common. We were too nice for our own good. Too content to be doormats.

"Well..." I say, trailing off.

"I'm sorry," Claire blurts out, her eyes pleading. "I'm so sorry, Lennon. I had no idea...There's no way I could have known...I'm so sorry."

I tilt my head and survey her.

I search my heart for any sort of sympathy, but I find none.

All I can think of are the times she wasn't a friend to me growing up, despite claiming to be my best friend. All the ways she took from me, draining me dry, never giving anything unless it benefitted her. All the horrible things she said about Macon. Even the shitty way she treated me just a few weeks ago when I saw her for the first time in four years runs through my head.

For my dad's sake, for Drea's, I try to find forgiveness, but I can't.

"Okay," I say, and Claire sits up straighter.

"Really?"

"I can accept that you couldn't have known the damage you would cause by taking that letter. I can even accept that causing this much pain wasn't your intention—"

"It wasn't. I swear."

"But you still did that to hurt me, Claire. It doesn't change the fact that you wanted to cause me pain. And then on top of everything, even after taking that letter, you could have told me the truth when you replied to my email. You didn't even have to tell me about the letter, but you could have at least been honest about Macon being in rehab. I emailed you *begging* to talk to him. It was obvious I had no clue what was going on, and what did you do?"

She winces, and her eyes close, tears seeping through her eyelashes and soaking her face.

"You told me he was better off without me. That he didn't want to talk to me. You *lied*, Claire. You lied because you wanted to hurt me. You wanted to cause me pain, and I will never be able to forget that."

"I know," Claire whimpers.

"Maybe someday I'll be able to forgive you, but that day isn't today. I'll tolerate you for our parents, for Evie, but we will never be friends again. You're my stepmother's daughter, and I'm not going to pretend that I like you. And when Macon and I get married—because we will—you'll be invited only so you can sit in the audience and watch a love that you tried so hard to kill thrive, and I hope you feel insignificant. I hope you feel like a failure. You tried to hurt me, Claire, but in the end, all you did was hurt yourself."

Claire cries harder and she nods with her eyes closed, but she doesn't say anything else. No more apologies or excuses. For once, Claire has nothing to say, and it feels good.

I turn around and leave, pulling the door shut behind me, and head back down the stairs to find Macon.

"How'd it go?"

He's leaning on the counter, drinking a glass of orange juice, but when I step in front of him, he puts the glass down and pulls me into a hug. I wrap my arms around him and hold him to me. I breathe him in, spearmint and spice, and press a kiss to his chest.

"As good as can be expected. But I feel better."

"Good." He pulls back and hits me with a mischievous waggle of his brows. "Now should we go break it to Harper that she's been demoted to number two on your list of favorite people?"

I laugh and shake my head. I take a step back, so his arms fall to his sides, and match his smirk with one of my own.

"It's gonna take a lot more than good dick to demote Sam, Macon," I say plainly, and his smile grows.

"Just good?"

I laugh louder and roll my eyes.

"Maybe more than good."

"More than good?" He grabs my hips and pulls me back against his chest, pressing a kiss to my lips before whispering against them. "Let's go home and I'll show you *more than good*. Maybe even great."

"Oh, great, huh?"

"Maybe even fucking phenomenal."

"Hmmm." I take a step back, then turn and head to the door. "Let's not waste any more time, then," I call over my shoulder. "You show me yours, and I'll show you mine."

THIRTY-THREE

Macon

3 Weeks Later

"Wake up, Ms. Jet Lag," I whisper into Lennon's ear. "We've got to be at Mom and Trent's in an hour."

"Fifteen more minutes," she mumbles, and I laugh into her neck.

"You said that fifteen minutes ago."

She whines and rolls over, so she's on her back underneath me, which is one of my favorite places to have her.

"I'm so tired." She covers her mouth with her hand and yawns. "Why did I agree to this?"

"I told you to say no." I lean down and kiss her forehead. "We could have done this next weekend."

I knew she'd be too jetlagged for her belated birthday dinner. She only just got back from her seven-day goodbye tour of Paris, which consisted mostly of cleaning out her apartment, saying *au revoir* to friends, and sending a ton of boxes of clothes back to my place. Lennon could easily sleep for three straight days.

"Ugh, I know." She gives my chest a light shove so I'll roll off her, then she sits up. "I just..."

She shrugs.

She doesn't have to explain any further. It's her first birthday celebration at home, with all of us, since she turned seventeen. She spent her eighteenth birthday in England with Sam and her Aunt Becca in a hospital, and she's spent every birthday since trying to run from that memory.

I can only hope this one will be different. Maybe this birthday can be the first good one. The healing birthday.

Slowly, she pushes herself up from the bed and moves to the closet. I lie back on the pillows and watch as she pulls off my t-shirt, showing me her naked back, and my dick hardens.

She doesn't even have to turn around to turn me on. Just knowing she's naked does it for me. Fuck, just knowing she exists is enough.

She pulls a dress off a hanger and slips it over her head, hiding her body from me. My dick stays hard, though.

She turns around to face me and flashes me a smile.

"How do I look?"

"Gorgeous."

"Thank you," she says softly, and I push off the bed and close the distance between us.

"You're welcome." I kiss her, then tug on her hand. "Now, let's go."

Lennon drives my car to the house. She's missed driving since living in Paris, so I told her she could have free rein of my car until she gets one of her own. You'd think I'd told her she was being featured in the MoMA for how excited she got.

As she drives, we listen to Fleetwood Mac, and I draw stupid, little hearts on her thigh with my index finger. I know the moment she realizes what I'm drawing, because her lips turn up softly at the corners, and when she flicks her eyes to mine briefly, they're full of everything I've been hoping for years.

"I love you," she says, and I smirk.

"I know."

She rolls her eyes and turns the radio up, and I lay my head against the seat and look at her for the rest of the drive.

"Hey, it's the birthday girl," Trent calls from his spot on the couch, when we walk into the living room.

"Hey, Daddy," Lennon says, bending down to give him a hug.

He's already looking ten times better than he did last week. One hundred times better than the week before that. Nic's in charge of his PT, and I know she's taking good care of him.

"Macon." Trent sticks out his hand so I can shake it.

"Sir."

Lennon snorts out a laugh at our formalities, and I wave her off, just as my mom comes in with Evie on her hip.

"Noh nah, noh nah, noh nah," Evie starts to chant, reaching out her grabby hands for Lennon and bouncing in my mom's arms.

"Oh, my goodness," Mom says with a laugh. "Here's your Nona."

"Say *Macon*," I tell Evie as Mom hands her to Lennon. "May-con. Maaaaay-conn. You can do it."

Evie laughs, but she doesn't even try to say my name. Instead, she just slobbers up Lennon's cheek with one of her baby kisses, and I scowl.

"I'm with her nearly every day for months, and nothing. Then you come in and she says your name after just a few weeks."

"Aw, are you jealous?" Lennon pats my cheek, and I narrow my eyes at her.

"Nona doesn't even sound like Lennon."

"Stop pouting." She reaches up and tugs on my lower lip. "You're cuter when you're cocky."

At that, I grin, and she laughs. She opens her mouth to say something, but another voice calls through the house from the front door. We all turn to find Sam and Casper, arms filled with balloons and gift bags.

"I said I didn't want gifts," Lennon says, and Sam rolls her eyes.

"Open 'em, and if you don't want 'em, I'll keep them for myself."

"You're not keepin' mine," Casper says, and Sam gives him a side-eyed glance that says *watch me*.

I'm not sure what's been going on with those two lately, but they've been showing up everywhere together. Casper has been tight-lipped, but we've never had the kind of relationship where we talk about girls or hookups or whatever it is they might be doing. If Sam's said anything to Lennon, Lennon's kept her secret.

I bounce my attention between the two of them.

They'd certainly be an odd pair. Poor boy from the wrong side of the tracks. Rich daughter of a senator. Hell, they even look wrong for each other, what with Casper's tattered jeans and plain black tee next to Sam's pressed designer everything. The only designer Casper's ever owned is the WeatherTech floor mats he bought for his truck.

"You can put those over here," Mom tells Casper, and I watch as he takes the gifts he's carrying and the package from Sam's arms and sets them all on the table.

Sam gives Lennon a hug and boops Evie on the nose.

"Say *Sam*," Sam says, annunciating her name. "Ssss. Aaaa. Mmm."

"Ssssssss," Evie says, hissing like a snake and then giggling, making everyone else laugh, too.

"I'll take it," Sam chirps, sending me a smug grin.

I flip her off and hear Trent huff out a laugh. I don't look at him to confirm he caught me, though. I just grab Lennon's hand and lead her to the couch, then I sit down on it and pull her and Evie onto my lap.

"Oh, this is too cute," Mom says when she sees us, whipping out her phone and snapping a picture. "I'm going to frame this one."

I give Lennon's hip a squeeze, and she winks at me, and I watch as she talks with everyone. Her friends, her family. She dyed her hair back to her natural color a few weeks ago when she couldn't ignore her roots any longer, and ever since then, I've had to pinch myself a few times.

She's my Lennon, again. My *Astraea*.

We've both changed in some big ways during the past four years, but at our core, we're still us. She's still my Lennon. I'm still her Macon. We're at our truest when we're together.

My mom says something about dinner being ready, and she lifts Evie out of Lennon's arms and heads into the kitchen. I keep my hand on Lennon's thigh, holding her on my lap while everyone else filters out of the room.

When we're alone, she looks at me.

"What's up?"

I reach up and tuck a strand of hair behind her ear, then trace my thumb over her jaw. This feels like healing. It feels like we're going to be okay. Better than okay.

"I love you."

She smiles and presses a soft kiss to my lips.

"I know."

It's almost midnight by the time we get back to our apartment.

Dinner was great. The cake was better. Evie still won't say Macon or walk. We talked and laughed and had a great night.

I can't remember the last time I was this happy, but I'm certain it was a time that involved Lennon.

Lennon is in all of my happy memories.

We drop the gift bags by the door, shove the leftovers Mom sent home with us in the fridge, and strip naked before crawling into bed.

Lennon curls into my side, her head on my chest and my arm wrapped around her body.

I used to joke that my left side was unlucky. Broken wrist, broken femur, broken heart. But it turns out, Lennon likes the left side of the bed, and her head fits perfectly on the left side of my chest.

My left side wasn't unlucky. It was just waiting for Lennon. She heals my hurts. She strengthens me. I'm so stupidly in love with her.

"Did you have a nice birthday dinner?"

I brush my fingers back and forth over the soft flesh at the curve of her hip, and she purrs. I love that fucking sound.

"It was wonderful." Her breath dances across my chest as she speaks. "I was a little worried, to be honest, but it's been great being home."

I smile. I haven't heard her call it that yet. Just before she left to pack up her apartment, she was still referring to Paris as home. But just now, it came freely.

"Home?"

"Yeah, home. Here with you. With Dad and Drea and Evie. Home."

She has no idea how strongly I feel those words. The absolute joy they give me. I bring my free hand to her chin and tilt her head upward, then I kiss her lips gently.

"*You're my home, Astraea.*"

She smiles and kisses me again before laying her head back on my chest.

"You want to know a secret?" she whispers, and I nod.

"Yes," I whisper back. "I want to know all your secrets."

She pauses for a moment, just the sounds of our breathing in the dark bedroom, and she gently draws hearts on my chest with her index finger. I'm sure she can hear my heart racing.

"I was scared that we'd missed our chance."

Her voice cracks, and I wait while she takes a few deep breaths.

"I was worried we'd changed too much. That we wouldn't work anymore. That there wasn't a place for us in this life. I never gave up, Macon. Not really. I was just scared I'd have to wait until the next life to find you again."

Gently, I slide my arm and roll up on my side, so Lennon and I are face to face. I kiss her lips once, then trace my knuckles over her jaw. I look in her eyes and hold them.

"This life. The next life. Every life after that. I will love you in all of them, Lennon Capri. It doesn't matter who you become or how you change. My soul will always belong to yours."

I wipe a tear off her cheek with my thumb. She turns and kisses my palm, then kisses my wrist, then my lips.

"I love you, Macon Andrew Davis, in this life and all the rest of them. I love you."

Macon

EPILOGUE

1 Year Later

FUCK.

I'm going to be late. I check myself in the mirror one last time, sliding my hand down the lapels of my suit jacket. The knot in my tie is smooth, my slacks are creased, my shoes are scuff-free.

I'm going to be late, but at least I look good.

The last time I wore something even remotely resembling a suit like this was at senior prom. This one cost a little more than that one, though.

I grab my keycard off the desk next to the elaborate arrangement of flowers Franco sent. He wanted to make it tonight, but I'm glad he couldn't. I'm coming around to him, but I still harbor some jealousy. He'll always be the French twat to me.

I shove the keycard into my wallet, then stick the wallet in the little hidden pocket thing on the inside of my jacket on the way out the door. I shoot off a text to Trent as I push the elevator button, telling him to tell Lennon I'll be there in ten minutes, then I pace.

I pace as I wait for the elevator car, and I pace the whole time I'm in the elevator car.

The moment the doors open on the ground floor, I'm sprinting through the lobby, out to the street, and down the block. At least this gallery isn't far from the hotel.

I stop running once I hit the street, then check myself in the window of a corner building. Knot, lapels, creases, shoes. All still in good shape. Then I take a deep breath and walk briskly to the *Galerie D'atelier*, an artist-owned art gallery in Washington, DC. And despite the name, it has no ties to France.

When I get to the building, my heart swells with pride when I see Lennon's name on the signage, signifying her as the gallery's featured artist. Last month, *Galerie D'atelier* offered Lennon membership to their prestigious gallery. The honor is huge. The artists accepted into this gallery have gone on to have museum exhibitions and global acclaim. Of course, she accepted the invitation, so tonight is the opening night of her week-long new member exhibition.

My eyes settle on her the moment I step through the door. I hang back and watch her. She's gorgeous, dressed in a black dress with her hair in soft waves at her back, and her beauty is amplified when she's in her element. I watch her chat up the patrons. People stop and ask her questions. She smiles and answers. I can always tell when she's talking about her work because her face grows serious, but her eyes dance.

I catch sight of Trent, Mom, and Sam chatting in a corner, but instead of going to them to say hi, I trail Lennon as she moves through the crowd. She stops to discuss her paintings and smiles whenever she receives praise, which is constantly.

That's the biggest reason I have to thank Paris. Lennon

knows her talent now. She accepts compliments because she believes she's worthy of the praise. She wasn't like that before.

I've got a list of things that make me grateful for Paris, even if it meant I had to lose Lennon for a while. In Paris, she blossomed. She grew into her independence. She mastered the use of her voice.

Could she have done those things here in Virginia with me? I don't think so.

I was too much of a mess to help her grow. I had to do my own growing. We had to be apart before we could be stronger together.

Lennon breaks off from a group of people and heads to the back of the building, so I follow. She waves and smiles, but she doesn't stop to talk, and then she's rounding a corner and disappearing from view. I slow my steps and stroll toward the hallway, so it doesn't look like I'm stalking the featured artist, but when I round the very corner Lennon turned, I'm snatched by my lapels and pinned to the wall.

"You're late," Lennon whispers in my ear, her whole body plastered to mine. Because I'm a glutton for punishment, I thrust against her just slightly, and I have to stifle a groan.

Fuck, she's sexy in this dress.

"I've been here," I tell her, and she smirks.

"I know."

She moves to take a step back, but I grab her shoulder and spin her, reversing our positions, so I'm the one pinning her to the wall. The look in her eyes sparks fire in my veins. I kiss her jaw, then the soft spot behind her ear, then her neck and collarbone. She's pliant for me, her breaths coming hot and fast.

"You nervous?" I drag my hands to the hem of her dress and inch it up, until it's just under the curve of her ass. "Need me to take the edge off?"

"I'm not nervous," she whispers as she reaches for my zipper, "but you can still take the edge off."

I waste no time sliding her panties to the side and slipping my fingers into her as she squeezes and pumps my dick. I rub her clit and finger-fuck her until she's ready for me, then I hitch her leg on my hip and slide my hard cock deep into her pussy.

"Yes," she breathes out when I'm fully seated.

"Be quiet now."

I pulse deep inside her, covering her mouth with mine every time she whimpers or gasps. I cup her breast and tweak her nipple through the fabric of the dress. When she clenches around me, I have to bite my lip to keep from groaning.

She's so fucking sexy.

"Rub on your clit for me," I tell her, and she snakes her hand between us. "Atta girl. Rub it nice and fast so you come on my cock, okay?"

She nods and whimpers, and I speed up my pulsing, fucking her until she's clenching around me and quivering from her orgasm.

"How's that edge?" I ask as I pull out of her and tug her dress back down over her ass.

She smiles. "Gone. Took it clean off."

"Good."

"Did you want me to..." She drops her eyes to my hard cock and licks her lips, and I groan as I fasten my pants back up, tucking my dick inside.

"Nah." I grab her hand and press it over the bulge in my pants. "But later tonight? I'm fucking you in the shower in the hotel room, then again on the bed, and again on the terrace at midnight."

"Promise?"

She gives my dick a playful squeeze, and I blow out a harsh breath.

"Promise," I tell her. "Now go schmooze those artsy people into buying one of your paintings so you can pay rent."

She rolls her eyes and presses a kiss to my lips. We both know she doesn't need to sell any paintings here. She makes a killing on commissions.

"I love you."

"I know."

She giggles and slips back around the corner, and I take a few minutes to get my shit under control. I do the *Friends* method and think about Casper's various body parts. His hair, his ears, his toes. Within a minute, my erection is gone, and I'm good to mingle.

On the way out of the random dark hallway, I find a man dressed in all-white holding a tray covered in an array of champagne flutes.

"You got any sparkling water?" I ask, and he pulls a flute filled with clear, bubbly liquid and a single raspberry, and hands it to me. I sniff it, and sure enough, it's sparkling water. "Thanks, man."

I weave back through the gallery, sending Lennon a wink when I see her, and find my way back to Trent, Mom, and Sam.

Claire is at home babysitting Evie. She knew she wasn't invited, but I guess she wanted to be helpful anyway. She's trying. It's not enough, but it's something.

"You made it," Mom says, giving me a hug.

"Yeah, I've been here a bit already. Been exploring."

"Isn't she brilliant?"

I nod, because yeah, she is. No words can really capture just how talented she is, though I know some art critics tomorrow will try.

"How do you think this one will look in the living room?" Trent says, gesturing to a large painting displayed on a side wall.

It's a colorful piece, the outline of a woman's figure standing amongst bursts of purples, blues, reds, and pinks. I remember when she painted this one. It's titled *La Petite Mort*, which is what the French call an orgasm. I glance at Sam, and her eyes are wide trying not to laugh.

"It's a great piece," I say slowly, "but I don't think you'd want it in your living room."

"No?" Trent looks at it again. "Too bright?"

"Sure," I hedge, which causes Sam's composer to slip, and she snorts out a loud laugh.

My mom has her hand propped under her chin, and she's watching Trent and me with amusement. She does this all the time when we're together. I still don't understand why.

"C'mon, old man." I put my hand on Trent's shoulder. "I know just the painting for your living room." Then I walk him toward something less... orgasm-y.

We're standing in front of a safer piece, one simply called Homesick, when I catch Trent watching Lennon.

"Look at our girl, Macon," he says softly. "Did you think she'd be doing something like this when you first met her?"

My lips quirk up, and I answer immediately.

"I did."

Trent chuckles and pats me on the back.

"Me too."

The End.

Want to know more about Sam?

She gets her HEA in *The Love You Fight For*, and it's available now!

Macon

EXTENDED EPILOGUE

6 Years Later

"Baby! Let's move!"

"We're comin'!"

The sound of feet pound on the floor above me. Light, quick steps followed by longer, heavier ones. I hear Lennon yell, *gotcha*, and then a fit of high-pitched giggles, and I can't help but smile at the ceiling.

"What're they doin'?" Gabe asks, and I shrug. I never know. I just roll with it.

Moments later, a single pair of feet come skipping down the stairs, and Lennon slides into the kitchen with Charlie slung over her shoulder. Charlie is giggling like crazy, her little feet kicking excitedly, and Lennon's face is flushed.

My girls can be a handful. I fucking love it.

"Ready?" I ask with a laugh, and Lennon nods.

"Ready," she sings, and we head out the door with Gabe in my arms and Charlie in hers.

"Not bad," I say, checking my watch. "We're only going to be fifteen minutes late."

EXTENDED EPILOGUE

"Can we be late if the party is for us?" Lennon says playfully, and Gabe nods.

"Yes, we can," he says seriously.

Lennon gives me an amused side-eye, and I wink.

Gabe's been ready to go since six a.m. Got up and dressed himself and everything. He's been excited to see his Auntie Evie all week. He might be a few years younger than her, but they've been best friends since Gabe could crawl. A soon as Gabe was born, he became Evie's favorite person. Me and Lennon were immediately demoted.

"No worries, bud. They won't start without us."

I strap Gabe into his car seat while Lennon does the same with Charlie on the other side, then we head to Mom and Trent's across town.

Or Neenee and Teetee, as Charlie calls them.

No clue where she came up with those.

Gabe's squirming out of his buckle as soon I park in the driveway, and I have to hustle to haul him out before he has a meltdown. The moment I set him on the ground, he takes off sprinting into the house.

"Whoa," I say as Lennon steps up next to me with Charlie in her arms. "You think he's excited?"

She hums in response, and when I look at her, her eyes are staring at the street. I follow her gaze and find a familiar grey Toyota parked at the curb.

"We can tell her to leave if you want. She doesn't have to be here."

She shakes her head slowly, then drags her eyes to mine.

"No. I told her she could be here. I'm staying true to my word."

I nod and give her a soft smile, then lean down and press a kiss to her lips.

"I love you," I whisper, and she smirks against me.

"I know."

I kiss Charlie's forehead, making her laugh, and we head into the house, running smack into Sam.

"You would be late for your own party," Sam teases, then turns her attention to Charlie. "Charlotte Grace, you little monster, come to your Aunt Sam."

Sam scoops a giggling Charlie into her arms, then does a double take at Lennon's simple white dress. Lennon looks down and sighs.

"*Merde*," she says under her breath. "I don't even know what that is. Toothpaste, maybe? Candy?"

I look at the stain on Lennon's dress.

"Maybe it's playdough?" I suggest, and Sam shakes her head.

"C'mon," she says, wrapping her free hand around Lennon's. "I prepared for this."

Sam whisks my girls away, so I make my way into the kitchen.

"You're late," Casper calls from his place in front of the fridge.

"Oh, cut him some slack," my mom says, rounding the kitchen island to wrap me in a hug. "They've got two kids under five. They're allowed to be a little late."

Casper rolls his eyes and hits me with a sly grin. He knows it wasn't exactly the kids' fault we were late. I wink at him, and he barks out a laugh.

"Where's Gabe?" I ask, and my mom points to the ceiling.

"He's upstairs with Evelyn and Trent. They'll be down in time. Just head out back."

Her excitement is brimming, her eyes dancing, and I feel it too. I'm trying to play it cool, but inside, I'm turning cartwheels. I've waited years for this moment.

I walk slowly through the living room and out the sliding glass doors to the backyard. My eyes fall on Claire, then flit

EXTENDED EPILOGUE

away quickly. It's been seven years since everything was revealed and I still haven't forgiven her.

I don't know if I ever will.

She's allowed at holidays now. She knows my kids, but Sam is more their aunt than she'll ever be. Me and Claire? We will never be okay.

I ignore her and walk toward the arch Trent built. Lennon told him it wasn't necessary for the small ceremony, but I love it. She will too. I don't think there's anything Trent can't do. This intricately crafted arch is proof.

I stand underneath and survey it, then a hand comes down on my shoulder.

"Ready, dick?" Casper asks, and I laugh.

"Yeah," I say honestly, eagerly. "I've been ready."

He smiles, then takes a step behind me, positioning himself in the middle of the arch. He runs his hands down his suit jacket, then adjusts his tie. Then he glances at me and reaches out to adjust my tie. I laugh, but I let him do it.

"I thought you were all starched up since the Marines," he says. "Civilian life's got you slippin'."

I roll my eyes.

"Gabe was tugging at it. I haven't had a chance to fix it."

Casper grins at the mention of Gabe, then glances around the yard.

"Ah, Gabriel Christopher Davis, my namesake. Where is my boy?"

"With Trent," I start to say, then a DAD! is shouted from the deck.

I look up to find him standing on the stairs, waving at me and grinning proudly in a little suit—not the khakis and polo we dressed him in before we left—and I get choked up. He looks just like Lennon, but she thinks he looks like me. He's got my hair, but he's got her eyes.

Casper laughs, and I glance at him.

EXTENDED EPILOGUE

"Did you do this?" I ask, and he nods.

"We took him two weeks ago to get it fitted. I'm surprised the little rascal kept the secret."

Me too. Gabe is terrible with secrets. I take a deep breath to calm myself, then pat Casper on the back.

"Thanks, man."

"Don't thank me just yet," he says cryptically, and then he checks his phone. "Showtime."

He stands up straight, then turns me so I'm looking down the makeshift aisle. Music starts to float from speakers attached to the arch that I didn't notice before, and I smile immediately. "In Your Eyes" by Peter Gabriel plays, and I immediately think of that night in the rec center when Lennon found me at the pottery wheel.

God, we had no idea what we were getting into.

I glance at Casper.

"What's all this? I thought we were just saying vows, then blowing out candles."

"Blame Sam," he says with a grin, then he nods forward. "Focus."

I turn my head just in time to see Charlie in a lavender dress, toddling down the aisle throwing petals, with Sam following right behind in a matching dress.

She winks at me when she gets close, then scoops up Charlie and moves to stand across from me.

Thank you, I mouth, and she grins, nodding back to the aisle.

Gabe comes next, strutting in his suit, with a little box in his hand. I chuckle. A ring bearer and a flower girl. This is much more than just reciting some vows. I should have known they'd plan something. Sam and Casper are always making bigger deals out of these milestones than Lennon and I do.

Gabe stands next to me, and Casper reaches out and ruffles his unruly curls. I hear laughter, and I look up to find my mom smiling with tears in her eyes. There are only ten people sitting on folding chairs in the yard. My mom, Evie, and Claire, then some volunteers from the rec center and artist friends of Lennon's. Franco isn't here, but he sent us a gift.

I'm warming up to the twat.

When the chorus to the song kicks up, I glance back down the aisle, and my breath wooshes from my lungs.

Lennon, in a white lace dress I've never seen before, stands with her arm threaded through Trent's. I'm nearly knocked on my ass by the sight. She's gorgeous, and she's mine.

"Fuck," I mutter, and Charlie gasps.

"Bad Daddy," she scolds, making everyone laugh. I flick my eyes to her sheepishly.

"Sorry, Pumpkin."

Charlie grins, and my attention finds Lennon once more.

She's already crying, and now so am I.

I've never seen anyone so stunning. I can't tear my eyes from her as she walks toward me. I've dreamt about this so many times. At one point, I thought that's all it would ever be —a dream. I'm almost afraid to blink for fear it will all disappear.

The last seven years haven't always been easy. We've had more than our fair share of challenges, but we've pulled through together, and there is no place I'd rather be than by her side.

The closer she gets to me, the harder my heart beats. I use my hand to wipe away some tears so I can see her clearly once more. She laughs, and I laugh, and we can't stop smiling. Smiling and crying. I love her so much.

When they're standing before me, Trent passes me Lennon's hand. His eyes mist when they meet mine, and he nods. It's a simple gesture, but the meaning behind it fills me with pride.

He trusts me. He appreciates me. He loves me.

I'm the good man he's always known I'd be, and he's proud to have me as a son.

We didn't rehearse any of this, so I have no idea what to do once Trent moves to the side. I just pull Lennon to me and drink her in. Her rose scent. Her gorgeous hazel eyes. Her beautiful smile.

She squeezes my hand.

Hi, she mouths with a shy smile.

Hi, I mouth back.

I don't take my eyes off her as Casper starts to speak. His words fade in and out of my consciousness. All I see is Lennon. All I hear is Lennon. All I know and want is Lennon.

I repeat after him when I'm supposed to.

In sickness. In health. In this life and the next.

When I kiss her, it's with all I have. It's a reminder of every good memory, and a promise of infinite more to be made.

We pull apart just slightly, and I reach up to brush away one of her tears. I barely register the sound of people clapping. Someone whistles, but I can't look away from Lennon.

"Happy birthday," I whisper, and she hiccups a laugh through her tears.

"I love you," she says back, and I smirk.

"I know."

The Official End
(for now)

SNEAK PEEK

THE LOVE YOU FIGHT FOR

Sam

I sit up with a gasp.

The bedsheet falls to my waist, the air-conditioning calming my sweat-slicked skin, and I take deep gulps of cool air into my lungs. My eyes burn, and my hands press on my chest to feel the rapid thrumming of my panicked heartbeat.

The dream.

It was just the dream.

It's okay. I'm okay. It was just the dream.

I squeeze my eyes shut and fist my fingers in my hair, tugging at the root, willing myself to feel something else—to focus on *anything* else—but flashes of memory still paint the darkness behind my closed lids.

The sudden drop. The crunch of bone. The chase. The fear. The desperation. The pain.

My gut roils and my head throbs.

I kick off the bedsheet and climb out of bed, hurrying my way through the darkness toward my en suite bathroom. I don't bother turning on the light. I just rush to the toilet, drop to my knees, and empty the meager contents of my stomach into the bowl. I heave until sparks dance before my eyes. Until my throat feels raw and my face is wet with sweat. Then I flush the toilet and stand, forcing myself to face my reflection in the mirror.

I reach over and flip the light switch, wincing at the shock of the sudden brightness, then look at myself in the mirror. My skin is red-splotched and shining. My blond hair sticks to my forehead and neck. I stare into my own bloodshot eyes, the blue stark against the red tint, and I don't like what I see.

A scared, vulnerable little girl. A damaged woman. A *victim*.

My lip curls in a snarl of disgust. This is who I promised myself I'd never become.

I open the cabinet under the sink.

With practiced movements, I pull out the bottle and the shot glass, then uncap the bottle and pour some of the amber liquid into the glass. I will my fingers to stop trembling as I bring the shot glass to my lips and swallow back its contents.

The bourbon burns, and I welcome it, breathing through my nose to try to calm my still racing heart. But when I close my eyes, I still see it. I'm right back there, picking up where it left off before I jolted awake.

I pour another shot and choke it down, gritting my teeth against the desire to cry.

When my eyes start to well anyway, I slam my fist on the quartz countertop. Once. Twice. I relish the vibration that shoots up my wrist and forearm. I pound once more just to feel the ache in my shoulder.

I swore I wouldn't let them take up any more space in my head. That I wouldn't spend another second feeling scared. I force myself to feel anger instead, then will that anger to swallow my fear, and thoughts of revenge, of getting even, fight through the haze. I latch onto them.

I pour a third shot and swallow it as a single tear breaks

past my lashes. It rolls down my cheek and falls onto my chest. With the back of my hand, I wipe it away, then meet my own eyes in the mirror once more. I glare at my reflection until the panic starts to fade. Until the scared, vulnerable child I've outgrown is gone. Until she's tucked back safely where she belongs.

I return the bottle and shot glass to the shelf under the sink, then slip on the silk robe hanging next to my shower. Back in my bedroom, I turn on the light. The guy in my bed flinches but doesn't wake, so I round the bed and pull the blanket off him, giving the mattress a shove in the process.

"Get up. Time to go."

He cracks open a confused eye. "What?"

"I said it's time for you to leave. I've got a schedule to keep."

I don't give him a chance to question me, and truly, it's not too far out of the realm of possibility for someone to be starting their day at 4 a.m. on a Sunday. Especially not in this city. As he sits up, I gather his clothes from where they've been discarded on the floor and hand them to him one by one. Designer boxer briefs. Perfectly pressed button-down. Bespoke navy-blue slacks and jacket. Brown Italian leather belt. No tie, though. He was too trendy for that.

The metal bracelet jangles as he slips on his Cartier watch. His eight-hundred-dollar cap toe Oxfords are downstairs by the front door where he took them off. The shoes are what caught my eye last night. I'm a sucker for a stylish shoe.

"There will be a car waiting for you downstairs," I say flatly as he stands and starts to dress. I grab my phone off the charger and head to my walk-in closet. "Turn the lights off when you leave, please, but don't worry about locking up. Security will take care of it."

"Can I call you?" he asks my back, and I pause.

My hand flexes on the knob of my closet door and my lips

purse before I force my face into a soft smile and glance at him over my shoulder.

"I'd rather you didn't."

I push open the door and step inside, then shut it tightly behind me. With my ear trained to the noise coming from my bedroom, I listen to him dress. The bedroom door opens. The soft click of the wall switch is paired with the disappearance of the light beam seeping under the closet door, plunging me back into darkness.

I send my security detail a text, telling him to let the gentleman out of the building, then wait for the *all clear* before I use my app to relock my door and reset the alarm.

In the comfortable darkness, I make my way to the back of my closet, to the section of racks that hold cocktail and evening gowns. Hundreds of thousands of dollars hang delicately on display, but I don't bother looking at them. Instead, I drop to my knees and crawl through them until I'm nestled in the corner behind a wall of long protective garment bags. Then I put my phone on speaker and dial my only emergency contact.

"Hey," my best friend answers, and her knowing voice is warm with concern.

It's around 9 a.m. in Paris, so I close my eyes and picture her sitting at the window in her small apartment with a croissant and a coffee surrounded by painting supplies.

"Hey," I reply. "What are you working on?"

"A commission piece. Landscape. I'm almost done."

I hum in response and listen to her soft movements on the other end of the phone. Clinking of what could be a coffee cup or a pastry plate. Rustling of fabric. Shuffling of papers. The faint music that I heard when she answered gets louder, then shuts off completely.

"Where are you?" she asks, and I smile grimly to myself.

"Hanging out with my friends, Oscar de la Renta and Tom Ford." I sigh and force a weak laugh as I run my fingers over one of the garment bags hanging next to me. "Donatella and Vera are here somewhere, too."

I hear pages of a book, then, and the tension in my neck and shoulders loosens. Tears of relief prickle the backs of my eyelids, and I inhale deeply through my nose.

"I think we were on chapter fourteen," she says smoothly, her voice low but free of pity.

All I hear is love and unwavering support.

Her tone suggests that there is absolutely nothing wrong or shameful about me calling her up at 4 a.m. my time while cowering in the back of my luxury walk-in closet. I don't need to be embarrassed or sorry for interrupting her painting. I know she knows about the shots of bourbon that came before this phone call and the vomiting before that. She knows about the nightmare. She doesn't ask, but she doesn't have to.

And anyway, none of it matters anymore.

"Chapter fourteen is perfect."

I rest my head against the wall as she inhales smoothly, then starts to read out loud from *Pride and Prejudice*, picking up exactly where we left off the last time.

In only takes a few sentences for my muscles to relax, a couple paragraphs for the threat of tears to abate completely. As she ends the chapter and begins a new one, my body sags with exhaustion, but the panic and fear are gone.

"Hey, Len," I interrupt.

"Yeah?"

"I love you."

I can't see it, but I can feel her soft smile. I hear her sniffle, then chuckle lightly before she responds.

"I love you too, Sam."

Read *The Love You Fight For* today in KU!

BONUS CONTENT

My Astraea,

I'm sorry. If you're reading this, that means your luggage got to your aunt's house and you're an ocean away from me. Fuck. I miss you already. Prom was the best night of my life. That memory is going to fuel my recovery, Astraea. I promise. I have to go to rehab. I'm leaving today after Trent drops you at the airport. I'm sorry I couldn't tell you sooner. Please don't be mad at your dad. I asked him to send you early. I promise I'll explain in detail when I get out and you come home in the fall. Enjoy England. I know it's been your dream since you were little. Take lots of pictures because I want to hear all about it. Don't give up on me, Astraea. Just wait for me a little while longer. Then when I get out, it's you and me. For real. Out loud. Forever. I love you. Lennon Capri Washington. See you soon.

ACKNOWLEDGMENTS

This duet has wrecked me, and I plan to read for three weeks straight now that it's finished.

I love Macon and Lennon. I love them so much. Their story is heartbreakingly beautiful and larger-than-life, and they wouldn't exist in this capacity if it weren't for a few crucial souls. Here are my heartfelt, shouted from the rooftops, all the way from my toes, thank-yous.

First, to my MFing Street Team! Macon's Madams, I fucking love you ladies so much. Your love fuels mine. Your enthusiasm gasses me up. You are my people. I'm so happy to have found you. PLEASE NEVER LEAVE ME!

To the ARC readers and bloggers, for once again taking a chance on me and this story. It was a gamble for me. It was out of my comfort zone and a giant step away from what I'd released previously. THANK YOU for showing me my risk was worth it.

To Jessie, for being a beta, a sounding board, and my emotional support pirate. Macon and Lennon almost broke me. Thank you for being my IRL Samantha Harper (post-bitchy rivalry, of course).

To Haley- you're one of the best. You loved Macon even before I did, you stepped up every time I needed you, and you single-handedly saved Trent's life. I literally could not have done this without you. I love you so, so big, friend.

To Kara, for always giving me the most honest feedback, and always being down to hear my rambling voice notes complaining about my pain-in-the-ass characters, I thank you.

You're the reason I was confident enough to lean into the edge. You encouraged the grit (and the Casper) in this duet, and it made all the difference.

To Caitlin, for feeling this story so deeply. You have no idea how much it means to me that you experienced these characters in their rawest forms and still loved them. You helped make these babies real. Thank you.

To my editor, Becky at Fairest Reviews Editing Services, my Comma Queen and Raise/Rise Expert, I owe you so much for this duet. Thank you for working with my mess. Thank you for your patience and honesty. Thank you for so willingly chunking it up for me because I was STRUGGLING. You're brilliant and I love you.

To my proofreader, Sarah at All Encompassing Books, for putting up with multiple emails and updates and additions, thank you for standing by me through this epic disaster of a love story. I'm proud of this HEA, and I owe a lot of that to you.

To Murphy Rae for getting these covers and the first try. Are you kidding me right now? They're perfect. I want to stare at them forever. Thank you, thank you, thank you.

To my husband Jonathan, for once again carrying my mental and physical health on your shoulders while I trudged through this duet. You're a serious trooper. Thank you for being my person, and for never putting me through the shit Macon put Lennon through. I love you the biggest.

To Julia Michaels for dominating my playlist and giving me all the love and angst that I needed to finish this duet.

I love you all.

ABOUT THE AUTHOR

Brit Benson writes romance novels that are sassy, sexy, and sweet.

Brit would almost always rather be reading or writing. When she's not dreaming up her next swoony book boyfriend and fierce book bestie, she's getting lost in someone else's fictional world. When she's not doing that, she's probably marathoning a Netflix series or wandering aimlessly up and down the aisles in Homegoods, sniffing candles and touching things she'll never buy.

Printed in Dunstable, United Kingdom